# to catch a wolf

A *three seventeen* NOVEL

Kerri L. Bennett

Savannah Street
P U B L I S H I N G

First Print Edition, 2014
Published in the United States of America

**ISBN-13: 978-0692343982    ISBN-10: 0692343989**

## Dedication

This novel is dedicated to my Daddy, Bobby Bennett, for all the nights spent coloring in the living room floor, the bedtime stories of his childhood adventures, the Saturday morning rides in his pickup truck down the gravel roads of his youth, the Sunday morning walks to the coffee shop before church, and all the other uncountable things he did every day so that I've never once had to question the kind of man he is or the depth of his love for me.

It was too late for guilt. She'd thrown her lot in with Logan's, and now she'd face the consequences. *Besides, maybe there's hope for him yet . . .*
~Lillie Thackery
*Three Seventeen*

# Contents

Prologue ....................................................................7

Chapter 1 ..................................................................9

Chapter 2 ................................................................12

Chapter 3 ................................................................20

Chapter 4 ................................................................28

Chapter 5 ................................................................39

Chapter 6 ................................................................46

Chapter 7 ................................................................53

Chapter 8 ................................................................63

Chapter 9 ................................................................73

Chapter 10 ..............................................................86

Chapter 11 ..............................................................93

Chapter 12 ............................................................112

Chapter 13 ............................................................123

Chapter 14 ............................................................136

Chapter 15 ............................................................146

Chapter 16 ............................................................158

Chapter 17 ............................................................171

Chapter 18 ............................................................185

Chapter 19 ............................................................194

Chapter 20 ............................................................202

Chapter 21.................................................................209

Chapter 22.................................................................220

Chapter 23.................................................................229

Chapter 24.................................................................235

Chapter 25.................................................................240

Chapter 26.................................................................250

Chapter 27.................................................................261

Chapter 28.................................................................273

Chapter 29.................................................................291

Chapter 30.................................................................303

Chapter 31.................................................................312

Chapter 32.................................................................320

Epilogue...................................................................325

## Prologue

*Manteo, NC, 2008*

She was sitting on the porch, watching the sun's light fade orange into the horizon. The streaks of red and pink mingled alongside it, and she wondered if she'd ever seen anything as pretty, even with all the places she had been. Sighing, she decided in the contrary, especially when she looked up at a small sound and was met with his handsome smile and steel gray eyes.

A sharp pain had Lillie bolting up in the darkness. Gone was the dream, soft and shimmering as it had been; gone with it was the face that haunted even her waking hours, though she hadn't actually seen it in six months. She wished it could be gone entirely from her memory as instantly, but it could not, and would not vanish completely so long as the child she carried lived and breathed.

She laid down again and tried to get comfortable enough to go to back to sleep, but even in the familiarity of the bed she'd slept on her whole life, doing so was a struggle. She was inclined to curl up on her side as she'd been told to do, but couldn't seem to fall asleep that way. She settled flat on her back and willed her mind and body to relax, but there was another flash of pain. She rose and woke her parents. For a moment, her excitement

7

overshadowed everything, even the hollow ache that never quite went away. *He's coming. He's coming at last.*

## Chapter 1

*Ann Arbor, MI, 2021*

Lillie Thackery was not the kind of person who joked about anything. And she sure as heck didn't take off work on her PhD stuff for anything that wasn't majorly important, but if he didn't know any better, he'd think his mom was playing some sort of joke on him. It also wasn't like her not to gripe him out over the currently super-gross, mud-covered state of his room.

He stared at his mother in disbelief. He had always known her to be the most logical person in his life, but now she had read to him from a book he had never seen before, and she wanted him to believe it was true, even though every word of it sounded to him like some fairy story by one of those authors trying to capitalize on a fad that was popular ten years ago, or even worse, some crappy horror movie for teens, except in those kind of movies, the virgin girl died once she'd Done It with some guy. In *this* story, which his mom claimed wasn't a story at all, but an historical record of the events leading up to his birth, it wasn't the girl who died, but the guy who was supposed to save the day. *On second thought, it **can't** be a crappy horror movie because the story line's too lame for even that.*

If he hadn't been so freaked out when he woke up this morning naked and dirty all over, Lo would have been even more freaked over how long he would be punished for destroying his bedroom; as it was, he didn't stop to think about the consequences. He just yelled for his mom because the throbbing in his head wouldn't let him do anything else.

She came running, of course. It was just the two of them, and it had been as long as Lo could remember, so she was the one who kept the monsters out of his closet and from under his bed. He'd had his eyes shut so that maybe his headache wouldn't hurt so bad and didn't see her come in, but he felt her arms around him and heard her murmuring softly in his ear, "It's all right, baby. It's okay." She rocked him close until he could think enough to be embarrassed about still crying in his mother's lap at thirteen.

"What's happening?" he asked when he'd opened his eyes.

"Let's get you cleaned up, and then we'll talk about it," she gave him one last squeeze before pushing up from the floor and pulling Lo into a standing position with her.

On the way to the bathroom, he tried to guess what she was thinking from the look on her face, but he couldn't. She seemed just as calm as she was when he'd seen her lecturing her Intro to Anthropology students. *Any other mom would be screaming her head off right now, but not my mom.* He hadn't made up his mind whether he thought that was a good or bad thing when she handed him a fresh bar of soap, a towel, and some p.j. pants as they reached the bathroom. "We'll talk about it as soon as you're clean," she promised, giving him a nudge and shutting the door behind him.

True to her word, as soon as he was out of the bathroom and had found a shirt, she called him into the living room and asked him to sit next to her on the couch. When he was comfortable, she looked him in the eye and said the words that he'd never seen coming, "Lo, my love, there's something you need to know."

## Chapter 2

"So you're saying you actually know who my dad is?" he asked the only question that he felt it safe to concentrate on.

His mother sighed. "Yes. His name is Philip Logan Michaels."

"Then why have you always told me that you had no idea who or where he was?" Lo raised a brow. Lillie had never allowed dishonesty between them.

"Because *he* has no idea that either one of us exists, and if your grandparents had known who he was, they would've stopped at nothing to find him and make him take responsibility for us." There was something in her green eyes that Lo had never seen before.

"And that would've been a bad thing, how?" he demanded.

"It would have been a disaster because Philip would have disinherited him the minute he heard about you, and then there would have been law suits and hatred, bitterness and pain—"

"Philip? You mean my father?" This whole same-name thing was getting complicated.

"No, Philip, your grandfather. Logan is your father's name, as is yours. Anyway, I couldn't be responsible for ruining your father's life, not when he was just beginning to possibly find faith in someone other than himself."

"Forget finding faith! What about us? What about Ma and Pa? What about him, even? Didn't he deserve to know the truth?"

"Logan Daniel Thackery. Don't speak to me that way. Whatever else I am, I'm your mother. Do you understand me?" The lack of emotion behind her words had him wincing.

"Yes, ma'am. I'm sorry, Mom, but really. Don't you think we had a right to know the truth?" he lowered his tone and stared at his p.j. pants.

"I think you're missing the point, baby. I didn't tell you the story so you could know who your father is. I told you so that you could understand what's happening to you, to your body."

"You told me because I'm . . . like him . . . because I'm a werewolf?"

She laughed. "Your father was always uncomfortable with that term. He preferred 'lycanthrope,' but yes, that's exactly what you are."

"That means I'll wake up tomorrow morning the same way I did this morning?"

"And the next morning too," Lillie nodded. "You'll phase for three days each month, every month from now on, unless the wolf inside you is killed. If and when that happens, the human inside you will survive, but you'll have no memory of the time when the wolf lived in you." It had never been her way to shelter him, and she wasn't about to start now.

Lo fought to keep color in his face when his mom mentioned the word "killed." He had been the man of the house as long as he could remember, and as soon as he was old enough to understand the responsibility that came with the title, he'd done his best to live up to it.

13

Bravery in the face of the unknown was part of that responsibility, so showing her how scared he was wasn't an option. Instead, he changed the subject. "If I'm a lycanthrope, or whatever, because he passed it to me through the gene pool, then why haven't I phased before now?"

~

Lillie had been pondering the answer to Lo's question since he was fifteen days old, and she spent that first night before the full moon waiting anxiously for the newborn in the bassinet to phase into a pup. When the second month and then the third passed without a transformation, she ceased to watch for lupine behavior. By the time he was one, she was fairly certain that Logan hadn't passed the curse to their son.

The older Lo got, the more he resembled his father, which caused twin claws to tear through her. She missed Logan, even after so much time and distance lay between them. She missed him at night when she couldn't shut her brain off enough for sleep. She missed him when Lo smiled. When he frowned. When he laughed. And she worried. Worried that the lycanthropy, like the features that were hauntingly Logan's, was hiding somewhere within her boy, waiting to appear seamlessly and catch her unawares.

"I don't know, Lo. If I had to guess, I'd say that the delay could be a result of the differing conditions of exposure. In your father's case, he contracted the curse after birth, when coming into contact with an external contagion—Sarah Abbot in wolf-form. Presumably, *you* were born with it. If so, it lay dormant in your system until your body entered puberty, and then, for whatever reason, manifest itself visually for the first time last night

14

because that was the first occurrence of the condition that triggers the phase since the curse became active."

"So I changed from a boy to a wolf last night because tonight is the first full moon since I hit puberty?" he reviewed, proving that he was quick enough to follow her scientific explanation.

"As far as I can tell," she agreed. *Other thirteen-year-olds would be whining or crying by now, but not my son.*

"Could I hurt you tonight . . . when I'm a wolf?"

"Only if the wolf feels threatened by me. When your father phased, he had roommates sleeping right down the hall, and they never even knew." She saw Lo exhale. Always thinking of her. For now, he retained the sweetness she had known since his personality began to develop. She didn't like to think of the time in the near future when his teenage angst would have him pushing away from her. "How about some breakfast? I can make pancakes."

~

Lo ate six pancakes even though his head was killing him. That was no excuse to turn down food. Besides, his mom looked like she needed something to do to keep from freaking out, even if it was only on the inside, and he couldn't blame her. Raising a kid and being a college professor were hard enough jobs for just one person. Now she had to deal with him being a werewolf too.

"Thanks, Mom. They were great," he smiled as he took both their plates to the sink to wash them. He let the water heat up and shook his head. *If we'd stayed in North Carolina, Ma and Pa could help out.* It wasn't the first time he wished that his mom hadn't wanted to get a PhD in Michigan, but he knew that she wouldn't have been happy without it. And that's what he wanted most. That and a father.

"You're welcome, baby. I'm going to see about that mess in your room," she reached over and brushed her fingers over his hair. Lo winced just thinking about all the stuff that was destroyed in there. "How's your head? Do you want some Tylenol?"

"Yes, ma'am," he grabbed a dishcloth and some liquid soap and swallowed the pills she handed him. "I'll help with my room as soon as I finish the dishes."

~

By the end of his first phase on Monday morning, Lillie had no idea what to do. She had told herself long ago that she was doing this alone, and she had been okay with that. More than okay with it, especially after watching Logan walk across that stage and receive his business degree. As her mother liked to say, he looked like he was going places, and she wasn't about to take those places from him.

She would have been as firm now about that decision as she had been on graduation day, if Lo had been only human. *And really, why should Lo's lycanthropy change anything? It isn't like they could share horror stories about the mornings after.* But that was only the logical part of her talking.

Her son was hurting and she knew it, despite the pains he took to keep it from her. *How can I watch this happen over and over again?* But as soon as the question registered, she knew the how was unimportant. It didn't come down to "how." It came down to "I will."

~

When his mom dropped him off at school on Monday, Lo had to stifle a yawn. For three nights, he had lived as a wolf, and while that was pretty cool when he sat down

16

and thought about it, it would have been much cooler if he could actually remember what living as a wolf was like. Oh, he'd seen his share of horror flicks when he'd camped out at a buddy's house, but watching a movie about werewolves wasn't the same as *being* one.

He'd only been thirteen a little over a week, since his birthday was November 13th, and if he'd been asked before then what he thought about being a teenager, he would have answered that being a teen was going to be awesome, definitely much cooler than just being . . . whatever it was you were when you were only twelve. But that was before.

*Now*, he'd say that being a twelve-year-old kid was way cooler than being a teenage werewolf. For one thing, the movies didn't tell you how much it sucked to wake up the morning after and have to shower for a good fifteen minutes before you were sure you had all the mud off. They also forgot to warn you about the massive headache that made you want to puke so bad that you had to be careful what you did or how much light you let into your room, if you knew what was good for you.

Lo saw that Alex Thompson was waiting for him in their usual place in front of the school. They had been friends since a week after Lo and his mom had moved to Ann Arbor three years ago. Alex had been born in Michigan and had lived there all his life, except for the summers he spent with his grandmother who lived "down South."

"What's up, man? You never came over for some Xbox on Saturday."

"I felt kinda cruddy this weekend, dude," Lo shrugged.

"I think it was 'cause you didn't want to get annihilated by my awesome shooting skills," Alex grinned.

"I think you ought to be glad I didn't because *you* would've been the one getting annihilated by *my* shooting skills and on your own game too!" Lo replied solemnly.

"I doubt that," Alex answered, and then the conversation was ended by the approach of their friend J.J. Well, he was actually more like Alex's friend, but he hung out with Lo because Lo hung out with Alex.

Though Lillie and Lo had been in Ann Arbor long enough for her to be nearly done with her classes, there was something about living here that made Lo feel separate. When they had first come to the North, his mother had told him that it might take him a while, but he would get used to the life here. He would adapt, she knew, because she studied human culture. She said it was natural for people to resist change, but over time, the change in environment actually brought about change in the people themselves. Lo was still waiting for Ann Arbor to become home.

He was still waiting for people to stop asking him where he was from the moment he opened his mouth around anyone new. He was still waiting for the time when the cooler temperatures no longer seemed extreme to him. He was still waiting for the time when he didn't wish he were back in North Carolina, back in Raleigh or even in Manteo, in the land of crab bakes and country music. Somehow, life seemed faster here. There was more to do, of course, but there was less time to do it.

"What's your problem, Thack?" Jeff Jones stopped talking with Alex to ask. "You're just standing there, staring, with your mouth open like a zombie or something. Has the apocalypse started, or is there a cute chick over there somewhere that I'm not seeing?"

"Nope. You don't have to worry about the undead.

I'm just still half asleep." Lo answered, which was true.

"I wasn't really worried about the undead, man. I've seen enough movies and games to survive, as long as I have enough ammo. I was just really hoping you'd seen a hot girl." Jeff sighed. "I'm tired of looking at the same regular girls in our class all the time. Why can't they look like the babes in the movies?"

"Cheer up, J.J., if they were as hot as all that, they sure wouldn't have time for you!" Alex attempted to console him.

The bell rang before J.J. could do more than scowl, and Lo laughed as he moved inside the building, grateful to be out of the cold November air.

## Chapter 3

The one place Lo didn't feel isolated was school. It seemed that no matter where he was in America, school was school. He always did well in his classes, and he had always figured that it came from his mother. If she could have her way, she would never stop going to school. Lo wasn't that excited about learning, but he did know that he wanted to do well. *Mom will expect it, for one thing.* But also, there was his future. *I don't want to spend my life in college like she's doing, but I do want to get a degree and make enough to take care of her for a change.* Not that he had a clue what he wanted to do, but whatever it was, it would be something that allowed him to buy her a big, nice house and maybe a better car, and even send her on digs again.

When they still lived in Raleigh, Lo had spent a couple of summers with Ma and Pa while she had gone to South America to help excavate artifacts from sites of ancient civilizations. She was the happiest he had ever seen her when she planned for those digs. But leaving him behind for two months had been hard, and since they'd moved to Michigan, she hadn't gone, even though he knew she would have loved to.

What it was that she loved about crouching in the dirt for hours with a brush and a pick in her hands, he hadn't figured out, but he had to admit that when she'd taken him with her to Roanoke, it was fun to look around and imagine the colonists and what could have happened to them. But he couldn't spend hours at it like she could. It got boring after the imagining wore off.

It didn't matter how he felt about digs, though, because she deserved to go to those places and find those artifacts and publish articles in those journals she was always reading for her upcoming dissertation. She deserved it because she worked harder than anyone else's mom he knew. She taught, she went to class, and she was home when he needed her to be. She was everywhere at once and everything at once. Everything except a father.

~

Lillie drove away and wondered. Wondered if she had done right by Lo when she took him away from all he had ever known and moved to Michigan. She watched him carefully, as carefully as she did the potsherds she pulled from ground, looking for the damage that uprooting him from his foundation had done. He was a bright boy, clever in his studies and quick to read her. He knew without being told when she needed quiet, when she needed conversation, when she needed love. In many ways, he filled her heart like his father never had. In others, he made the hole Logan left feel even larger.

When she arrived at the University of Michigan, she headed to her office to prepare for the classes she would teach at 9:00, 10:00, and 2:00. They were freshman and sophomore level classes, of course, since the upper levels always went to the permanent faculty and tenured professors. Still, she liked to flip through her notes and read over the familiar material to clear her mind before she went into the classroom.

The people groups she covered in class had been real, and she always worried that she hadn't adequately translated the pictures and slides and lines of text into the living, breathing, feeling humans they represented. She

21

knew that most of the students were only taking her course to fulfill a gen ed requirement or perhaps as one of their electives, but she hoped that a small handful out of each class became interested in archeology because of an artifact she mentioned or a cultural reference she had made. There were hundreds of thousand stories that had been swallowed up by time, stories that could never be recovered, but she owed it to those people whose memories had been erased to ensure that those whose stories were still out there, hidden in the earth, were rediscovered and consequently remembered by future generations. Not everyone was as lucky as Virginia Dare and Tutankhamen, but everyone was just as worthy of remembrance.

~

Lo sat down at the laptop that he and his mother shared and Googled "werewolf." He had been itching to do his own research since the first morning of his phase, but he wasn't sure what his mom would think, so he read the diary she gave him at least three times over the weekend, but he still had questions. Why did the mirror kill the wolf? Was it that it was backed with silver, and silver is poisonous to werewolves, like the movies said? Was it that the wolf saw its human spirit in the mirror's reflection like the Native American legends claimed? Or was it the fact that jumping through glass and falling six feet would kill any wolf, even a normal one? And what the heck happened to Sarah Abbot? Did she ever find a cure like his parents had? Or was she still roaming around in the woods of Colorado, infecting more people with the curse?

When his first search yielded nothing, he tried "Sarah Abbot," and couldn't find anything other than the news article from a paper in Breckenridge from 2007, which said that she was the only person in that tourist group whose body wasn't found. *Well, that's it,* he thought and started to close the lid, when something occurred to him. He pulled up the Internet and held his breath as Google gathered results for the phrase "Logan Michaels."

When Lo had been a little boy, he had imagined what his father was like. At first, he had always thought of his dad as someone who was strong and powerful, like Wolverine from *X-Men* who would have loved to spend his days playing cowboys and Indians with Lo, but he was too busy defending the world from an evil super-villain, like Magneto. But then he got a little older and realized that grownups didn't actually have superpowers, so his dad couldn't be a hero, unless he was in the military. And then, he told himself that his father could very well have been in Iraq or Afghanistan, defending the country from terrorism, which would have been way cooler than being a mutant anyway. But now he didn't have to imagine a life for his father. Now he his own power, the power to find out who and what his dad really was.

Apparently, his father had taken over his grandfather's company because Logan was listed as CEO of Michaels Corporate Management. Even after reading about MCM on its website, Lo couldn't figure out exactly what it was his dad's company did to make money, but he did learn that Logan had moved the company's offices from Asheville to Raleigh two years before he and his mom had moved from there to Ann Arbor.

*We were in the same city* was the first thing he thought. *Have I seen him before? What if we were in the same store? We*

23

*may have passed each other on the sidewalk or on the road and never knew.* He pulled up a picture of Logan and found that his father had strong, hard features, ones that glared out of the screen at him, but the hair and the eyes were familiar, the same hair and eyes he saw in his own mirror as he brushed his teeth. Looking at Logan, Lo found that his father, like his mother, looked much younger than Alex or J.J.'s parents did. And yet he still seemed very much older than his mom did. *Maybe it's just the picture and the suit and tie he's wearing. Or maybe he's just trying to look serious on the company website so that people will trust him to do his job.* Never, in all his imaginings, had Lo pictured his dad as someone so stern. Suddenly, he shut the laptop, unsure that he wanted to know anymore.

Lo tried not to think of the approaching three days in December, but he couldn't help himself. He re-read the diary again, especially the parts about what happened to his dad when he phased. The problem with the diary was that his dad was never able to remember anything that happened while he was a wolf, and the few times that Lo's mother had come into contact with the wolf were too short for her to see exactly how Logan changed from man to wolf and back again. *Why hadn't he been willing to let her watch? Why hadn't she done it anyway?* was a better question. His mom never gave in when it came to something she wanted to do, which was why she was still in school and working on her PhD. But if that was true, why in the world had she let Logan tell her what to do?

When Lillie and Lo had finished supper one night about a week before Lo was set to have his second phase, he sat next to her on the couch and waited until she

24

looked up from her book. "Mom, are you worried?"

"Worried about what, my love?"

"Worried about what'll happen to me in a few days."

"Are *you* worried about it, Lo?" she asked, and he regretted bringing it up because if she hadn't been worried before, he could hear it in her voice now.

"Kind of," he admitted. "I just wish we knew more about it."

"You and I know a great deal more now than your father and I did thirteen years ago, baby," she reminded him gently.

"I know," he nodded and decided that he was going to change the subject, but his mom was speaking again before he could.

"It can be scary when we face things we don't fully understand, and it's ok if you feel that way. I'm scared too, Lo," she told him after a moment.

"I thought you said I wouldn't hurt you!" he exclaimed, and suddenly he had a brand new reason to be worried.

"Come here," she told him and opened her arms. She hadn't held him since that morning nearly a month before, and even though he was embarrassed about being too old for that, he saw the look in her eyes.

"Yes, ma'am," he answered and did as he was told.

When he was situated in her lap as best he could be, she smoothed his hair and smiled. "You've always been so grown up, Lo. Maybe I made you grow up too fast, and I'm sorry for that. I'm sorry, too, that you have to deal with the problem that your father and I passed down to you. I prayed so many nights that you wouldn't have to pay for our sins, but since it wasn't to be, I'm going to make you a promise. I promise that I will do everything within my power to help you cure this curse."

"I thought you already knew how to do it," Lo said without lifting his head from her shoulder.

"I do, but I have to find the wolf's den and the boundaries of his territory before I can set the trap, and I was unable to track it during the last phase."

"You went out after it?" Lo stiffened in her arms and felt real outrage at her for the first time in his life.

"Of course I did, Lo. How else am I supposed to find it and force it to break a mirror?"

"But what if it had attacked you? What if you had been hurt or killed?" He couldn't hide the panic in his voice and didn't really care that he hadn't.

"I was careful, sweetheart," she promised, "and I'll be careful this time too."

"I really think we should tell someone," he shook his head.

"Who can we tell, Lo? Who would believe us?"

"Anyone who watched me change would *have* to believe us, Mom."

"We can't take that risk, baby. What happens if the wolf sees whomever it is we've told as that person is watching the phase? What if it feels threatened and attacks or kills whomever we tell? I can't let you have anyone's blood on your hands. I've brought enough upon you as it is."

"And what happens if the wolf kills you, Momma? What would I do then? I can't go back home! What happens if the wolf hurts Ma or Pa? I can't have their blood on my hands either!"

"Then who do you think we should tell?" Lillie demanded in a louder tone than he expected.

"I think we need to tell my dad," he stated flatly.

"What in the world do you think he can do about it? He has absolutely no idea who we are! He doesn't remember *anything* about that whole year!"

~

Lillie had never been so furious with her son in all his thirteen years of life. She decided to blame this stubbornness on Logan, since he, too, had often refused to listen to reason.

"He won't come riding in on a white horse to rescue us, Lo. He isn't some knight in shining armor with an impeccable code of conduct. He's a regular person with flaws, and as much as I love him, he just won't be the man you think he is."

"How do you know? Have you even given him the chance?" Lo didn't bother to hide his temper, since she wasn't hiding hers.

"I know because I've lived through this one time before, son. He's a better person than he thinks he is, but there are limits to what you can expect from him. He doesn't think in the same terms that we do."

"He may not be perfect, but he still might be able to help us," he insisted. "I mean, you convinced him to believe it once before, didn't you? There's no reason you can't do it again."

"And you might have gotten more from your father than just his lycanthropy and his looks."

## Chapter 4

Lo was still angry with his mom, and he wasn't sure what he was going to do about that. Sure he had been aggravated with her before, when she didn't let him have his way or see things from his point of view, but those times only lasted for an afternoon or evening. They had fought about his father three days ago. It was now December 13th (which meant he'd been a teenager for a full month), and things were still weird between them. *I don't like it, but I can't listen to and obey her this time. I just can't. It's too dangerous for us to do this alone, and I still think that he has a right to know that I'm alive.* But Lo only had four days before he phased, *and "Hello, sir. We don't know each other, but I'm pretty sure I'm your son," isn't the kind of thing that you should tell someone over the phone, even if I could manage to find his cell number somehow.* But the four days left before his Second Phase began might not give him enough time to get back to Raleigh and find Logan before he changed. So there was no way he would be able to tell his dad before Christmas.

He really didn't want to think about his mom going out in the dark, searching for the path the wolf had taken from Lo's bedroom window to wherever its den was. Too much stuff could happen to her. *Even if she does find the den this time, she won't have time to find the right kind of mirror and find the perfect place to put it, like she did last time with Dad.* It looked like he was definitely going to have at least one more phase before his mom could kill the wolf, and he really didn't want to think about that either. There was always a chance that something could happen the way it had back in 2008, and this time his mom might not be so lucky. According to her journal, she had escaped that time with nothing more than a few scratches and bruises, but they had hung around for a little while.

His mom had always taught him that there was no such thing as luck. Things happen for a reason, even if you don't know what that reason is, and you have to trust that things will work out according to a greater plan than your own. Her faith had never wavered once since he had known her, and he wished he could accept things as easily as she did, but he couldn't. He hoped that Ma and Pa and his mom were right, that there was a benevolent hand guiding their every step and helping them in times of need, but there were just too many times that he had seen his mom work through her problems on her own to believe that someone else was helping her, even invisibly.

Still, he would like to think that there was something to Mass and the sermons and liturgical readings, so he went with his mom on Sundays and waited there too, to feel whatever it was she felt that made her have so much faith. *If You're listening,* he thought after the Hail Mary, *it would be really great if You could keep my mom safe when I phase . . . and if it isn't too much to ask, could You please help my dad know what to do?* And then it hit him: his mother had no faith in Logan, but maybe Lo's own faith in him would be enough.

~

Lillie waited outside Lo's open bedroom window. The moon had risen and the sun had set, so any moment now, the wolf would bound out here and head for the nearest wooded area. There was a copse of trees that was a few blocks from their neighborhood, and she suspected that was the direction it'd be heading. *If I don't find the den tonight, then Lo'll have to go through this again*; the thought ran through her head as she crouched next to the side of the house. The similarity of her situation took her back to that cool Carolina night when she crouched in the trees, waiting for a different wolf to arrive.

She pushed the thought and a tear away and concentrated on the now. Dwelling on what had been and what she had lost that night would do Lo no good, and he was all that mattered now.

She held her breath as she heard a sound in Lo's room, a muffled thump and then scrambling and shuffling. A part of her wanted to peek inside and see the phase happen. It had been one of the mysteries of the curse since she'd taken an interest in the brooding guy, poring over his stack of medical books day after day in her section of the NCSU library. To this day, she had no idea what it was that made her ask him if he needed help. It was a mundane, yet defining moment in her life. And after all that had happened between the two of them, she still looked back on it with fondness and felt no regret for what had come later.

Her curiosity outweighed her cautiousness, and she inched closer to the open pane to peer inside. In the dimness of the room, she could make out a form convulsing in the shadows. It took her a moment, but she identified a fur-covered hand and arm. With the next thrash, she saw that human teeth were bared, but the wide, unseeing eyes were already composed of some wild, golden liquid, hot even as they remained unfocused. After another contortion, the hands and arms had become paws and legs. Yet another severe spasm had the head jerking back into the weak light to show a snout where a nose had been, and beneath it, sharp canines snapped reflexively in the air. Then the body was still in the darkness, and after the fury of those few minutes before, the calm seemed unnatural to Lillie.

She held her breath and watched the unmoving mound that had once been her son but was now fully lupine. Though fairly quick, the transformation had been a violent one, and she prayed that there had been no pain. When a quarter of an hour had passed, she wondered if she hadn't seen a tiny twitch. *Perhaps it was the tail, or even one of the paws.* She blinked and shook her head, in case it was only wishful thinking, but when she looked again, she saw a glint of light, which then became two. And suddenly there were two coals of burning amber that flashed briefly in the dark before the wolf was on its feet, and she could risk it no longer.

She backed quickly from the window and slipped around the corner of the house to the scraping of claws on Lo's wooden floorboards. Seconds later, the wolf sailed out into the night, landing in the soft dirt where she had just been, without a sound.

Despite what Lo had feared, the wolf loped away without looking back, seemingly searching for shelter or food. Lillie meant to follow it and track the trail that led to its bed, but the smooth efficiency of its unhampered gait had her losing it long before they had reached any place suitable for its safety.

When she was sure it was gone, and there was no way to tell where it had headed, she went back inside to wait for the sun to rise.

~

Lo came to himself abruptly, and regardless of the throbbing in his head, he was acutely aware that something was pinning his arms to his sides. Unwisely he opened his eyes and the vicious, blinding light seared everything until he couldn't stop himself from screaming.

"It's okay, baby," her voice filled his ear and pressed in on the pain, amplifying it until he wished he could pass out. "You're all right, my love," and this time the sound was so terrible that the world around him began to move, which made him notice the unsettled state of his stomach.

"Momma," he heard his own voice whimper and felt her cool hand on the side of his cheek. It was then that he realized what was holding him.

"I've got you, Lo. I'm right here," her arms were tight around his torso and she was rocking slowly, forward and back, forward and back.

He forced his eyes open again and looked up at her. It was a little better this time, but it was still hard not to squint. "You shouldn't be here," he whispered. "It's too dangerous."

"I'm fine, sweetheart," she smiled. "Can you move?"

Lo pushed out of her arms and tried to sit, but thought better of it. He laid his cheek on the floorboard and saw that they were in the middle of his room, and it was totally trashed. "Did you find the den?" he wondered.

"No. The wolf was too fast for me, and I lost it, but I'll try again tonight, and tomorrow night too, if I have to," she answered, and he noticed how soft her tone was.

"How long have you been holding me?" The ache was easing a bit now, and he could think clearly enough to worry that she had tried to grab the wolf and restrain it as he phased into himself again.

"Since the moment you came back to me," she said.

~

The next two nights weren't any easier for Lillie with what she had seen on the first night. If anything, it was harder for her to accept that he had to relive the transformation twice more. It was no wonder that Lo had such a terrible headache when he awoke. Every part of him had ceased to be, and yet every part of him had become something different. Even his brain had likely morphed into the compact size a wolf's skull required, and then converted back again to fit the more complex needs of the human body all in the span of one night. That he was even able to survive the phase was absolutely miraculous and something she had never considered before.

*We took so many things for granted*, she thought, remembering again those long afternoons of researching in the stacks and the even longer nights she had spent lying awake in her bed, waiting on the call that allowed her to breathe freely again. She recalled having been afraid that some outside force, like a hunter, or a game warden, or even another animal would take Logan's life, but she had never supposed that the phase itself might end him.

Because Lo was in the shower, meticulously scrubbing off the filth, she knew she would have a bit of time to herself. It was safe now to worry about how she was going to track the wolf, since it had evaded her for five nights. It was safe now to wonder if Lo was still angry with her about refusing to tell Logan. It was safe now to wonder what would happen if she did.

~

When Lo got out of the shower, he was glad he wouldn't have to be doing that kind of cleaning again for

33

a whole month, but he was also glad that he was out of school now for the rest of the year.

He and his mom would be heading home to see Ma and Pa in a day or two, and they'd spend Christmas Eve and Day together as a family. If his mom followed her traditional plan, they'd come back to Ann Arbor on December 26, which gave him a whole week before school started again.

"Hey, Mom, is it okay if I go hang out with Alex and J.J. for a while this afternoon, since we're going home pretty soon?" he called as he left his room after getting dressed.

"Sure," she told him as she looked up from her laptop with a smile. "Have a good time, and text me if you need anything," she said as she held up the cell phone he had gotten for his birthday, but was only allowed to use when he was hanging out with friends or his grandparents and without her. She promised that when he was sixteen he would be allowed to carry it all the time as long as he didn't run up the bill or get in trouble with it in school. That was the thing about his mom. She may have been a single parent, but she was way stricter with him than the other single parents he knew of were on their kids.

Even when she had to take her night classes on Tuesdays, she didn't leave him at home with the TV and a bowl of leftover spaghetti to microwave for supper. She paid a grad assistant in the master's program twenty-five bucks an hour to stay at the apartment with him. Lo didn't like to think that he needed a babysitter anymore, especially now that he was thirteen, but once he had refused to let her get someone, and he was never making that stupid mistake again.

34

He had thought that hanging out in her office while she was in class would be way cooler than being at home with a sitter, but she refused to give him the password to the desktop in her office, and after spending an hour trying to crack it, he realized that it was impossible. That left him with absolutely nothing to do for the rest of the night but homework or read one of the archeology books from her shelves. So now, he always chose the sitter, and most of the time she tried to get a guy to do it so that they'd be more likely to have something in common. Plus, he was allowed to do whatever he wanted once his homework and chores were done, so more often than not, he ended up beating the crap out of a college dude on whatever Xbox game they happened to pick, and that gave him awesome bragging rights with J.J. and Alex.

Lo took the cell phone from his mom and kissed her on the cheek as he did. "I know, I know. Be back before supper or text if I'm eating with them," he quoted her usual instructions before she could.

"Be careful, Lo, and let me know when you get there," she was looking at the screen again.

"Yes, ma'am," he opened the door but turned back to say, "Bye, Mom. Love you."

"I love you, too," she looked up just in time to see him send her a smile as he shut the door.

Lo walked the few blocks to Alex's house and texted his mother when Mrs. Thompson let him in. Her response reminded him to be polite and to text if he needed her.

"How's it going, Thack?" Alex called from the den. He and J.J. were already playing a game, and they pressed pause so that his entrance wouldn't cause any casualties.

"Not too, bad, man." he answered, as he picked up a third controller, and they started a new game to make room for him. "How are y'all?" he made sure that he included J.J., who had yet to say anything.

"Well, we've got Christmas at the end of the week and no school until January 3$^{rd}$, so I'm great." Alex answered. J.J. just grunted in Lo's direction when he could afford to look away from the screen. That was his way. He was better with video game characters than actual people.

They continued playing until Alex had thoroughly humiliated both of his opponents. But by that time, they had already begun speculating about Christmas presents, and no one really cared who had accumulated the most kill points, except maybe J.J., but if he did, he didn't say.

"This year I'm asking for a bigger flat screen, since the one I got for my birthday two years ago pretty much sucks," J.J. announced.

"What's wrong with it?" Lo wondered.

"It isn't the new 3-D kind, and *that's* the kind of movies they're making all the time now." If J.J. wasn't playing a video game, then he was watching a comic book movie, which Lo had to admit, did look a lot cooler in 3-D than on regular film. "What d'you guys want?"

"I was thinking of asking for a new iPhone, but then I wouldn't get anything for my Xbox, so I'm not sure, yet" Alex admitted.

There was really only one thing that Lo wanted for Christmas this year, and it was something that couldn't be bought, something he was sure his mom wouldn't allow him to have. So he told the guys the exact same thing that he had told his mom: "I just want money. There isn't anything I really want, right now, so that way, I can start saving up for something bigger, and maybe by the time I do figure out what I want, it won't take me as long to get it."

"Thack, you're one weird dude, you know that?" Alex asked.

J.J. looked at Lo like he agreed with Alex. "Why not just ask for something flat out, if you're looking to speed things up. Waiting a week for Christmas to come is a heck of a lot shorter than having to wait until you save up for something."

Alex's mom called the boys for supper, and her timing saved Lo the trouble of trying to explain the fact that the one thing he wanted for Christmas didn't come from a store, so he was grateful. To keep himself out of hot water with his mom, he sent her the mandatory text, and then took a seat at the table with the Thompsons.

Eating with Alex's family was the closest thing to being home that Lo had found in Ann Arbor. Maybe they didn't pray before they ate, but they did have a big meal together at night, which is exactly what Lo would have been doing, if he had been in Manteo with Ma and Pa tonight.

When Lo was really young, he and his mom had lived with her parents, and so even though they had moved out of Ma and Pa's house when he was seven so his mom could go back to NCSU and get her master's degree, he still thought of it as home. He even had a bedroom there that he still kept some of his stuff in, but he had to share it with his cousins if they came over when he was in Ann Arbor.

Before he and his mom had moved to Raleigh, he saw his mom's siblings pretty often. She was the second baby that Ma and Pa had, and she was the oldest girl. Only Uncle Tommy was older than she was, and after Lo's mom came Uncle Jude, Uncle Matt, Aunt Sylvia, and finally Aunt Cathy. None of them lived at home anymore because they were all grown up and in college or married now, but they all came back whenever they could. Even Aunt Cathy had gotten engaged at Thanksgiving this year, and that only left Lo's mom unmarried.

Mrs. Thompson had made pot roast, and when he had filled his plate and set it down again, the sight of the roast with gravy and vegetables on the side only made him miss Ma and Pa more than he already did. Alex's family was smaller than the Thackerys were when they got together, but he and J.J. made the group seem a little bigger.

As he took his first bite, Lo looked at Mr. Thompson, Alex's dad. Lo hadn't spent much time with him, but from the few words he had spoken to Lo, he seemed to be a nice guy. Of course, when Alex talked about his dad, it was always to say that he had done something really lame or annoying, or both, but Lo had never heard Alex say anything terrible about him either.

"Lo, are you and your mom going back down South for the holidays?" Mrs. Thompson wondered.

"Yes, ma'am. We'll be leaving tomorrow, probably," Lo answered her, and wondered how long she had been married to Alex's dad.

Divorce was pretty common with Lo's friends' parents, so his mom wasn't the only one on her own, but she was always careful to avoid questions about Lo's father.

"It's good to hear that you guys'll be back home for the holidays," Mr. Thompson added, smiling at his family and then Lo before passing him another roll.

## Chapter 5

Lo was seriously excited when they loaded the car at seven the next morning and headed south. He had been home a month before, but for some odd reason, it felt more like it had been the three-month wait between Christmas and Easter. He wanted Ma's food and Pa's aggravations, his own warm bed and the loud, crowded atmosphere that came with fourteen people sharing a four-bedroom house.

What Lo wasn't excited about was the fourteen-hour drive from Ann Arbor to Manteo. His mom split the trip in two, since he was old enough now to occupy himself in the car with his iPod, which she had reminded him to charge last night. He also had a car charger, just in case. They'd stop for gas and lunch, and then they'd drive five more hours before they stopped again for supper and got a hotel. Then they had another three-and-a-half hours left to look forward to when they got up. *But it'll totally be worth it because by tomorrow afternoon I'll be eating Ma's party mix by the handful!*

~

Lillie glanced over at her sleeping son. She'd been driving for about three hours and was getting a little groggy herself, so she planned to take the next exit and buy some coffee. *Of course, gas station coffee is nothing like the coffee from Hill of Beans,* she thought before she could stop herself.

Though she had become seriously addicted to it by the time she was a college junior, and her daily rendezvous with Logan there only exacerbated the problem, she never went back to Hill of Beans after Logan was cured and was lost to her. It hurt too much, sitting there without him. Remembering what she had had, if only for a short time.

And it was about this time of year when she had made the decision that had determined her fate and that of Lo. Thinking back, she could admit now that before it happened, she had been hoping it would for days. Once she'd discovered that he was more than his carefully constructed hedonistic image implied, she couldn't help but fall in love with the same gorgeous face that so many others had. But there was more to Logan than his good cheekbones and dark hair. He was inherently kind and unfailingly loyal, and he could love unreservedly, even though he would never admit it, and she doubted that any other woman who'd come before or after would agree. For all those reasons, she had chosen the campus playboy, Logan Michaels.

Even after thirteen-and-a-half years, she could still feel her hand in his and hear him whisper a warning: "I don't want the same things you want. I can't give them to you." And with full knowledge of that, she had vowed to take whatever he could give her and make it be enough.

She wiped the tears with the back of her hand as she drove, since he wasn't there to brush them away with his thumbs as he had that first time. If she let herself, she could still feel the warmth that surrounded her as she lay wrapped in his arms beneath the covers. She could breathe in his cologne, as if her nose was still nuzzled in the crook of his neck and shoulder. She could taste his kiss as if his lips had just left hers.

All it took was closing her eyes and drifting back. She was twenty again. Her biggest worries were finding a cure and what she would do when graduation came. *And that, more than anything else, was why there had never been another.* In spite of all the time and distance, Logan was still close enough to touch.

From the corner of her eye, Lillie saw Lo stir and smiled. She may have given Logan a big part of herself, but he hadn't left her empty-handed.

~

Lo opened his eyes and saw that they were still driving. "Where are we?" he wondered once he'd stretched and yawned like a lion.

"We're on the turnpike, not too far from Pennsylvania," his mom laughed. "I'm planning to take a break for coffee at the next exit."

"Good! Latte or Frappuccino?" he teased. His mom had a weird thing about only drinking coffee at certain temperatures during certain times of the day.

"I'm thinking latte, since we haven't eaten lunch yet. Frappuccino feels like dessert today," she grinned.

"Can I have one too?" As a general rule, Lo wasn't allowed to drink much coffee with his mom, but she let it slide on Saturday mornings and chilly winter nights when they weren't going anywhere, or they had no plans the next day. Ma always told him no because, she said, it would stunt his growth.

"You may . . . so long as you promise not to get too antsy. We still have about an hour to an hour-and-a-half before we stop for lunch, so you'll have to wait until then to get out and walk around."

41

"Yes, ma'am," he agreed. He knew his mom was serious about him behaving in the car. He could still remember her pulling over on the interstate to spank him about four years ago for throwing a fit because he wanted out of his seatbelt, and she wouldn't let him. Plus, the fewer stops they made, the quicker they would get home, which was fine with Lo.

When they'd gotten gas and two lattes, his mom pulled back onto I-80 and turned on the radio. She loved music from the '90s and early 2000s, so it was no surprise to Lo when the station started playing Aerosmith's "Don't Want to Miss a Thing." What did surprise him was that when he looked over at her, expecting to see her smiling as she was singing with the chorus, he thought he saw a tear on her cheek. But it couldn't have been a tear he saw; his mom never cried.

~

After a night in Comfort Inn and breakfast at IHOP, Lillie and Lo reluctantly returned to the car for the last few hours of their trip. They were the hardest for Lo and subsequently the hardest for Lillie. By this point, her usually easy-going son became moody and had a hair-trigger temper for the last leg of the journey, but as she had always done in the past, she bit her tongue and told herself that she would hardly have behaved any better on a fourteen-hour drive.

About ninety minutes in, Lo reached over and turned down Savage Garden, right in the middle of "Truly, Madly, Deeply."

"Hey! I was singing to that," Lillie protested.

"I need to ask you something," he informed her.

The tone had her playful rebuke dying before she

spoke it. "Ok," she said instead. "What is it?"

"Why are you so sure that my dad wouldn't want to help if he knew about our situation?" He looked her in the eye without blinking.

She took a breath before answering to keep from losing her cool. Two testy people trapped in a car for another two hours would be seriously dangerous. "I've already told you that we can't tell your father about the situation because he has no reason to trust or help us, and even if he did believe us, there would be nothing he could do to improve the situation."

"You can't know that, mom! You just can't! I think you don't want to tell him because you're afraid!"

"Logan Thackery, don't you raise your voice to me, young man."

"It's true, mom," he insisted, albeit in a lower tone. "You're afraid of what will happen if he knows about us."

"What on Earth would I be afraid of, son?" Lille couldn't keep her voice even anymore.

"Maybe you don't want to lose me," Lo shrugged.

"Lo, I don't care how much money and power your father has now; there is absolutely no way he would ever be able to take you away from me if I was still breathing," she told him with an arched brow.

"Well, then will you take me to Raleigh on the way back to Michigan?" She heard the eagerness in his voice and was sorry for it.

"Don't you think it's a little out-of-the-way for us to do that? The trip's pretty long as it is," she tried reasoning.

"What's another hour or so? It's nothing compared to THIRTEEN YEARS!" He was close to crying, so she didn't chide him for raising his to her voice again, though it was tempting.

"My love, I know that it's been hard on you growing up without a father, and I'm sorry that it had to be this way, but I'm not going to apologize for making the choice I did before you were born. I did what was best for all three of us, and if I could do it all over again, I would. Your father would have done right by us, even if he didn't understand how it happened. He would have done it because that's the kind of man he is, but he would have also felt trapped and hopeless, and soon enough, he would have resented both of us for it. When I got pregnant with you, he was just beginning to figure out who he was in the world and who he wanted to be. If I had told him about us, he would have had to sacrifice all that and work for his own father to provide for us, and he would never have found his place. I couldn't do that to him. I couldn't do that to *you*."

"But he *did* go to work for his father!" Lo cried. "So you kept us apart for nothing!"

"What did you say?" she took her eyes from the road to glance at him and found his cheeks wet and red.

"I looked him up on the Internet. He took over his dad's company not too long ago. *That's* how I know he lives in Raleigh."

"Why did you do that, Lo? I told you not to contact him!" She was too stunned by Lo's defiance to think.

"I *haven't*! But I have a right to know who my dad is, and he has a right to know about me!" Lo was screaming now. Lillie looked for a wide shoulder and pulled off the interstate.

"You may be a teenager now, Lo, but I am still your mother, and until you're old enough to be on your own, you will do as I say. Do you hear me, young man?" She unbuckled he seatbelt and leaned over so that her face was inches from his. "I said, *do you hear me?*"

"Yes, ma'am," he whispered, staring at his lap.

"Look me in the eye and promise me that you will not try to call or email your father until I say that you may do so." Lillie's tone brooked no argument. She watched as he slowly raised his head and met her eyes.

"I promise."

"Good. Now, let's not talk about this anymore until we figure out what to do about your lycanthropy. Once that problem is taken care of, *then* we'll see about finding the best way to tell your dad about us. Okay?" Strangely, Lillie found herself smiling at the thought of seeing Logan again and sharing the son they had made with him. *They're so much alike*, she shook her head.

"Okay," Lo sighed.

As she pulled carefully back onto the road, Lillie turned the radio back on and deliberately put it on the heavy metal that Lo was so fond of. When they had ridden a few miles in silence save the pounding from the speakers, she put her hand on his. "I'm sorry I yelled at you, baby."

"It's okay, mom," Lo mumbled. "I'm sorry I yelled at you, too," he said as he took her hand and squeezed.

## Chapter 6

Lo had a great time at home for Christmas. Somehow, his mom always managed to surprise him on Christmas Morning, even though he had helped her put their stuff in the car. He still couldn't figure it out, but he wasn't sure he wanted to. The whole day was almost like some kind of movie. All the Thackerys were together, and everyone was excited about seeing each other again and opening gifts and eating Christmas dinner, which, he had to admit, was even better than presents, especially when it had been ages since he'd eaten Ma's dressing.

The fact that it had been such a good day made what he was doing that night even harder than it might have been if he and his mom had fought again like they had in the car on the way down.

He felt bad, but honestly, there was no other way. His mom was dead set against him finding his dad, and she was so upset by the idea that she didn't even make any sense when she tried to explain why he couldn't do it. *If I leave it up to her, I'll never get to meet him.*

Lo checked the watch that Pa had given him last year. It was a nice one that had a button you could press to make the face glow in the dark so that you could always read the time. *12:15. That meant it was now December 26ᵗʰ, and his mom would be up in about five hours, so he'd better hope that he could find some rides between now and then.* The glow from his watch faded, and the only lights he saw were the ones lining the streets.

For the past fifteen minutes, he had been walking at a steady pace away from home. If he could make it the thirty miles to Elizabeth City, then he could buy a ticket and ride a Greyhound from there to Raleigh, he hoped, but he wasn't too sure if Raleigh was a stop on that route or not. *But there weren't any other options tonight, and if he didn't leave before his mom headed out of town in the morning, there would be absolutely no way to get away from her long enough to catch a bus.*

Manteo was normally a quiet little town, but it was even quieter when it was the middle of the night. He hadn't even seen one car since he sneaked out the door and shut it carefully behind him. *What if it takes hours to find one?* he wondered.

After another thirty minutes, Lo was getting chilly, despite the coat he'd snagged before he left and the Thermos full of coffee he stole from the pot when none of the adults were looking. That the cold kept seeping in was what made it worse than the walking.

He had his backpack on, but he had only put one change of clean clothes, a pair or two of extra socks and underwear, his map, a charger cord, a bag of party mix, *The Zombie Survival Guide* and all the cash he'd gotten for Christmas inside. He'd thought about blankets and a flashlight, but then decided that they would make his bag unnecessarily heavy, which would be a problem if he had to walk most of the way. His pockets were stuffed too. He had his phone, his keys to the apartment in Ann Arbor and Ma and Pa's, and a pocket knife that he had gotten one summer a few years back when Uncle Tommy realized he didn't own one.

He kept moving and tried not to run. Running would

make him tired, and also it might seem suspicious to anyone who happened to see him. And he figured that people wouldn't want to give someone a ride if that someone looked like he had just committed some kind of crime, like shoplifting, and was trying to get away.

He watched the clouds his breath made in the cool winter air and wondered what the temperature was. It seemed to be getting colder, but that could be his imagination. He checked the time again. *12:56.*

Time seemed to be moving slower than normal. He guessed that was a good thing . . . unless he was just making really slow progress, which would be a bad thing.

As he walked, Lo tried to entertain himself by imagining that the reason he was out here own his own was not because he was deliberately disobeying his mom and running away, but because the zombie apocalypse had taken place, just like in his favorite video game series *Left 4 Dead.* Anything was better than knowing he would have to face his mom sooner or later, even the rise of the undead.

There were a lot of different scenarios he could think of that could cause people to turn into something other than human, but his favorite was the one in the book *I Am Legend.* They had made a movie based on it back in the day, when Will Smith was still doing lots of movies all the time, but Lo liked the book way better. *I guess I get that from Mom.* Not that she didn't like movies. She was a collector, but her kind of movies and Lo's didn't even feel like the same things. His mom preferred to watch movies so old that they had been filmed in black-and-white for Pete's sake, and by now, they had to be almost a hundred years old. Her favorites were *Gone with the Wind* and

*Casablanca*, and for some crazy reason, she cried every single time she watched them. Why a person would like a movie that made them cry, Lo couldn't understand, but then again, she was a girl, and even at thirteen, he had come to realize that girls made no sense whatsoever most of the time.

He imagined that the abandoned streets and shadowed houses were that way because he was one of the last surviving humans, and he had to find his way to one of the compounds up north that were rumored to be populated with uninfected humans. His Thermos was actually a rifle that he had found in an abandoned house a few towns back, and his backpack was loaded down with enough shells to double-tap a horde of zombies. He watched carefully for any movement that was larger than a squirrel or rabbit. If one of those dead heads saw him before he saw it, there would be no hope. He decided that his zombies were kind of like Robert Neville's vamp-zombies, and they could be harmed by sunlight, but he vowed then and there not to let a girl make him lose focus. After all, look what happened in the book. Lo would be legend all right, but he would be a *living* legend.

He smiled as he walked, imagining being smarter than the Robert in the book *and* the one Will Smith played. *That* **would** *be legendary, if I could best Will Smith!* But even Lo, whose imagination had always been active, couldn't sustain that one, so he was back in North Carolina, walking in the dark, with no gun, no ammo, and no garlic-hating, undead monsters on his trail. There was only his mother's wrath behind him and his father's unknown reaction in front.

By the time he saw the flash of headlights and a car

actually pulled over, Lo had been walking for three hours. It was three a.m., and his first thought was *Oh, crap! What if this is mom?* He had barely made it to the Virginia Dare Memorial Bridge, which meant he had gone about two miles out of Manteo. That wasn't very far at all for someone in a car, but he was already tired.

When the Honda's window came down, Lo could see that the driver was young. Older than he was, since the guy had a license, but way younger than his mom.

"Do you need some help?" the dude asked.

"I'm headed for Raleigh, which is where my dad lives," Lo answered. He had already decided to stick to the truth as much as possible. It just seemed easier.

"How did you wind up in the Outer Banks, kid?" the dude was beginning to look a little nervous.

"My grandparents live in Manteo, and I was supposed to catch a flight back home at the Dare County airport, but something happened, and the plane never came, so I'm walking back home." Lo hoped it didn't sound as ridiculous to the dude in the car as it did to him when he heard it come out of his own mouth.

"Don't you know that hitchhiking is illegal? Couldn't you have called your grandparents to come and get you until your dad arranges for another flight?" *Yup, it sounded ridiculous to him too.*

"Look, I've been pretty much on my own for a while now. I'm not scared of the dark, and I can find my own way back to Raleigh if you aren't gonna give me a ride." Lo stepped back from the window and walked a few paces away from the car, still heading out of town.

"It isn't a good idea to be walking on this bridge at night, kid. You could have easily been hit," the dude shook his head and sighed, like he knew better than to be doing what he was about to.

"It also isn't a good idea to pick up strangers at night," Lo warned. "You could have easily invited a teenage serial killer into your car."

"You have a point," the dude grinned ruefully. "And I can't let a kid walk all the way back to Raleigh in the middle of the night," he said as he leaned over and opened the passenger door from the inside.

Lo climbed in despite the warning bells in his head screaming that he knew better than to get into a car with a stranger; then he shut the door and pulled on his seatbelt. They drove for a few minutes in silence until the dude spoke. "You gonna tell me your name, since I'm gonna be stuck in the car with you for the next three hours?"

"Phil," Lo told him, and was glad that the interior of the car was dark, so that the guy couldn't see his face. "What's yours?"

"I'm Ben."

The car was quiet again, and in the dark coziness, Lo had almost fallen asleep when he remembered to ask, "Where were you going in the middle of the night before you stopped and picked me up?"

"Back to Raleigh, too. I'm from Nags Head, and I'm heading back to NCSU."

Lo was able to pry his eyes open a little wider at that. NCSU was his parents' alma matter. "Doesn't your break last until after New Year's?"

"Yeah, but I got kinda bored at home and decided to go back to campus. The others'll be back soon enough, and until they are, I'll have the apartment to myself and the Xbox too, for that matter," Ben said.

"Do you ever play *Left 4 Dead*?" Lo ventured. That was

a safe enough topic, and one that wouldn't give Ben anything to tell the police, if they ever asked him.

When Ben shook Lo awake, it was still dark, but it was 6:30 in the morning on Sunday, December 26th. They were coming into Raleigh, and Ben wanted to know his dad's address. Lo yawned, and blinked confusedly over at him while debating telling him the truth again. *What difference does it make now? I'll likely never see this guy again, and by the time he figures out I'm a missing kid, I'll probably have called mom anyway.* Besides, if he got Ben to drop him off at his dad's apartment, he wouldn't have to pay for a taxi and would have made the entire trip for free.

He gave Ben the address he'd memorized from the Internet white pages, and it was one of the really swanky ones downtown. Ben's face had that suspicious look again, but there was little Lo could do about it now.

"Are you sure this is the right place?"

"Of *course* it's the right place! I've lived in the same apartment for the past three years!" Lo fished the keys out of his pocket and pulled out twenty bucks. "Here," he said, passing the bill to Ben. "For my part of the gas."

Ben looked at the money hesitantly and shrugged. "Looks like your dad won't miss it."

"You're right. He won't," Lo agreed, grabbing his bag and getting out of the car. "Thanks for the ride, man," he called, slamming the door quickly so that Ben didn't have time to ask any more questions. He headed toward the entrance as calmly as he could.

Lo stood in the entryway with the street to his back. It was a little after seven in the morning. If he took another step, he would finally know his father, but if he took that step, there was no going back.

## Chapter 7

Logan Michaels was enjoying the soft warmth of his bed. It was empty this morning, but that was only because he had just come back from Asheville last night, and after two days with his family, he just wanted some alone time. If he wanted company, there were plenty he could call tonight, or even tomorrow. For the moment, he was debating whether he wanted to get up and take a shower or sleep a few more minutes. Nobody would blame him if he slept in until 7:30. Everyone was still on Christmas vacation anyway.

He was coaxing himself out of the sheets with thoughts of coffee, when he heard his buzzer. That had him on his feet and grabbing some clothes on his way to the door. He wasn't expecting anyone, and he didn't have any meetings scheduled until after the first of the year. Because it was early and logic wasn't working at the moment, he pressed the button and demanded, "WHAT?"

"Can I please come up, Mr. Michaels?" a young voice asked.

Logan couldn't figure out if it was a boy or a girl, but he felt a twinge of guilt that he had yelled at one of the neighbor's kids. "Fine," he said a little softer and let the kid in.

A few minutes passed, and he heard a knock. By that time, he'd put a shirt and jeans on, just in case the kid had gotten locked out and he had to go downstairs. He opened the door and suddenly found that he couldn't breathe.

~

Lo stood on the other side of the door that his father just opened. For a minute, he had to work super-hard to breathe. This man looked exactly like the picture Lo had found on the Michaels' Corporate Management website, except now he was wearing a t-shirt and jeans instead of an expensive suit. *It's really him!* was all Lo had time to think.

"Who are you?" Logan bellowed.

"Hello, sir. My name is Lo Thackery," his words came out barely louder than whispers.

"And why exactly are you at my door this early in the morning, Lo Thackery?" His father wasn't smiling. In fact, he was frowning really hard.

"I had no other place to go," Lo admitted.

"Do I *know* you?" The scowl on his father's face didn't seem to be a very good sign.

"No, sir, but you knew my mother once," Lo said to the floor.

"Did I?" Logan raised a brow.

"Yes, sir, you did," Lo swallowed and tried to decide how to get it over with. "Her name is Lillie Thackery, and you met her in 2007, while y'all were students at NCSU."

"And I'm just supposed to help a kid I don't even know because I dated his mother thirteen years ago?" Logan questioned with frustration.

"No, sir," Lo made himself meet Logan's stare. "You're supposed to help me because you're my father."

~

"What did you say?" Logan heard the strangled words come from his mouth as he continued to stare at what could have been his own face from twenty years ago. If he didn't know for sure that Preston's voice had changed and he'd gotten taller, he might think this was his younger brother standing in front of him.

"I said you're my father," the kid repeated firmly. Logan stepped back and opened the door wide enough for him to come in. This conversation did not need to continue in the hallway.

He watched as the boy walked inside and stopped just past the door. Logan gestured to the couch, and the boy sat down. Logan sat on the edge of his favorite leather recliner, steepled his hands in front of his mouth, and waited.

The boy eyed his shoes like he had never seen them before.

Logan cleared his throat. "Why are you here? Are you looking for money?"

The kid's chin came up at that. "Mom and I don't need your money. We get by on our own."

"So, what **do** you want?" Logan didn't care if his tone was cold. The little liar deserved it.

"To meet my dad." The kid's eyes, *his own* freaking eyes, stared back at him with fury.

"You keep saying that, but how is that even possible? I don't have a clue who this Lillie chick is, and in case you didn't know, for what you claim to have happened to be true, I'd have to know her pretty well." Logan smirked, and the boy was on his feet.

"You knew her all right! Better than any other guy ever did!"

"You sure about that?" Logan cocked a brow.

"Look in the mirror, dude! What other proof do you need?"

"To attest paternity? How about a DNA test?" Logan countered.

"Are you saying my mom is a liar?" The boy was boiling.

"I'm saying you can't be right about this, so yeah, if she told you that I'm your dad, she lied." Logan, on the other hand, was cool, deliberately so.

"So it's just a coincidence that we look like the same guy, only at different ages, and we both have the same name?" the kid bit off.

"I didn't tell you my first name, pal." *Now we're getting somewhere!*

"Your first name is Philip. But I wasn't talking about that one. I meant that we're both named Logan." Now Lo was the one smirking.

"Looking alike means nothing. Haven't you heard of doppelgangers?" Logan watched the boy deflate and moved in for the kill. "And having the same name means even less than that. The last time I checked, this was a free country, and people could name their kids whatever the crap they wanted to."

"Yeah, and that means my mom *chose* to name me after you because you're my father!" Lo was still standing and glaring up at Logan.

"Prove it." Logan crossed his arms and scooted a bit further back into his chair.

"I c—" Lo was interrupted by his cell phone ringing and buzzing away in his pocket.

~

"Logan Daniel Thackery, *where on Earth are you?*" Lillie cried into her phone. When he wasn't in bed, she hadn't been too worried, but since no one else in the house had seen him after bedtime last night, and his backpack was missing, Lillie had become irate.

"I'm in Raleigh," Lo answered bravely.

"*Raleigh?* Why would you go to—" she began, but then there was no need to finish her question. "Lo, please tell me you didn't. Tell me you did not try to find your father." She covered her face with her hand and prayed that she was wrong while she waited for her son's response.

"I did find him," Lo swallowed.

"Is he with you right now?" She knew the answer to that one too, yet she still hoped to be wrong. When Lo didn't respond, she said, "Pass him the phone this instant, young man."

There was a slight pause and an exchange she couldn't quite make out, and then she heard what she hadn't heard in Lo's lifetime except when she was dreaming. "Logan Michaels speaking."

"Logan." Her throat closed with the word.

"Yes?" There was impatience in his voice, but she was still struggling to form any sort of sentence.

She cleared her throat and pulled out her professor mode. If she could talk in front of hundreds of freshmen every week, she could talk to Logan over the phone. "L-Mr. Michaels, let me apologize for my son. It was very rude, not to mention presumptuous, for him to show up at your door with no preamble. I'll leave right away to come and get him, but I'm afraid it will take a few hours to get there because I'm in Manteo at the moment."

"Wait a minute. Are you telling me that this little boy came all the way from Manteo *by himself? In the middle of the night?*" Logan sounded incredulous.

"He's quite resourceful when he wants to be," Lillie tried not to sound proud as she said it.

"Apparently so," Logan agreed. "He claims that I'm his father. Do you know anything about that, Ms. . . . ?"

"Lillie. Call me Lillie. And, yes, I do." *Oh, boy.*

"Would you care to explain that to me, Lillie?" Hearing Logan say her name again, even in his annoyed tone, was almost too much.

At last, she managed, "Not at present, if you please, Mr. Michaels. I think my son's paternity is something better discussed face-to-face."

"Bu—"

"I do promise to explain everything to you just as soon as I get to Raleigh, Mr. Michaels," Lillie interrupted before he could protest.

"Fine," Logan told her, and the way he said it sent her back to NCSU when they were quarrelling once more over something in the stacks. She shook herself back to the present in time to take down the address he gave her.

"Thank you for being so understanding. I can appreciate how much of an inconvenience my son has been to you already." She was careful not to let her professionalism slip. If it did, she would have no way of continuing the conversation.

"I'm not sure you do, but if you aren't here by noon, I'm calling the police, and you'll have them to deal with." The smooth charm that he had skated by on was still there, but she knew all too well the potency of the venom underneath.

"I understand. Will you put Lo back on, please?" Lillie kept her voice as neutral as she could.

"Certainly. Goodbye, Lillie," he told her, and she knew exactly how he looked as he did.

~

Logan handed the phone back to the boy and had to admit that he was being pretty mature about the fact that he was about to get reamed for what was probably the first of multiple times today. Even though the kid paled as he took the cell, his hand was steady as he brought it to his ear. "Yes, ma'am. Yes, ma'am. I understand. Yes ma'am. I l-love you too, Mom," he said before hanging up and sitting back down on the couch, where he proceeded to hold his head in his hands.

They were both quiet for a few more minutes before Lo wondered aloud, "Do you think she'll calm down any by the time she gets here?"

Logan almost felt sorry for the little guy. Almost. Then he remembered that the kid had run away from home in the middle of the night and presumably hitchhiked the two hundred miles to Logan's door, and he believed that he was Logan's son. "Probably not."

~

When Lo had been sitting on the couch for a little while, his dad turned on the flat screen that he hadn't even noticed before.

"You hungry?"

"A little," Lo admitted. "But Mom says I'm not supposed to bother you about anything other than to use the bathroom, and that if I do, things will be 'even worse' when we get home."

"Well, what if I said that I was going to the kitchen to get myself some Cap'n Crunch anyway, and making an extra bowl wouldn't count as bothering," his dad offered. "Would you eat some?"

"Yes, sir," Lo nodded and watched his dad walk off to where the kitchen must be. He came back a few moments later with two bowls and handed one to Lo. "Thank you, sir," he said as he took it.

"So where is home for you, anyway, kid? Manteo?" Logan asked around a bite of cereal.

"No, sir. We used to live there, when I was real little, but now we live in Michigan so Mom can finish her PhD," Lo was careful to wait until his mouth was empty to speak.

Logan whistled. "Michigan is a long way from North Carolina."

"It's fourteen hours from Manteo to Ann Arbor," Lo agreed. "That's why we aren't home very often, but Mom promised that when she passes her comps, she'll try to find someplace that's a lot closer to work at while she finishes her dissertation."

"So, it's just you and your mom, then?" his dad took another bite.

"Yeah—I–I mean, yes, sir," Lo's face turned red as he realized that he had just committed another error that might compound his punishment.

"Why did you come looking for me, Lo?" Logan pressed mute on the game he had stopped on.

"To meet you," he repeated.

"No, I mean, why did you come looking for me *today?*" For the first time, his dad actually didn't look mad. Instead, he seemed curious.

"Because it was the first time since I found out who you are that I could." Lo took another bite and was careful not to drip milk on the couch or the hardwood floor.

When Lo finished his cereal, he asked the way to the kitchen so that he could clean it up, but his dad said there was a dishwasher, and adding one extra little bowl and spoon in the next load wouldn't be a bother. So he and his dad watched ESPN together for a little while before Lo saw that his dad had an Xbox in the cabinet his flat screen was sitting on.

Lo cleared his throat. "Um, sir . . ."

"You can call me Logan," his dad chuckled.

"Mr. Logan, sir, what games do you have for your Xbox?"

"Have you ever played *Call of Duty*?"

~

When Lillie buzzed the apartment a few minutes after eleven, Logan almost jumped out of the recliner and dropped his controller. He also took a hit on-screen, which gave the little twerp even more time to get kills. He paused the game and rose to get the door, casting an I-wish-I-could-say-I'm-sorry-it-sucks-to-be-you look Lo's way. He saw Lo set his controller carefully on the couch beside him and swallow hard. Logan managed to turn to the door before he broke into a grin.

For the second time that morning, he opened his door to a stranger's knock, but this time the person on the other side could not be considered a child. She was small but athletically built and had seemingly long, dark hair pulled into a loose bun on top of her head. She had a pointed chin and nose, and she was giving him a practiced smile. He took his time looking, wondering if they really had been together in college. She was wearing a white knitted sweater and deep green leggings, and she seemed both cozy and stylish. Her eyes, he saw, were as sharp as her chin and as deep green as her pants, beneath the slightly smoky makeup she wore on them.

He had to admit, as she stood here in his doorway, that there was something studious about her that would have put him off her instantly, had he considered seeing her. And there was nothing familiar about her.

"You must be Lillie," he sent her his own prepared smile and extended a hand.

"Hello, Logan," she shook his hand firmly and followed him inside. He gestured to the couch and watched Lo flinch as she sat down right beside him.

"May I get you something to drink?" he offered to keep himself from laughing.

"No, thank you," she answered. "I suppose that I've kept you in suspense long enough."

## Chapter 8

Lillie reached into her brown leather satchel and retrieved an old journal and a faded expandable file folder that was stuffed to the brim. She laid them on the coffee table, within easy reach for Logan. "How much do you remember about the time between the Spring Break of your junior year and the one during your senior year?"

"Absolutely nothing. Why do you ask?" He didn't know what his amnesia had to do with anything, or how she even knew about it.

"Don't you ever wonder what happened to you during that year and why you can't recall a thing about it?" Logan found that Lillie was watching him closely while she waited for his reply, and the kid hadn't said a word since she came in.

"I did, right after I first woke up in those woods without a stitch of clothes on, scratches all over myself, and a migraine that hung on for days, but after you've seen about three dozen neurologists and shrinks, and none of them can figure anything out, you just chalk it up to the unexplained and move on. And, I don't see how that has anything to do with why your kid thinks I'm his father." It was Logan's turn to watch closely.

"Because it was during that time period that you happened to swagger into my section of the stacks for the first time with those eyes of cool steel and that quick, cocky smile. And it was during that time period that your

63

son was conceived." Logan watched as something flashed in her eyes that seemed to dare him to contradict her.

"Don't take this the wrong way, Ms. Thackery, but I'm going to need a little more than just your word that he's mine . . . since I have no memory of you before you walked in here a few minutes ago," he was careful with his tone, making sure to remain polite.

"I thought as much. You haven't changed," she almost smiled. "That's why I'm agreeable to a DNA test as soon as we're able to get one."

That she hadn't faltered one bit at the prospect of irrefutable evidence against her claim took him aback. *I bet that woman's a killer at cards.*

"Until that time," she continued, "I brought along quite a bit of other evidence, should you be interested. This, for example," she tapped the journal with her index finger, "will probably answer a vast majority of the questions surrounding your missing year."

Until that point, Logan had been able to control himself, but there was something maddening about the way that woman spoke, and he was raising his voice to say, "Seriously? Seriously? Did you *seriously* just claim to know what nearly fifty medical professionals unanimously do not?" He laughed, and the boy jumped at the rough sound. "Not only that, but you *also* expect me to swallow this nonsense about fathering a child! I just told you that I can't remember a thing from that year, so who's to say that you aren't making up our supposed past acquaintance entirely? I'd be a fool not to question it, and only another fool wouldn't expect me to see that. No, you strike me as a sensible woman, so you couldn't possibly be saying that." The edge of his voice was sharp, but he didn't care if it sliced.

"Always so logical," she sighed. "I'd tell you to ask Andrew or Mark for corroboration, but I doubt they were even aware of me." *If she knows the guys, maybe we really did spend time together.*

"Okay. You know who I roomed with in Wolf Village. That still doesn't prove we had a relationship," he refuted his own thoughts as well as hers. "And if we were together, why wouldn't my closest friends know who you were?"

"I'm not exactly your type of girl, Logan. I imagine you didn't want them to know you were temporarily monogamous, especially with someone so . . . shall we say, scholarly."

That much was true. Even now, Logan avoided going out with the women who were more concerned with their IQs than their dress sizes. It wasn't that he had anything against them. Beauty could still have brains. The terms weren't mutually exclusive. He had women on his board of directors who were Ivy Leaguers. But he drew the line at dating them. They were too much work, with their unfamiliar set of rules and penchants for creating new ones. What was the point of learning all that with no guarantee of a win, when he could pick up a socialite and have the upper hand five minutes after meeting her? And the socialites already knew the game. There were no messy strings to get untangled from at the end of a night or two. With the smart ones, you never knew what they were thinking, so you never knew what they were expecting the morning after, and there was nothing more risky than calling their bluffs.

"It is true," he admitted, "and because it is, I wonder what it was about you that made me interested in the first place; and I've never been 'temporarily monogamous' to my knowledge, so that begs the question, why I would agree to be exclusive with you?"

"I can only guess at the reasons, Logan, but I still think things would make more sense to you if you looked at the journal," she reminded him.

"Why can't you just *tell me* whatever it is you want me to know?" Because the boy jumped, Logan realized that he had spoken louder than he meant to. He waited a moment, and when she said nothing, he asked in a quieter tone, "What's all that other stuff?" Logan indicated the file folder that looked like it would explode any moment and send its contents fluttering all over the apartment.

"That's the research we collected, which is the reason you came to the library and why we even met in the first place." She smiled warmly when she said this, which made him wonder what exactly she meant when she used the word "research." *Which reminds me of something . . .*

"Something about your story still isn't adding up. If you knew that I was the father all along, why did you just recently tell your son?"

"What good would it have done, Logan? Fatherhood's a heavy responsibility for someone who's just graduated college and is trying to find his place in the world. I didn't want you to be stuck in a job you didn't want because you suddenly had two other people depending on you. You meant something to me, Logan, and I just couldn't do that to you." She sniffed softly when she stopped speaking.

"Well, if what you say is true," and even though he didn't want to, he was starting to think it might be, "then that wasn't your choice to make. If he is my son, you shouldn't have kept him a secret from me for the past thirteen years!" He could feel his volume rising and tried again to lower it.

"And what was I supposed to say? Yeah, I know you have no idea who I am, but I was your lover, and I'm pregnant with your child? You wouldn't believe it then any more than you do right now. So I decided to do what was best for you and let you go. You think it was easy for me to let you walk out of my life, knowing I'd never see you again? It tore my heart out, Logan."

"So what changed?" he asked before he did something he might regret later.

"Nothing has changed for me," she pulled a tissue from her purse and dabbed the corner of her eye. "If I could, I would walk out of your door right now, and you would never see me or Lo again, but you're right. It wasn't my choice to make alone, so it's up to you and Lo now."

Lo had spent the past several minutes listening to his parents argue, and even though they weren't exactly peaceful conversations, they somehow made him feel good. *I wish Dad would just do what she says and read the story. Then maybe he could stop challenging everything she says, and we could keep hanging out.*

Those few hours that they'd played *COD* together were pretty awesome, even though his dad wasn't very much competition. He imagined what it would be like living here in his dad's place and spending all his Saturdays like that. But he couldn't be happy, even spending time with his dad, if his mom wasn't okay with it, and right now, she didn't look very happy. She seemed to be either really sad, really tired, or both.

"Mom," Lo made sure to wait until she was finished speaking.

"Yes, my love?" she turned to him.

"Are you okay?"

"Yes, I'm fine, Lo. I'm just tired. And after your adventure last night, I'm sure you are too. Why don't we go find a hotel and leave Mr. Michaels to look at the journal?" She stood and smoothed her sweater, then picked up her purse and the now empty satchel. "Come on, Lo."

He stood immediately because he had a feeling his dad had been right about her not getting any calmer while she was driving. His dad stood too and walked with them to his door.

"If you'll give me your cell phone number, I'll call you when we've settled into a hotel," his mom was speaking really formally, the way she did when she lectured her classes.

"Sounds good," his dad agreed, and she entered the numbers as he told them to her.

A few seconds later, his phone dinged. "And now you have my number as well," she closed her phone and dropped it into her purse. "Goodbye, Logan. It was nice to see you again after all this time." His mom reached for the door, but his dad was quicker, and had it open before she could. Lo felt her nudge his arm.

"Bye, Mr. Logan. Sorry for causing so much trouble today, but I had a good time playing Xbox."

"So did I, kid," the corner of his dad's mouth turned up a bit, and that was the last thing he saw before the door closed, and they were walking away.

~

Lillie stayed quiet until they were out of the building and in her car. She buckled up and turned to ensure that Lo did the same. *Then* she did what she had wanted to do since she'd hung up with Lo this morning. "LOGAN DANIEL THACKERY! I could just shake you! Do you have any idea how worried I was when I couldn't find you? Do you?" When Lo was wise enough to be silent, she continued. "I have never been so scared in all my life! If you ever, *ever* do something like this to me *ever* again, you won't be able to sit for a week. I don't care how old you are!"

"Yes, ma'am," he answered quietly, and again was wise enough to look meekly at his lap.

"When we get back home, you are grounded from Alex's and J.J.'s. You are also grounded from your Xbox," Lillie looked briefly in his direction before looking back at the road in front of her.

"Yes, ma'am," she heard him say.

She didn't say anything else to him as she drove to the Comfort Inn that was only about twenty minutes from Logan's. She was still quiet when she returned to the car with the room key card and remained so even after they had unloaded the car for the night. Lo flopped face down on his bed after turning down the comforter, and then she called Logan.

~

Lillie appeared on Logan's phone about forty-five minutes after they had left his place. He had thought of calling Andrew to check her story when she and the kid were gone, but who knew what the guy was doing to someone's brain at the moment. There was also Mark, who was less likely to be doing something life threatening, since he was a research analyst, but why would Mark remember some chick that Logan was supposedly sleeping with thirteen years back? So he had resorted to the only method of corroboration that he had: the journal she'd left. *And how trustworthy will this be, since she wrote it herself?* He had made it to the part in her story where she'd described his drunken search for firewood by the time she called.

"That was fast," Logan said as he picked up after a couple of rings.

"I know my way around Raleigh. I spent six years here all together, between my undergrad and master's," he thought he heard a smile. "We're at the Comfort Inn on Glenwood, in room 321."

"Good to know," he walked to his desk and wrote the information on a Post-It.

"Lo and I are going out for food in a bit, and while we're out, I'll pick up a home DNA kit. That way we can take the samples and mail them out tomorrow. Hopefully we won't have to wait more than a few weeks for conformation."

"Are those things admissible in court?" *There's no need to pay for a home kit if it has to be redone by a lab tech later.*

"Some of them are, so long as you have a notary sign that the swabs are from the correct people, but I'm not looking for child support, Logan. You don't have to worry about that. I've always known who Lo's father is and was content to raise him alone. It's Lo who came looking for you, and he doesn't want your money either. All he wants is your love."

Logan was quiet.

"But, if you feel it wiser to pay for an agency to conduct the test, I have no problem with that, so long as you cover your part of the cost," she continued after a beat.

"I'll talk to someone in my legal department and get back to you. If he is mine, I want to do right by him, but that means more than just monetary support," he warned.

"Ann Arbor's pretty far from Raleigh . . . I don't even make it home to my parents' more than three or four times a year right now," her voice had become protective, and Logan got the sense that she didn't want to think about sharing her son with anyone.

"Like I said: *if.* And that's a pretty big if. Let me make some calls and get back to you. You and the kid have specific plans for dinner?" he asked before he knew what he was saying.

"I was planning to be on the way back to Michigan tonight, so no." The end of her answer trailed off, as if she was unsure.

"Well, I've been flipping through this journal, and I don't think you could have written those things if you hadn't known me pretty well, so I was thinking maybe we ought to start over . . . since it looks like we'll be dealing with each other frequently in the near future." *Let's see your reaction to that!*

"Are you admitting that you believe I'm telling the truth?" Her surprise carried through clearly.

"About the fact that we knew each other, yes. But I'm withholding judgment on the other issue until we get the test results," he hoped he didn't sound like he was smiling.

"What changed your mind?"

"I remember that drive to Breckenridge. I remember that lodge. I remember getting drunk, but that's *all* I remember anything about until I woke up a year later.

There's no way you would have known about the things I do remember if I hadn't told you." And that was the plain truth of it. It was uncanny the way she had captured his relationships with his former roommates Mark Malone and Andrew Stevenson. And somehow, she'd even gotten that jackass Rob Norton right. No stranger would have picked up on all that on her own.

"You believe me because, right now, logic dictates that you must," she didn't try to hide her own laughter. "Do me a favor and stop reading before you get to the part where I talk you out of going to the shrink because I have a better idea."

"Why?" The woman could tick him off faster than anyone he had ever met, even his father, and that was saying quite a bit.

"Let's just say, you didn't take my idea so well the first time, and I doubt you'll handle it any better this time, since things are even more complicated now than they were then." *Lillie's having fun with this. She has to be.* He could just imagine her lips curving into a smiling sickle and those knife-like green eyes laughing along with them.

"Are you ever going to give me a straight answer?" Now that he thought about it, this felt a lot like flirting, and he wondered if it was the way she could wield words that enticed him to give her a chance.

Sometimes he liked a good challenge. And his primary complaint about the bookish ones was that there wasn't enough in the pot at the end of the night, compared to the work he had to put in to win all the previous rounds when he played their kind of games. *But maybe Lillie was an exception to the rule.* Maybe she would be worth the effort.

"Perhaps, when you let me get to know who you are again."

## Chapter 9

Lo and his mom met his dad at Red Robin a few hours later. The restaurant wasn't too far from their hotel, and he was always up for bottomless fries, so Lo was happy that he didn't have to wait until the next day to hang out with his dad some more.

He had been asleep when his mom called his dad, so he didn't know what they talked about, but whatever it was, his mom was in a way better mood than she had been before he fell asleep.

Oh, she was still mad; he could tell because she kept reminding him how much trouble he was in, but she was smiling when she thought he wasn't looking, and she let him pick the music in the car on the way. *Good job, Dad!*

Logan met them in the lobby, where Lo enjoyed the TV screen that was set into the floor for a few minutes before a waitress showed them a booth. When he slid in next to his mom, he noticed that this one had a good view of another TV, which was on the wall across the aisle from them. "Hey, look, Mom!" he pointed at the framed Beatles poster on the wall near his dad.

"Do you like The Beatles?" Logan wondered, as he followed Lo's finger.

"Yeah, she does. It's one of the only real groups she listens to, unless we're in the car. When we're at home and she's working on her dissertation, or whatever, she always listens to folk songs!" Lo made a face as he said it.

"Lo," his mom said and gave him that look that said he had just been rude to an adult.

"I mean, yes, sir. She does," he amended.

"So you have an appreciation for things of the past," his dad observed, and Lo wanted to bang his head on the table and say, you think?

"Apparently you haven't gotten to the part of the journal where you discover that I'm an archeology major," she buried her grin in the menu.

His dad smiled, "Apparently not."

When the waitress came and took their drink order, Lo wondered if she thought they were a real family like the Thompsons.

When they were alone again, his mom asked, "What did you do with your business degree?"

"I went in with my father, and now I run things," his dad didn't take his eyes from the menu.

"Oh," the way she said it, like she was catching her breath, made Lo look over at her, and he saw that his dad was looking too. Her cheeks reddened as she explained, "The last time we talked about it, working for your father was the one thing you didn't want to spend your life doing. I had hoped you escaped that fate."

His dad looked surprised. "Well, escaping the family business is a little challenging when your old man paid for part of your education."

"I thought you had everything covered," Lillie protested.

"Sure. If 'everything' means tuition, meals and a dorm room, but there are books and fees and living expenses too, not to mention the money for Kappa Sigma. After four years including summers, I owed him, and going in with him was how he called in the debt."

"I'm sorry, Logan. I know that isn't what you wanted," her voice was even again.

"You're right about that, but I wasn't exactly in a position to tell him no. Like I said, I did owe him, and then there was that whole extensive head trauma/amnesia thing which had me messed up for a couple months. I had no other prospects, so I did what I had to do. I'm sure you would have already earned your doctorate and be working toward tenure by now if things had been different for you," his dad pointed out.

"I'm sure I would have, but I'm glad things turned out the way they did. It would have made leaving Raleigh much harder if I hadn't known I was going to have a baby." It was sort of weird to hear his parents talk about him as if he had never been born, but at least he knew where his mom stood.

When the waitress brought them their drinks, and they had ordered their food, there was a pause in conversation. His mom was staring at the cardboard sign for some special burger that was only available for a limited time, and his dad was looking at his mom.

She must have felt his eyes because Lillie set the sign down and said, "How's your little brother? Preston, right?"

Logan nodded. "Pres is good. He just finished at Dartmouth in May, and I expect he'll be going back for an MBA in a couple of years, but he's got a job with the company right now, since my father didn't seem to want him to work anywhere else."

"Do you think he's any happier about working for your father than you are?" she asked.

"He and Dad always saw things similarly, and for whatever reason, Dad and I never did," his dad shrugged and caught the attention of their waitress so they could order their food.

Lo had to admit that as far as family meals went, this one was great, especially since it was their first one. Sure, there were two checks at the end of the night, and he watched his dad pull away in a different car, but the fact that the three of them had eaten together, at the same table, was pretty cool.

"Don't get too excited about this, Lo," his mom warned when they had both gotten into their beds, and she was doing some background reading for her dissertation.

Lo set the TV remote on the nightstand. "What do you mean?"

"Just because Logan didn't send us packing today, that doesn't mean he's going to be the World's Greatest Dad to you. He won't even admit that you're his son, even though the two of you look more alike than you and I do." Lillie sighed and put her book down too.

"Why do you automatically think that, Mom?" Lo knew he was whining, but his mom wasn't being fair. *She can't tell the future.*

"Because I know him, baby. He can be very charming, and he's capable of being kind as well, but he is also stubborn and bitter, and distrustful of others. In other words, he isn't the kind of man your Pa is." When she looked at Lo, he could see the sympathy in her eyes, and he didn't like it.

"But he loved you once, didn't he?" Lo tried again.

"Well, he did care more about me than he had about any other woman, but I'm not sure if he ever loved me. Not the way you're thinking of." That stupid sadness was back in her voice, and he was tired of his mom not making any sense, so Lo turned off his lamp and rolled to face the other way and go to sleep.

~

Logan drove back to his apartment and wondered how he'd gotten here. *There's no way in the world that I have a thirteen-year-old son with that woman!* And yet he hadn't dismissed the boy immediately. He had spent the morning playing Xbox with the kid and getting schooled. He hadn't called his lawyer and figured out some way to ensure he didn't wind up paying the chick child support for the next five years. He'd met them for burgers and fries. *I'm losing it!* Apparently, those few days in Asheville had affected him more than a trip home usually did. *This calls for a bottle.*

He shoved past the Jäger that he always kept in his cabinet and opted instead for Jameson. He was feeling more Irish than German tonight. He poured three fingers into a whiskey glass and sat down at his computer to continue the investigation he had begun earlier in the day.

Lillie Danielle Thackery had grown up in Manteo, earned a bachelor's in archeology from NCSU in 2008, and then a master's in 2017, and since then, she'd been studying for her PhD at the University of Michigan in Ann Arbor. But, he knew all that from talking to her and the boy. What he wanted was to know about her personal life. How much did she socialize? How often did she date? What were the odds that Lo wasn't his?

Unfortunately, he had never been all that good at research. This was why he had people who worked for him who did all the digging. He didn't expect them to disseminate anything, of course, but the finding of the information was always pawned off on someone else.

When he was in college, he always asked a chick to help, but he couldn't very well pick some woman up and ask her to find info on another. Even Mark Malone wasn't as ignorant as that.

She had published a few papers and articles about chronological archeology of medieval England, but other than that, she didn't appear on the results page. He checked Facebook, though he had to reactivate his account to do so. If she currently or had ever had a page, he couldn't find it.

He was at a loss as to where he might locate any personal info on Lillie, so he stopped typing and took a second to sip and think. Logan's eyes landed on the journal, and he decided that her own biased portrayal of herself was better than nothing.

He read through almost the end of Chapter 4 (breaking the story into chapters seemed pretentious to him, but whatever) before he came across any description that seemed to be about Lillie. She had described herself very similarly to the way he himself had observed when she came to his door that morning:

SHE HAD STICK STRAIGHT HAIR THAT WAS A RIVER OF INK FALLING PAST HER SHOULDERS, BUT IT WAS UNEVEN ON THE ENDS, AS IF ODD PIECES OF THE PUZZLE WERE MISSING. HE COULDN'T SEE THE COLOR OF HER EYES, AS SHE SEEMED TO BE READING, BUT HE BET THEY WERE AS SHARP AS HER CHIN. SHE WAS SMALL AND THIN, BUT THE SET OF HER MOUTH TOLD HIM THAT SHE COULD HOLD HER OWN WHEN THE NEED AROSE. IF HE HAD FOUND HER IN ANY OTHER SETTING, HE WOULD HAVE APPROACHED HER, BUT HE

KNEW HOW INTENSE THE STUDIOUS ONES WERE AND DECIDED TO BACK OFF.

It was unnerving the way she had chosen the same adjective to describe her eyes in her journal back when she was writing in it as he had this very morning. It didn't make sense that out of all the descriptive words in the English language, they had both chosen the same one. *But then how would she know my first impression of her? Either she's guessing or I told her at some point.* When he thought of it that way, the word choice didn't seem as strangely coincidental. After all, people did have certain patterns of speech, and if both of the descriptions were his, repetitive word choice was to be expected.

*But when is it ever safe to tell a woman the truth about your first impression of her?* No sane man would ever do it of his own free will because that was a guaranteed way to tick her off and lose the opportunity to take her to bed later. *It doesn't make any sense.* But then, nothing really had since that kid appeared at his door that morning. *This is why you should never have actual relationships with the women you fool around with.* But he couldn't really blame himself for breaking one of his personal rules when he didn't even remember doing it. He drained his glass and kept reading. *It isn't like I'm going to be able to sleep tonight anyway.*

Logan was able to finish the journal at about 4:30 that morning, but only with the help of the Jameson. *Lord, but the woman is nuts!* She had to be if she actually expected him to believe that crap about him being a werewolf. And not only that, but if he had read the ending correctly, she seemed to imply that she was in love with him and that's why she had chosen to defy her conservative family and keep her baby instead of giving it up for adoption.

*I need another shot.* He reached for the bottle and found that his whiskey was gone. That was a simple enough problem to fix, so he went to his liquor cabinet and found the familiar dark green bottle.

Jägermeister had been his drink of choice since his late teens, but sometime in the last six or eight years, he had developed a taste for Irish whiskey. Logan still made sure to keep a bottle of it, but he rarely drank any. Part of him had always wondered if the Jäger had contributed to whatever accident he'd had in the woods that night. Against his will, he thought back to waking up in that hole for what felt like the millionth time.

It was cool out, and he remembered coming to himself suddenly and panicking because he had no idea where he was. It was morning, he knew, since the sun shone in from above, causing the pain in his head to pulse. He shut his eyes for a moment to think, and that was when he realized that he was lying at the bottom of a rectangular hole. There was dirt all around him. He could smell it. He stood and felt to see how deep the hole was. His bare toes pressed into the earth beneath them. He was naked. Logan looked up and saw the woods around him. The hole he was in must have been about six feet deep because when he was standing, he could just see over the edge, which meant he could pull himself out, if his head would quit pounding long enough for him to do it. He had no way of marking time, so he wasn't sure exactly how long it took him to get out, but when he did, he saw that he was covered in tiny nicks and cuts, some deeper than others.

He took a step and winced, feeling the shards of glass for the first time. *Maybe this is some kind of prank*, he thought as he took a few more steps and tried to remember where he had been. After thinking for several minutes, he was fairly sure that the last thing he had done was get totally wasted with the guys. But this didn't look like Colorado. *It doesn't make any sense.*

The more he thought about it, the more he was sure that they had been in their cabin in Colorado. They'd had a few girls, had several bottles, and everyone had passed out. Now he was in the woods, naked, and scratched to pieces. *What the crap did the guys do to me?* But it was too warm to be Colorado. *So where the freak am I?*

Logan looked around for landmarks, but there weren't any that he could see. He walked a bit farther, but he didn't have a clue where he was going. He retraced his steps, and by now, the glass was really starting to bother him, but he had to find his clothes or phone or car or something. Otherwise, he could be wandering out here for days. Plus, it wasn't exactly pleasant to be outside and fully exposed.

*There's no need to freak out. If I'm not in Breckenridge, then there's only one other place I can be,* he told himself. *I'm somewhere on campus, and the guys have just played the mother of all pranks on me . . . and they're gonna pay for it too, just as soon as I find my way back to 317,* he vowed. While he was seething, he chose a random direction and trudged that way, hoping to find some clothes before he ran into anyone he knew.

The anger drove him forward, and he went without feeling the glass anymore. He only focused on finding clothes and a way back to the apartment.

After about thirty minutes, he found what he hoped was Trailwood Drive and kept walking. *Sooner or later, I've got to meet a car.* He told himself that as he moved. He wasn't going to be stuck out here forever. There just *had* to be someone on campus.

*Is it still Spring Break?* The thought came to him, and he hoped that it was. *How long was I out?* But without a phone or watch, there was no way to tell. He gave up trying to figure it out because he couldn't remember a single thing after they started drinking in the cabin, and the more he tried, the more his head felt like it was being ripped apart from the inside out.

With each breath he took, Logan could feel the ache, and he hoped that a headache fit for a wooly mammoth wasn't one of the signs of alcohol poisoning. *How much did I drink?* he wondered. Jäger never did that to him, but then again, he had no idea *how much* Jäger he'd actually consumed. Logically, he knew that everything had a limit, and maybe this was what happened when you found it with Jäger. He had to stop walking because the headache was suddenly blinding. It actually made his ears ring. He shook his head to clear it, but that was a massive mistake as he almost puked. He closed his eyes, leaned over and braced his hands on his thighs so that maybe the world would stop spinning. When he stood up and opened his eyes again, he saw the flash of a cop car's lights. *This sucks!*

Resigned, he raised his hands in the air and waited for the cop to pull up and get out. *How in the crap am I gonna explain this?* He had just enough time to realize that the cop's siren was what was making the pain in his head so much worse, and then everything was dark and quiet.

Logan shook his head. If the crazy chick was right, it wasn't the Jäger that had nearly killed him. It was her! Apparently, the reason he had come to in a hole big enough to be a grave was because she had set a freaking trap for him. But not him, really, just the lupine version of him that supposedly posed a threat to her. He was also supposed to believe that she hadn't done it for selfish reasons. No, she had done it out of fear for his immortal soul.

He took a swig and considered. Granted, there were parts of her story that were certifiable, but if he thought about others, they did make a little sense. *For one, if she used a mirror, that explained how he got so many small cuts. For another, if he did contract some kind of disease during his junior Spring Break, and she was somehow able to cure him with that mirror crap at the same time the next Spring Break, that would explain the year-long amnesia and the severe head trauma that the doctors had all agreed on.*

~

THIS IS LILLIE THACKERY. ARE YOU AWAKE? Lillie texted Logan's phone at about nine thirty the next morning. She figured that he had spent most of the night reading the journal and the rest of it drinking, so she hoped by that hour, he had been able to sleep most of it off.

NOW. Lillie burst out laughing when she got his one-word response a few seconds later.

"What?" Lo yawned at her from his bed. She ignored her sleepy son and sent his sleepy father another text.

HOW'S YOUR HEAD?

ARE YOU PSYCHIC ON TOP OF BEING PSYCHO? His second response had her cracking up even more.

NO. JUST KNEW YOU VERY WELL ONCE UPON A TIME. She smiled when she imagined how aggravated he would be over that.

KNOW A MAGIC SPELL FOR HANGOVERS, PRINCESS? Somehow, she could hear his sarcasm even though the text wasn't spoken and smiled again.

NO. AFTER WE EAT, WE'LL COME OVER FOR DNA SWABS. WANT ASPIRIN? She remembered how bad his and Lo's headaches always were on the mornings after each night of the phase and hoped this particular one came nowhere close.

GOT IT. LATER.

Lillie slipped her phone in her pocket, knowing that Logan's end of the conversation was over. "Come on, Lo. Get up," she called as she walked to the mirror to do her face.

~

Lo laid still and pretended he'd gone back to sleep. He had never seen his mom act like this before. She was smiling and giggling and blushing and acting like a . . . well, a girl. *Not that she didn't always act like a girl, but now there was something different.* She had always been a mom who happened to be a girl, and now it was almost like she was being a girl who happened to be a mom.

He made sure to stir when she called to him, and he added a groan or two for effect. Then he watched her through the slits of his eyelids. She was putting on her make-up, which she almost always did, but it seemed like she was doing something new, though he didn't know why.

"Lo! Get up now. We have to go meet Logan soon," she raised her voice a bit and began to do her hair. Lo watched her as she sprayed something on it and then brushed it, he guessed, until she liked the way it looked. She walked over to his bed and jerked the covers off. "Get up, lazy," she shook his shoulder, and he did his best not to smile.

"Yes, ma'am," he pretended to stretch and then rubbed his eyes. Lo got up and brushed his teeth. When he was done, he went to the bag his mom had brought from Ma and Pa's for him and got out some clothes, then went into the bathroom to change.

When he came out, his mom was sitting on her bed, holding a book in her lap. She looked up at the sound he made, and before he knew what he was doing, he told her, "You look really pretty today, Mom." And it was true.

## Chapter 10

Lillie had to fight to control her nerves as she drove to Logan's apartment. Unlike yesterday, there was no concern for Lo to distract her. It was hard not to fidget, but she couldn't let Lo see that anything was different, *wouldn't* let him. **That** *was something to think about.* She was still angry that he had disobeyed her and come to Raleigh, and she couldn't bear to consider what could have happened if he had run into the wrong person. She suppressed a shudder. But dang if he hadn't melted her heart earlier when he told her that she looked pretty.

*It doesn't matter what Logan thinks of me. Lo's the most important person in my world,* she reminded herself. And Lo was why she was doing this, not because his father still meant anything to her. She repeated it over and over, and by the time they pulled up to the curb near Logan's building, Lillie no longer noticed her nerves.

Lo had been pretty quiet during the ride, since he had his ear buds in, but as she put the car in park, that was over. "Do you think he finished the book?" he asked as they got out of the car.

"Probably," she almost laughed again when she pictured Logan's reaction to finding out he was a former lycanthrope.

"Do you think he'll believe us now?" Lo wanted to know, just as she was about to buzz his father.

"No, Lo. I don't," she said, and shook her head because she could tell he had more questions coming.

"We'll figure it out when we get upstairs," she added firmly before pressing the buzzer.

The latch clicked, and Lillie ushered Lo inside. As they went upstairs, she steeled herself for the shock of seeing him in close proximity again. She had hoped that after so much time had passed since the last time she'd seen him in the library, she wouldn't feel anything when they were face to face again. She learned rather quickly yesterday that she had no such luck.

There was just something about the man that made her temper hot and her heart ache, and there was no way on Earth she was ever going to let him know it. So by the time she was knocking on his door, she had become ice, as that was the best way to combat heat.

She was careful with her expression when Logan opened the door, making sure there was only a slight curve to her lips. "Good morning, Logan."

"I wouldn't go that far," he told her as he stepped aside to let them in. "Hey, kid," he acknowledged Lo when the boy passed.

"It's Lo, sir. That shouldn't be too hard for *you* to remember," Lo told him politely, and Lillie caught the giggle just before it came out of her mouth.

"Right," Logan shut the door and turned back to them. He walked to his recliner and sat, then glanced back at them and rolled his eyes. "Y'all just gonna stand there in the doorway all day?"

"Can I take that as permission to sit?" Lillie arched a brow.

"Lillie, according to what I read last night, things haven't been that formal between us in a long time."

"So, you've finished?" she ignored his tone.

"Yes, I did. What else would have kept me up all night and driven me to drink a whole bottle of Irish whiskey and half of another of Jäger?" That familiar glint was in his eye.

"The answer to that question could have been a lot of things thirteen years ago," she smirked, sliding back into the familiar banter.

He blinked and looked at her for a moment, as if to be sure he had heard her correctly. Then the glint turned deadly, and she knew to brace for the anger. "Just what are you trying to say? Because from where I'm sitting, you come off as a grasping, manipulative little shrew! Do you really expect me to read about my own life from a book in *your* handwriting and just accept that you're telling the truth when you claim I'm a freaking werewolf? Why would you think that I would believe *anything* you say after that? Especially when you're also claiming to be the mother of my illegitimate son? . . . Which is something I highly doubt, seeing as how I *always* use protection, and for me to forget about that, I'd be too drunk to need it in the first place!" Logan made the mistake of stopping for a breath, and she took aim.

"Yes, Logan, I'm sure you do think of me as some ill-tempered, money-grubbing whore, but that's where you'd be mistaken. No, I don't expect you to believe a word I tell you, which is why I brought this," she drew the DNA kit out of her bag and tossed it at his face, "which will prove to your infuriatingly logical mind that I am indeed the mother of your illegitimate son, whom we conceived because you made exceptions for me, which didn't involve inebriation." *I can still shoot to kill,* she thought as his mouth opened slightly in surprise.

"What exactly do you mean by 'exceptions'?" he demanded.

"I'm Catholic, Logan. You figure it out." She crossed her arms and pinned him with that intimidating, unbreakable stare she had been able to perfect through years of practice both in motherhood and in the classroom. She'd only just begun to experience and appreciate its power when she had used it on him before. Now she was a master, and he could do little more than avert his eyes before he withered under it.

"Somehow, I have a hard time believing you were that persuasive," he murmured.

"You want to call? You go ahead," she smiled broadly. "But remember, I already know all the cards you have in your hand."

~

Lo wasn't sure what to think about the vibe between his parents, but it was totally different this morning than it had been yesterday. Both of them seemed to be really mad at each other, though he had no idea why.

"It's true, Mr. Logan. Somehow my mom *always* turns out to be right."

"Oh, does she? We'll see," his dad told him, opening the kit and looking at the contents. "You ready to do this?" he waited for Lo's nod and handed him one of the swabs that were incased in their own little packages.

While they were getting the cheek cell samples, his dad was careful to follow all the directions and make sure each swab went into its own envelope without being contaminated. He also made sure each envelope was correctly labeled. "Just so there are no questions," he told Lo and Lillie. Then, once the paperwork was all complete, he put everything in the larger mailing envelope and sealed it. "I guess that does it."

"Yeah," Lo agreed. "Too bad we have to wait a month for the results.

"Lo and I could drop it off in the mail, if you want," his mom made her first friendly statement to his dad of the day. *Maybe whatever they were mad about is over with*, he thought.

"I'll do it, if you don't mind," his dad was polite.

"Of course," his mom was too, but Lo knew by the look on her face that she wasn't happy.

Unfortunately, the awkward feeling between Logan and Lillie only got worse after that, and when he and his mom left the apartment a little while later, Lo was so mad that he didn't say a word to his mom until they had gotten in the car and started the drive back to Michigan.

Lo clicked the radio off the oldies station, which made his mom frown, but he didn't care. "What was going on at Dad's?"

"What d'you mean?" she asked as if it was a completely normal thing to leave your dad in Raleigh with no idea if you were ever going to see him again.

"I'm not a kid anymore, Mom. I know y'all were mad at each other, and I want to know why," he was determined to get some answers.

"Your father was angry with the situation he is in, and I was angry with him for being so stubborn and refusing to believe that we're telling him the truth," she answered after a moment.

"But you warned me that he would be hard to convince, didn't you? And he can't argue with science, so we can always try again when the DNA test comes back,"

Lo saw that it was more than anger. It seemed like her feelings were hurt. Now that he wasn't confused, Lo discovered that his mom wasn't the only one who was angry.

~

What Lillie didn't tell her son was that things wouldn't go any better with his father the next time they met. Presently, Logan was too much the guy she had first met than the one she'd fallen for. And she couldn't really blame him. *She* had been the one who killed that Logan, the one who held her as they slept. The one who bought her coffee and didn't expect anything in return. The one who would have committed suicide to save her if she hadn't stepped in.

Lo's father was never going to be the person he had dreamed of, and it was her own fault. *Why, why does he have to be so stubbornly logical?* But she knew that if she had grown up the way Logan had, she might very well have come to depend on logic too. She knew that family wasn't the same thing to him as it was to her and Lo, and part of her ached for the small boy inside of Logan who still felt alone in the world. She ached for him just as she did for her own son.

When they stopped for the night at a hotel just off the interstate, Lillie was glad that Lo was a teen and still needed a lot of sleep. It meant that once she'd turned out the light, she only had to wait about thirty minutes before he was snoozing.

Once she knew he was out, Lillie reached for the book that she took with her almost everywhere she went. It was about of one of the medieval princes of England, called *Royalty For Commoners: The Complete Known Lineage Of John*

*Of Gaunt, Son Of Edward III, King Of England, And Queen Philippa.* It was now very much out of date, as Lillie knew of at least one newer edition, and Lillie had read its nearly four hundred pages all the way through three times since Lo had been alive. It wasn't the sweeping romance of Anya Seton's novel *Katherine*, but she loved that book just as much. It was the only thing besides her son that Logan had ever given her.

## Chapter 11

Lo's third phase began on the Sunday night before Martin Luther King, Jr. Day, which was fortunate for him and Lillie since neither of them had to go to school the next morning. On those three nights, she was barely able to get any sleep, though she had decided it was too hard to track the wolf right now with the weather the way it was. *It isn't worth me getting sick*, she thought as she looked out the window at the snow. But then there was the problem of Lo, and the ever-present notion that the longer it took her to kill the wolf, the more of Lo's memories she would be taking away from him. Three months didn't seem as bad as a whole year, but Lo was still a kid, and who knew how he would react if she tried to explain all this to him again after he had been cured?

It was starting to make her think of *The Vow*, a movie where Rachel McAdams and Channing Tatum's characters are a married couple in a car accident that causes the female to forget the last five years of her life, and during that time she had met, fallen in love with, and married the male. It was basically Lillie's own life in reverse. *At least in the movie, Rachel McAdams isn't pregnant.* Or there was also one called *50 First Dates*, from when Lillie was much younger, where Adam Sandler's character had to make Drew Barrymore's fall in love with him all over again every single day because of a traumatic brain injury she had experienced before they met, and they did have kids.

Three months ago, she would never have dreamed that Lo would still be a lycanthrope at this point. She knew what she was doing this time around, after all. *If only Logan wasn't so freaking rational about every little thing in his life!* But if he weren't that way, he wouldn't have become the person he had once been.

As she sat on the couch in the living room, waiting for the wolf to return and phase back into her son, she wondered what his father was doing right then.

~

Logan was in bed, looking up in the darkness to where he knew his bedroom ceiling was. It was the second or third time this month that he had had insomnia. He checked to make sure that Julia, the blonde beside him, wasn't having the same problem. Her breathing was even, so he took that as a sign that she wasn't.

It annoyed him when he couldn't sleep if there seemed to be no reason for it. It was already after one in the a.m., and he'd just made Julia feel very good, so he should have had no problems drifting off. But here he was, unable to sleep and somehow still feeling extremely tired. *What sense does that make?*

Julia snuggled closer to him, and he let her. He thought back to a simpler time when all it took were a few shots of Jäger and a willing woman to have him sleeping through the night.

~

*This really sucks!* Lo thought as he woke up on his floor for the third morning running. His mom was sitting a few feet away and offered him a smile. "We made it through another one, baby."

"Thank goodness for that," he whispered since it hurt his head too much to talk in a normal volume.

When he was able, Lo got up and took a shower, and his mom vacuumed the room and put his sheets on to wash. Since this had happened six times now, they had developed a routine, so he knew that when he walked into the kitchen, a cup of decaf and some Tylenol would be sitting on the table next to his bowl of Cinnamon Toast Crunch.

It was getting harder and harder for Lo to keep the Phases a secret from Alex. The guy was too smart for his own good. "Dude, you look like crap!" he declared.

"Thanks, man. I didn't get much sleep last night." Lo said.

"Seriously, I swear you must have been up all night playing that stupid zombies-take-over-the-world game again. Or maybe you finally turned into one yourself."

"You know, I have been feeling pretty strange the past few months. I haven't been able to sleep much, and my arms and legs are sorta stiff. And now that I think about it, I haven't had much of an appetite lately, except for these strange cravings I've been having," Lo grinned ominously and took a few lumbering steps toward Alex.

"That's freaky, Lo," Alex laughed a little nervously.

"I still don't see why you think zombies are lame. You liked all the *Underworld* movies! And zombies're the undead too, which means they're, like indestructible, you know? They're much cooler than vampires. They aren't limited by the sunlight, and they don't have to depend on human blood to reanimate them. And if there was some sort of outbreak, you *know* there'd be no way to stop it from spreading all across the world. Think about it."

"What about their need for brains and the slight problem of being able to off them with a head shot? At

95

least with vamps, you don't have to worry about something as easy to come by as a gun. It's a heck of a lot harder to kill something by driving a freaking steak through its heart than by shooting it. And how many vamps do you know who would be slow or stupid enough to let a human get that close?" Alex countered. "I mean, really. Zombies are so slow that even blind people would have time to take kill shots. How is a mindless brain muncher who's probably missing half his limbs scarier than a former human with mad reflexes and uber-sensitive sight, smell and hearing? A vamp could stalk and kill you in the same amount of time it would take a zombie to drag his right foot six inches forward."

"But vamps don't have the potential to infect the entire human population in a matter of months," Lo insisted. "That's totally worse than turning people one bite at a time."

The thought of getting bitten by a bloodsucker made him think about the wolf that attacked his dad in the woods in Colorado. *If werewolves exist, does that mean that vamps do too? Holy crap, but that would suck!*

~

Lillie was in the middle of teaching her 10:00 when she felt her cell vibrate on her belt. She kept lecturing until she had covered what she planned and had gotten her students started on the activity that she assigned. When there were no more questions, she took a second and checked the text.

CALL ASAP.

That was it. And Logan was right back in the middle of her life, the place she had been trying to keep him out of. Ever since she had spoken to him on Lo's phone the day after Christmas, he had been creeping in from the periphery of her mind, getting closer and closer to her conscious thoughts.

But when he appeared there, she was incapable of performing even basic functions. She couldn't remember her place in her lecture without notes, she forgot to run errands that she had always run at specific times on specific days, and she even got behind on the readings for her classes.

*He's not that person. He never will be,* she reminded herself, but that didn't seem to help.

Somehow, she survived until the end of the class without looking like a clueless teaching assistant, but the moment she had shut her office door, she was dialing his number.

"Logan Michaels."

"You rang?" she answered.

"The test came back." There was no preamble, just the flat statement. "He's mine."

Lillie almost said I told you so, but was able to stop herself. "Yes."

"You were telling the truth."

"Yes, I was, Logan," she agreed.

"How?"

"Logan, I wish I had an explanation that was easier for you to accept, but I don't. We were together once. You cared about me once, and because you did, you were willing to take that risk for me."

"Why didn't you tell me, Lillie? I had a right to know! I had a right to be in my own son's life!" The shock-induced monotone had been replaced by outrage.

"I wanted to. But you would have never believed me. By the time I knew, you had already forgotten me, and there was no good way to tell you. You would have gotten angry and defensive, just the way you are now, and you would have struck out at me as you did on the day after Christmas. And I would have hated you."

"That's crap. You could have made me believe. You could have proven paternity then too. You just didn't want me to be involved. You wanted to keep him to yourself!"

"It wasn't like that, Logan. I never wanted to keep him from you. I never wanted to raise him alone, but I didn't want to stand in your way."

"You keep saying that, but if that was the case, then why did you ever tell Lo who I was? You had to know that as soon as you gave him a name he would start looking for me!"

"I had to."

"Why?" he was back to one-word questions.

"Because it started happening to him the same way it had happened to you, and telling him was the best way to explain it."

"Stop. Just stop. I can't believe you still expect me to believe that werewolf theory. Maybe I was wrong to doubt you when you named me as the father, since I have no idea what or who I did during an entire year, and that's plenty of time to father a child, but there's no way in hell that you can prove to me that I was a werewolf!"

"You have no reason to doubt me Logan. I've never lied to you."

"Right. I should just ignore the fact that what you're telling me contradicts science and common sense and accept it as the undeniable truth, just because I have no reason not to trust you." He was still angry, but he had dropped his tone, which Lillie knew meant that the fury was building to a dangerous level.

"Yes, that's exactly what I'm saying." That she was calm with her response seemed to make it even worse.

"What about keeping my son a secret from me? *That's* a stunning example of dishonesty. I mean what kind of mother keeps her son from his father intentionally, and for no better reason than that she wanted to keep her son to herself. It sounds like I had it right before. I think 'shrew' is a pretty accurate description."

"It isn't like that, Logan," she sighed. "I told you, I wanted better things for you than getting sucked back into your father's control, so I put what was best for you before what was best for me."

"I don't think you have the right to make that decision for me. And I hate to tell you this, but all your valiant self-sacrifice was for nothing. I run the freaking company for him now!"

"I know, and I'm sorry. I'm sorry for you, and I'm sorry for Lo, and I'm sorry for myself because all of us would be in totally different places right now if I had known that would happen, but I didn't, so I made the best choice I could at the time."

"That's a lie. You aren't sorry for anything except that Lo came looking for me."

"I cared about you Logan. I cared about you, and I am sorry for hurting you because I know how much you've been hurt in the past. Letting you graduate without telling you about us was one of the absolute hardest things I have ever done because I knew that once you walked across that stage, I would probably never see you again. But I cared about you, and I did it anyway."

"You cared about me? You had a funny way of showing it. By your own account, it was you who killed the werewolf! Why would you do that if you cared about me? You had no idea whether I would survive."

"You're right. I didn't have any idea. But I did know that you are a good man, and you would do the right thing, and I knew that you were getting close to killing yourself to protect me and any other human who might get in your way. So I decided to kill you myself, to save you from—"

"From what???" Impatience had him shouting.

"To save you from eternal damnation," she whispered.

~

"Excuse me?" Logan had to confirm what he thought he just heard.

"Suicide is a mortal sin, and I couldn't let you do that to yourself," her voice was still soft.

"Do what to myself?" He had known the girl was religious, but he had no idea that she believed there were categories of sin.

"If you commit a mortal sin and die before confessing it, then you don't even experience Purgatory. It's sort of like 'Go to Hell. Go directly to Hell. Do not pass Go. Do not collect $200.'"

Logan laughed. He couldn't help it. *Does she hear herself?* "You didn't want me to go to Hell, so you *committed murder* instead! What does that mean for your own soul?"

"I can do penance for my sin, and hopefully, after death, if I'm not yet worthy of Heaven, then I can go through Purgatory, or purification, and one day I will be worthy."

"That still doesn't sound good." Something about that situation didn't seem to make sense. Why did his soul matter, if saving it meant that hers was going to have to be "purified?"

"Oh, it won't be, but it's only temporary. . . I'm sorry, Logan, but I've got another class starting in about five minutes."

"Then we'll talk tonight," he said to make sure she knew that they weren't finished. Not by a long shot.

"All right. Until then," she agreed and hung up.

~

When Lo's mom came home after her office hours were over, he could tell that she had had a bad day. She was super quiet when she came in, and she went directly to her room after asking how he was. Then she came back wearing her pajamas.

He stopped doing his history homework. "Mom, are you ok?"

She had just settled into her place on the couch and turned on the TV. "Not really, Lo."

"What happened?" He got up from the table and went to sit with her.

"Your dad called today. The test came back positive, which proves that you're his."

"Then he knows that you were telling the truth, and I hope he feels really crappy for not believing you in the first place." *He deserves it for acting like such a scumbag.*

"Actually, he called me a liar when we were on the phone," his mom said, smiling a little when he must have made a face.

"Well, if he still doesn't believe that I'm a lycanthrope, that's no big deal," Lo shrugged. "We can prove that too."

"I know we can, Lo. That's not the problem."

"Then what is?"

"He's still angry with me, and I don't think he'll be content with an apology.

His mom was right. When his dad called after supper, she had turned pale not five minutes after they started talking. He could tell that she was trying to stay calm, but the way she held her lips meant that whatever his dad was saying wasn't nice.

"I understand that you feel like you've been cheated out of his childhood, Logan, but I can't just pull him out of school for an undetermined period of time. . . No. No, he can't start school in Raleigh . . . because he isn't—*we* aren't moving back home! . . . I'm in the middle of my course work, Logan! I can't just drop what I'm doing and come at your beck and call. I'm not that kind of woman . . . Of course, I'm not trying to keep you from seeing him! All I'm saying is that we can't come to Raleigh for any length of time until at least March. Our Spring Break is the week after your birthday, and that's the soonest we can come. Yes, I'm sure." Then she was quiet for a little while, until she took the phone from her ear and passed it to Lo. "He wants to talk to you."

*Oh, my gosh!* Lo took the phone and forced himself to say, "Hello?"

"Hello, Lo. I wanted to talk to you about some things," his father said.

"Ok. . ."

"I guess your mom told you about the test results."

"Yes, sir. She did."

"Well, I want you to know that even though we don't know each other very well right now, I want to change that as soon as we can. I want you to come to Raleigh."

"Really?" *Is he serious?* Lo couldn't hide his excitement.

"Yeah, really. I've got a lot of catching up to do," his dad laughed.

"That sounds cool," Lo grinned. It was a little late for Christmas, but he'd take a dad in January over none at all. "I can come for Spring Break, and we can hang out all week."

"I was hoping to see you before then, but your mom says she can't leave Ann Arbor for more than a weekend before then, so I have proposal."

"What?" Lo didn't see any way around that, since his mom had to work, and he had school until then.

"How would you feel about coming to Raleigh and staying with me for a while . . . without your mom?"

"I don't know, Mr. Logan—" Lo glanced at his mom. She was reading a textbook and apparently hadn't heard what he said.

"You came to Raleigh without her last month," his dad reminded him.

"Yes, sir, I did, but that was during Christmas Break," Lo agreed. "What about school?"

"Well, if you only miss one or two days, I don't think they'll mind." *That **does** sound like a good idea* . . . Lo looked toward Lillie again, sure that she would disapprove, but she was still glued to her book.

"Thanks for the offer, sir, but I'm not sure I want to do that. I don't like the idea of Mom being all alone here."

"So you'd rather wait two months?" Lo could tell that his dad thought he had said the wrong thing, but he didn't like the way his dad had treated his mom.

"Look, I really do what to hang out with you, but the last time I saw you, you were kind of a jerk to me and my mom, and she's the one who's always been there for me, so I'm not gonna blow her off just because you want to get to know me," Lo tried to explain.

"But she's the reason I even have to get to know you in the first place, Lo. If I had known that you were my son, you would have never grown up without a father."

"I know, but that doesn't mean that I'm going to go behind her back. She isn't crazy or a liar like you think."

"I never said that, Lo. But if you don't want to come without her, that's ok too. How would you feel about me coming there for a couple of days? That way you don't have to worry about leaving your mom alone or missing school."

"Great idea! How soon can you come?"

"This is Wednesday, so I can try for the day after tomorrow, and that way I can be there for the weekend. Give me back to your mom, and I'll see if we can figure something out."

"Mom," Lo took the phone to her. "He wants to talk to you."

Though she looked surprised, Lillie took the phone and talked to his dad again for almost thirty more minutes before they hung up.

Lo just thought he was excited when his dad had said he wanted to hang out. Now that it might be happening in two days, he couldn't sit still, so to keep himself from doing something crazy, like running laps all over the apartment, he went to his room, turned on his Xbox and started a brand new Singleplayer Campaign game of *Left 4 Dead*, since he already knew that he'd be too distracted to have very good luck on Realism Mode, and he didn't want The Director to take away any of the cool ammo it had been leaving him lately.

He had made it through the first chapter, though the Witches had almost caused him to lose too many Survivors, and he was now facing a swarm of the Infected along with a few Boomers. He doubted that he would make it all the way to chapter two. He had just managed to get a Jockey off his back, when his mom called him back into the living room.

"Your dad's booking a flight for Friday. He'll land in Detroit, and then I'll drive over and pick him up after I teach my 11:00 class. So, by the time you get home from school, the two of us should be back in town."

"You rock, Mom," he told her and went to her for a hug.

"So do you, my love," she squeezed him in return. "Your dad said you were adamant about not leaving me alone here while you boys are having fun in Raleigh."

"Yeah. I knew if I was going home, even for a little while, you needed to be able to come too. Plus, if you aren't there, who's gonna be my witness for when I beat the crap out of Dad on the Xbox," Lo smiled expectantly, already tasting that victory.

"I don't know about that, baby. If I remember correctly, your dad could hold his own against almost anyone on the Xbox, except Batu, but from what he told me, it seems like Batu was sort of a freak of nature when it came to video games. So beating your dad may not be as easy as you think it will be, pal."

~

Lillie watched Lo's eyes change just like his father's did, taking on that hard, cold look of determination when either of them made up his mind to do something, and she couldn't help but laugh. *If Logan had seen that expression, even he would have been able to do without the DNA test.*

105

On Friday, Lille made the hour-long commute from Ann Arbor to Detroit. Though Lo was nearly too ecstatic to contain himself long enough to finish getting ready for school that morning, she was anything but. It wasn't that she didn't want Lo and Logan to spend time together. It was just that she didn't relish the thought of being alone in the car with Logan for an hour, possibly longer if the traffic was snarly, and it probably would be. And if she did manage to survive the drive home, then she had the whole weekend to look forward to. It would be good for both of them, but a part of her knew how much it would hurt her to breathe the same air as Logan for the next forty-eight hours and be constantly reminded that he neither liked nor trusted her at all.

Unfortunately, that was not the only part of Lillie. *Why? Why did it have to be him?* She'd asked herself and God the same question so many times during Lo's life, but she had no more of an answer now than she did in May of 2008, when she first realized she was pregnant.

There was no way that Logan could have ever been the kind of man she would have needed, even if he hadn't lost all recollection of their relationship, and Logan himself had told her as much on the night they were first together. But in that moment, for the first time in her life, Lillie knew what it meant to want someone, really want a person, no matter what the cost.

It was a cost that she was still having to pay, and the only regret she had ever had about that night and the ones that followed was that she wasn't the only one who suffered because of them.

~

When Logan found his suitcase, he looked around the terminal for Lillie. She had been striking both times he had seen her before, and he didn't figure it would take too long to spot her here, even with a crowd.

It only took him a minute or two to find her slight figure and ink black hair. She had it down, cascading past her shoulders, but it was fastened away from each side of her face with a barrette. She looked almost like a schoolgirl except that she was wearing slacks and a ruffled blouse instead of a collared shirt and a skirt. He could tell that she was searching for him, but knew the instant she saw him because of the dramatic change in her face. Her lips curved into a quick, wide smile and her eyes lightened. Still, as he approached, her smile narrowed some, and her eyes became somber.

"Hello," she said when he was in earshot. "I hope you had a nice flight."

"It was ok, but I've had better."

"Have you got everything?" she looked at his suitcase.

"Yeah, I travel pretty light," he said.

"The car's not too far, and it shouldn't take much more than an hour to get back to Ann Arbor," she smiled again, and he saw that it was the same, careful one from a moment ago. *Apparently, she's decided to make nice.*

They climbed into Lillie's small black Corolla, and Logan immediately missed his MKZ. Once she started the car, she adjusted the radio volume and stopped on a station that was playing "You Shook Me All Night Long."

"You still like AC/DC, right?"

"I do," he grinned, though it was strange that she knew his music preferences. "I don't think that's the kind of thing you grow out of."

"Good to know." She turned it up a little more, and they drove in silence for several miles.

As she was driving, he had a prolonged chance to study her profile. She was calm and comfortable behind the wheel, and though her face gave him no reason to suspect it, he felt sure she was tense. *Maybe it's that she isn't prepared to share Lo.* It had sort of seemed that way when they were talking on the phone on Wednesday, but she had agreed to this weekend with hardly any nudging.

"Lillie, I think we should start over, if that's ok with you."

"What?" She hadn't taken her eyes off the road though there was no doubt his comment had surprised her. "We just did. Last month, actually," she glanced over now, possibly to see if he was serious.

"No. I don't mean from back then. I mean, from that day we took the DNA test. I was a bit edgy, and I—"

"I'm sorry," she broke in before he could finish. "Did you just say *edgy*? Because that's what I thought I heard, and edgy is not what you were that day."

He had to clench his teeth, but he managed to say, "Fine. I was asinine, but you weren't the picture of politeness either . . . Anyway, since we're gonna be spending some time together on and off for at least the next five years, I think things might be a little easier if we make up our make up our minds to try to be friendly."

"That is a very sensible plan, Logan. But I think I might have a little trouble maintaining 'friendly' with you as long as you refuse to trust me," she informed him primly.

"Can you blame me? You're trying to tell me that my amnesia is caused by the fact that I spent the year as a mythological creature! That sounds pretty freaking unbelievable to me," he countered before he could stop himself.

"I admit that it's unorthodox, but did you not tell me that there *isn't* a reasonable explanation? And if there isn't a reasonable explanation to be found, why *can't* you consider a supernatural one?"

"That's like asking why everyone doesn't believe that aliens exist, since there isn't a rational explanation for crop circles!" he threw his hands in the air.

"No, it isn't. Have *I* ever given you cause to think me a crazy alien conspiracy theorist? I'm a PhD candidate, for goodness sakes, Logan! I'm not some weirdo on the fringes of society," she was losing her temper, he knew, but there was little he was willing to do about it.

"But you sound like one when you ask me to believe that I was once a werewolf!" *How, how did I stand her long enough to knock her up?*

"But you *were* a werewolf for an entire year. Unfortunately, there's no way I can prove that to you with a swab test." The acid in her voice left no question of her sarcasm.

"Do you have anything to corroborate your story? Because I find it kind of suspicious that we had finally found the cause of my mysterious blackouts, but we didn't tell a single other person," he retaliated.

"Why would we have? They'd have reacted to the story the same way you have," She sent him a brief but exasperated look.

"So, why do you expect me to believe something that no one else would? The fact that I've slept with you doesn't mean that you automatically have my undying loyalty and trust. It only means that I thought you were attractive and that we would have a good time together," he smirked.

"And what about the fact that we were together exclusively for three months?" She sounded superior when she asked it.

"I'm almost never committed to one woman for more than a week at a time. And that reminds me, what about that girl at the lodge, Jenny? Can you even prove that happened?" He bet she couldn't.

"Ask Mark or Andrew. One or the other might remember her and the way they teased you for keeping the same girl for more than one night. And speaking of evidence, what about that scar on your right arm?" she raised a brow. "How do you explain that?"

"Mark and Andrew's version did actually agree with your journal, to a point. Both explain the scar by my drunken tumble in the woods when I thought it was a good idea to gather snow-covered firewood in the middle of the night." He ran his left hand over the scar on his forearm. Even now it was a faint pink ridge that zigzagged across the length of his arm, but he had no memory of how it came to be there. Occasionally he jokingly compared it to Harry Potter's famous lightning bolt, especially when he was trying to coax a slightly intoxicated woman into his bed, and about half the time, it worked.

During those first few months after he woke in the woods, he had stared at that scar over and over and wondered if it was the key to his lost year. The doctors said he'd carried it for a year, and that was about the time that his memories ended, so it made sense that it was connected, but since his accident happened when no one was around, there was no way to prove anything. Now,

110

after all this time, Lillie was telling him that he had been right. The amnesia and the scar came from the same source. *I only wish I could believe her.*

## Chapter 12

Lo was practicing his zombie-slaying skills on *Call of Duty* when he heard his mom's key in the door. He really wanted to drop the controller and run into the living room so that he didn't even have to wait one more minute before he saw his dad again. But that would make him look like some kind of overexcited little kid, and he didn't want his dad thinking he was lame. If he did, he might not come to visit very often. *That would seriously suck, since Mom basically said she wasn't going to take me back to Raleigh any time before Spring Break.* So he kept on playing, even though he had just taken a serious hit, and there was little hope he was going to finish the round.

"Lo," his mom's voice called out.

*Now I can!* He turned off his Xbox and TV, and then he walked calmly into the living room.

"Hey, Mom," he smiled and walked over to kiss her cheek.

"Hi, my love. How was school?" she asked when he stepped back.

"It was school," he said and turned to his dad. "Hey, Mr. Logan."

"Hey, Lo. It's good to see you again," his dad smiled at him, and he couldn't help but grin, though he still didn't like the way his dad had acted after they took the DNA test. But it was almost like there were two Los: the one who wanted to defend his mom and gripe at his dad for

112

being suck a jerk, and one who was just super happy to be spending the entire weekend figuring out stuff about his dad.

"It's good to see you, too," he agreed and put out his hand, since hugging a man he barely knew would definitely be something a little kid would do. As he took Lo's hand, his dad's smile twisted a little, but that was ok because when he shook Lo's hand, it was a real handshake, and not a silly one grownups gave to kids to make them feel big.

"Logan, you're in Lo's room for the weekend, so Lo'll show you where to go, if you want to put your suitcase down," his mom's voice was as close to happy as he had ever heard it when his dad was concerned, so he guessed they had figured out whatever it was that made them so mad at each other the last time they were together, and maybe his dad had even apologized, which meant that it was totally acceptable to be excited about hanging with *both* of his parents at the same time.

He had been pretty worried when his mom told him that she was going to pick his dad up from the airport. They had been so angry and upset with each other during Christmas break that he figured they would have gotten into a real fight while they were riding in the car if he hadn't been there. And since his dad's flight was coming in before Lo got out of class, that meant that he couldn't ride along and help the situation. It was just the two of them in his mom's little Toyota, and he really didn't want to wind up an orphan before the day was over.

But they both looked ok, so he didn't have to try to smile when he said, "Sure thing. My room's the one on the left," he pointed to three doors on the far wall. "And the one in the middle is the bathroom, and mom's room is on the right."

Last night, his mom had made him clean his room extra well since she didn't want his dad to have to sleep on the couch or in a dirty room, but for once in his life, Lo didn't even care that he had to clean. When his dad walked in, Lo wasn't embarrassed either. "I know the TV at your house is bigger," he said apologetically, "but I do have an Xbox, and *Call of Duty*."

"Well, as long as you have *COD*, I think I can make do," his dad winked and set his suitcase in front of Lo's closet. "You got a nice room here, Lo. It sort of reminds me of my little brother Preston's room at my mom and dad's house."

Lo had to work hard not to gasp. "I didn't know you had a brother."

"Yeah. He just graduated from college last year," his dad told him.

"Does he have a job?" Lo wondered.

"He works at my family's company," his dad nodded.

"You mean Michaels Corporate Management." Lo remembered. "What do you do there anyway, Mr. Logan?"

"Well, we do a lot of buying and selling, sort of like the stock market, except we aren't buying only stocks. We're buying whole companies at one time. We create and dismantle conglomerates," his dad answered. *I'm glad he talks to me like I know more than just two or three syllable words.*

"That's pretty cool, but I think it might be sorta risky, right? I mean, it is in the stock market," Lo was hasty to add on that last part, in case he had gotten confused about his teacher's lesson on bears and bulls or whatever animals they used to represent the way Wall Street was doing.

"It can be," his dad agreed. "But I have a financial team that helps me choose which companies to buy and sell and when to do it."

"Which means you can blame them if you lose big-time," Lo grinned. "That's pretty awesome."

"Yeah, sometimes it's good to be the boss," Logan laughed.

"I wouldn't know," Lo mumbled.

~

Lillie peeked into Lo's room to see what was keeping them. She saw that her son and his father were having a fairly serious discussion about how Logan made his money, and she was pleased to see that he wasn't patronizing Lo, despite his age. Logan was talking animatedly, and there wasn't a trace of acerbity in his voice. She smiled, and suddenly the two of them were blurred by tears.

She wiped them quickly with the back of her hand. *Neither of them would know what to do if he saw me cry.* She stood there another few seconds, watching before she knocked on the doorframe.

"Lo, did you show your father where the towels are?" she asked when they looked up at her.

"Oh! They're right here in the bathroom, Mr. Logan." Lo jumped up to take Logan to see the linen shelves behind the curtain in their bathroom/laundry area.

By the time they came back to the couch, she was sitting down, smiling fondly at both of her boys.

Lillie stood in the kitchen peeling and chopping the vegetables she was using for her stew. She could hear the sounds of a fierce Xbox competition coming from Lo's room. When she finished with the carrot she had been cubing, she paused. It had taken her a few potatoes and carrots before her hands were steady, but that wasn't an issue now. She was working mechanically, which was good, because if she let herself, she would panic at the thought of cooking for Logan.

Though they had been together for three months in college, she had never had the time or opportunity to make anything more substantial than coffee or cookies for him. Entertaining or impressing him hadn't been a concern back then. But now, she had gone back and forth a dozen times trying to decide what she would fix for him or whether she even wanted to. She had settled on stew as that would be hard to screw up, and hoped that he was open to the more rustic meal.

No, it wasn't the nerves that had her stopping the knife now. She tried to count the number of times she had imagined this. It wasn't possible. What had made her stop short was pure shock that a family dinner was actually happening.

She called Logan and Lo to the table when the meal was ready to serve. Lillie had put Lo at the head of the table, herself on his right and his father on his left.

"It looks good, Lillie," Logan said as he took his seat.

"Thanks," she managed to tell him and hoped she hadn't blushed, or at least that he hadn't seen it. To cover, she sat in her chair and made a show of scooting it up. When she could no longer delay looking up again, she fixed her eyes on Lo and nodded.

On cue, he took her hand and reached for Logan's. She saw that momentary flicker of surprise before Logan took Lo's hand, and then she bowed her head.

"Bless us, oh Lord, and these Thy gifts which we are about to receive from Thy bounty, through Christ Our Lord. Amen," Lo recited the prayer he had been using since he learned to speak.

As she looked up again, Logan caught her eye, and she could see the smirk. *So he lost that too.* She made sure that the sadness she felt didn't show and passed Logan the plate of cornbread bread.

~

Logan guessed he had been stupid not to expect that Lillie had raised their son in Catholicism. After all, that was her explanation for Lo's very existence. Still, it irked him. *Why do people feel compelled to force their children to be part of the same empty belief system that they are a part of?* As far as he was concerned, it was all a load of crap, and if parents knew it was crap, and they taught their children that it was a valuable part of life anyway, that seemed like deception. Then again, deception was pretty much all he and his brother had known from their parents. Still, that didn't make it right, and he didn't want that for Lo. It was a sure-fire way to guarantee that he was going to be jaded when he got older and realized things weren't as easy as a wish and a prayer.

Logan was under no illusions that he himself wasn't a bit on the cynical side, but he was not going to be the father that he had grown up with. He hoped he could at least say that for himself when Lo was grown. *I'll just have to talk to Lillie about that later.*

When he bit into the cornbread that Lo had passed him, all the inadequacies of religion left his mind. *Wow!*

was his only thought as he chewed. He hadn't had cornbread like this since he was small, and his mom still did some of the family cooking. Not that the cooks hadn't been good, but cornbread was something that not all people could make well. Lillie was obviously one of the few who could. He tried the stew next, and it didn't disappoint.

It wasn't the most sophisticated thing he had ever had in his mouth, but it was pleasant and filling and tasted of home somehow, though he couldn't recall ever having it at his parents'. "This is nice," he smiled genuinely.

"It isn't the type of food you're used to, but it was something hearty and warm, so I thought you might appreciate it after all your travelling today," she said without actually looking at him.

It was the second time she had avoided his eyes after he had given her a compliment today. *Surely she isn't embarrassed.* But he couldn't explain it otherwise, unless it meant that she was working especially hard not to make some sort of snide comment to counteract his praise. *The woman is a strange one,* he concluded. But Logan liked puzzles and the thrill of figuring out how all the pieces fit together, so he would keep working on her.

Maybe it was all her years of raising Lo on her own that made her so distant. She had probably had to go through some tough times, and her defense mechanism was most likely that icy exterior.

Because there was silence, he turned to Lo. "Does your mom cook like this all the time?"

"Pretty much, except for times like midterms and finals, and then she plans for it and freezes stuff ahead of time," he answered.

"Then I'm lucky that I'm usually so far away. Otherwise, I might come over for every meal and get too big to fit through the door!" Logan laughed along with his son, but watched Lillie's reaction carefully. She said nothing, only smiled slightly and continued to eat.

By his calculations, Lillie said no more than twenty words to him during the whole of dinner. She and Lo had a few short conversations in between bites, but she didn't seem inclined to say anything to him.

"Can I be excused, Mom?" Lo asked once they were finished.

"Yes, my love," she nodded.

Logan watched as Lo took all of their plates and went straight to the kitchen. Lillie was getting the soup pot, so he grabbed the platter of cornbread and pitcher of tea. By the time he had walked the few steps to the kitchen, Lo had the water for the dishes started, and Lillie was dipping the leftover soup into a plastic container. He slid into the narrow space and placed the platter on the counter.

"Excuse me," he moved carefully past her, opened the refrigerator, and put the pitcher in the door. When he had moved back past her again, he asked, "What do you want me to do with the cornbread?"

"I can just put it in a plastic bag," she closed the lid on her dish.

"Tell me where they are, and I'll do it," Logan insisted.

"There in the drawer, right next to the sink," Lo told him as he scrubbed the newly emptied pot.

Lillie reached for the drawer, but Logan was quicker and had the bag before she could get one. She gave him a long look, but she said nothing and began to dry the plates that Lo had washed.

Logan put the leftover cornbread into the bag and hoped that it would be just as tasty when it was reheated tomorrow. He watched as Lo and Lillie worked. They were efficient, and he figured that was because of the number of times they had done the dishes together. "Is there anything else you need me to do?" he asked, since it was clear that they had a system going.

"I think we're good here, thanks," she told him. "We'll be done in a few minutes."

~

Lo and his mom stood together and finished the supper dishes. It was pretty cool getting to eat with his dad, but his mom had been kind of quiet.

He waited until his dad had put up some things and walked towards the bathroom. "Are you ok, Mom?"

"Yes, baby. Why do you ask?" she glanced at him.

"Are you mad at Dad? You didn't want him to help us."

"He's our guest, Lo. It's rude to expect guests to help you clean up. Plus, you and I have it covered, don't we?" she smiled.

Lo and his dad decided to watch a movie when the kitchen was clean. Because he didn't want his mom to have any nightmares, Lo decided that he shouldn't suggest that they watch *Night of the Living Dead*, even though he was pretty sure his dad would like it. For the most part, his mom was pretty cool, even according to Alex and J.J. But her one weakness was that she was a chicken when it came to any kind of scary movie. The part he didn't get was that she could read all sorts of scary folktales and play with dead people's bones and all their stuff all day long, but she couldn't handle a monster on

120

TV. She always had to have a pillow to hide behind if she did agree to watch one.

Instead, he chose an action movie because he knew his mom liked those, especially if they had a hot dude and plenty of explosions for him to walk away from. So he put in *Raiders of the Lost Ark* because Indiana Jones was her favorite action movie hero, though she didn't count the Indy movie they made about the aliens.

But Lo wasn't stupid. He saw the way his mom tried not to look at his dad. She had been doing that ever since they got home today. And even though the lights were off, he knew that she wasn't watching the young version of Harrison Ford with the same kind of attention she usually did.

Over the credits, he heard his dad ask, "How much of that is real archeology?"

"Not very much at all, actually," she told him. "Unfortunately, none of my colleges are anywhere near that athletic, and none of them look that good in the field either."

"That explains why it's just the two of you, then," his dad teased.

Lo wished that there were some way he could talk to his dad telepathically. Mentioning the fact that his mom was single was the quickest way to make her mad, so he pretended to have to figure out where the movie went on the shelf.

"Yes, because I would only date men in my field and only those who masquerade as professors of archeology but never actually do any real archeological work," she crossed her arms.

"I was joking, Lillie," his dad explained. But it was too late. Lo could tell by the way she held her mouth that his dad was going to be in trouble with her for a while.

"It's just me and Lo because that's the way I want it to be. We get along fine by ourselves," she told him flatly.

"I can see that," his dad's tone had softened, Lo noted. *It sucks to be you*, he told his dad mentally, but at least he wasn't the one who was in trouble for his mouth this time.

## Chapter 13

Lillie went to bed that night knowing it was useless. *How can I even dream of sleeping when we're only separated by one room?* She laid in the darkness and thought back to the days just after Logan stopped coming to her apartment and how she wasn't able to sleep then either. At that time, she couldn't do it because she had become accustomed to curling up next to Logan's warmth and drifting off with the feel of his breath flowing lightly across her face.

The times when she woke during the night with him beside her were the ones that she had the hardest time keeping out of her head. Those were the times when she was sure he thought of her, maybe not in the same way as she thought of him, but he did think of her. In his sleep, he reached for her if she happened to move away from him, even fractionally, and sometimes, if he was particularly restless, he even said her name. It was those nights that she had measured everything else by, and when she did, those nights always proved to be worth the hard work and stress.

Now, it wasn't his absence that she had to worry about. It was his proximity. *Why did I ever agree to let him spend the weekend with us? Now I'm going to lose two nights of sleep and be too tired to function on Monday morning!*

Frustrated at her own emotions, Lillie rolled onto her side and clicked on her bedside lamp. She picked up *Katherine*, but after a few pages, it became evident to her that reading about John of Gaunt and his paramour wasn't the best way to put herself to sleep. She tried *Royalty For Commoners*, since it had no plot, but it had its own associations with Logan that overrode the dryness of its text.

She reread the first few pages when she thought about the inscription on the flyleaf. She had read the words repeatedly during those first few weeks after she'd lost him. She didn't even have to look at them now to quote what he had written:

To LILLIE,
FOR ALL THE LONG NIGHTS IN THE STACKS AND ELSEWHERE.
LOGAN

Lillie could have slapped herself in the face for her own stupidity. If the man needed concrete proof that he had contributed to the research in that file folder and that they had actually been a couple, then the words in his own handwriting should be concrete enough.

As Logan got into his son's bed, he had to admit that the night had been awkward, but it could have been worse. The kid had been so thrilled to hang out that Logan could have said or done almost anything, and he would have been happy. It was Lillie that Logan couldn't figure out.

She was polite most of the time, but there were others, particularly when he questioned her motives or truthfulness, when she was downright frigid. The entire time he had known her, which hadn't even been a month, she had kept her metaphorical distance from him, yet she expected him to take her at her word. *That's a double standard if I've ever heard of one.* For a woman who supposedly had been in love with him, she had an odd way of showing it. Then again, she had written that journal thirteen years ago, right after she had found out she was pregnant, if he was to believe her, so maybe she was still living in the glow of her first love back then, and by now she had gotten closely acquainted with reality, and when he didn't come riding in to the rescue, she had decided to be angry at rather than besotted with him. *If that's the case, it's just as well because this way I don't have to worry about any unwanted attachments.*

Lillie was still wide-awake when the clock on her nightstand told her it was six a.m. Because lying there for another two hours wouldn't help anything, she decided to get up and do some grading while she waited for the boys to wake up. She only had two courses of Intro to Anthropology this term, so the paperwork wasn't as overwhelming as it could be.

She wrapped herself in an afghan and padded to the kitchen in her warm, fuzzy socks to put on a pot of coffee.

When she had a warm cup in her hand, she grabbed her leather satchel, pulled out a stack of tests, and sat down at the kitchen table, since Lo was still snoozing on the couch. She was thankful that it wasn't yet midterms, which meant that she didn't have any essay questions to grade. She had almost finished the last of the stack when she heard the door to Lo's room open. Though she wasn't proud of it, she couldn't help looking up. Logan emerged and was wearing gray sweatpants and a white V-neck shirt.

"Good morning," she whispered, tucking the red pen she was grading with behind her ear.

"Morning," he nodded and headed to the bathroom with his shaving kit.

Lillie had a cup of black coffee waiting when he came out. He took a seat across from her, and she handed the mug to him with a pleasant smile. "You still take it like this, don't you? Because I have cream and sugar if you don't."

"I still like the taste of unadulterated coffee," his grin was quick, and it pulled at her, so she slid the hand that was very near to his back to her side of the table. She let him have a few sips in silence and watched as his steel gray eyes gradually lost the haze of sleep.

When Logan looked up at Lillie from his cup, she knew that he had something on his mind. Still, she pulled the pen from its perch and picked up another paper.

"Since Lo's still asleep, can we talk for a little while?" his voice broke in before she had read more than a sentence or two of the short answer.

"Sure," she set the paper back on top of the stack it came from and capped her pen.

"I'm not sure how we left things between us thirteen years ago, but it must have been hard for you not to have any closure." He was smart, she knew, and he was using those eyes of his to try to disarm her.

"I had closure, Logan. You came to my door, kissed me until I lost brain cells and then proceeded to tell me goodbye, just like I wrote in the journal you've already read."

"Well, that doesn't mean it was easy for you to watch me move on." His motive wasn't clear, but she knew he

126

wasn't at a place where he would be overly kind to her without one.

"It wasn't. What's this all about, Logan?" she raised a brow.

"I may not be the smartest guy on the planet, but I can tell when I'm getting the Big Chill, so I'm trying, once again, to make amends for whatever has made you so upset with me. Like I said before, the more we get along, the easier things will be for Lo."

"So you're apologizing for not believing me about the cause of your amnesia? Does that mean you also decided to believe that you were actually a lycanthrope?" She was careful not to use the word 'werewolf.'

He blinked at her for a moment, and when he answered, she knew he did so carefully. "Lillie, I'm sure that you believe you're telling me the truth, but I just can't get onboard with the idea. Besides, I wasn't talking about what I've done to upset you recently. I was talking about what I did before."

She knew he was changing the subject, but she couldn't resist responding. "You have nothing to apologize for as far as the past goes, Logan. Just because you don't remember anything doesn't mean that I don't, and the Logan who I dated was only ever good to me."

"So, you're pissed at me only because of what happened in December?" His coffee was getting cold, but she didn't bother to tell him that.

"I'm not pissed at you, Logan. I'm just disappointed in the person you are at the moment," she looked down at the table.

"What d'you mean?" She could hear his confusion and had to remind herself that his ignorance was no one's fault but her own.

"I mean, you may call yourself Logan Michaels, but the Logan who I knew–the one who is the father of my child–isn't the same man who's sitting across the table from me right now. And seeing your face, *his* face, makes me miss the man I knew. That man was my friend," she bit her lip.

~

He saw from her face that if he pushed the issue, she might crumble on him. *That's just what I need, to make my kid's mom cry.* "You've got to understand that I'm not the kind of person who lives with the abstract and the unknown the way you do. I deal with numbers and facts, and maybe living in absolutes for so long has killed my imagination, but it is what it is. I just can't explain my problems with a myth, and I'm sorry that the old me would have believed you, but you're right. The old me is gone, along with that year of my life, and there's nothing that I can do to change that."

"What if I can prove to you that, at one time in your life, you believed my theory?" she questioned suddenly.

"Then I'd say I'd be quite a bit easier to convince." *But that won't be possible.*

He watched as she pushed away from the table and went to her room. She came back almost immediately after she disappeared though her doorway. As she returned to her seat, Logan saw that she had a book in her hand. Lillie laid it on the table, opened it, and slid it to him.

On the inside cover, he could see an inscription that was in his own handwriting. *Apparently, we pulled a few all-nighters together.* "So we studied in the library. How does that prove anything? Wasn't that part of your job?"

"Yes, we spent many hours together in the stacks, studying possible cures for your condition, but most of that was off the clock for me."

Logan examined the lines of ink. *Why the freak can I not remember anything?* He tried to push past the blankness that he always ran into when he tried to recall anything about the time between the end of his junior year at NCSU and the end of his senior year. Like always, there was nothing there, no matter how hard he concentrated. There were no words, thoughts, or images of any kind.

He shook his head and vowed that he wasn't going to waste any more time trying to do what he couldn't. When he looked at Lillie again, her viridian eyes pierced him, and he had a sudden flash. It still wasn't a complete memory, but he did see one thing very clearly: green eyes.

~

"Logan!" Lillie had seen the change in Logan's face and knew that whatever he had just remembered wasn't pleasant. She covered his hand with hers. "Logan, are you okay?"

"You have green eyes," he said.

"Yes," she nodded. "That's right. I have green eyes, and you have gray ones."

"It's all I can remember. Just a pair of green eyes," he repeated and scrubbed his free hand over his face.

"Okay," she felt the hand beneath hers begin to tremble, and she squeezed it tightly. "It's okay, Logan. Are you sure that you're remembering eyes?"

"Yes, bright green eyes," he nodded.

"Here. Take a drink of coffee. I know it isn't what you want, but I won't be able to offer you anything stronger." She pushed his lukewarm mug into his hands, and he took a few swigs. He still looked a bit pale, but she hoped that he wasn't going to puke or pass out now.

"Your eyes. I'm remembering your eyes," he shook his head.

Though Lillie was trying to keep her emotions in check, she felt something come loose inside her. "We meant something to each other, Logan. The fact that you remember someone you once cared about isn't a surprise." She sent him a reassuring smile.

"But I *don't* remember you or whatever it was that I felt about you when we were together. The *only* thing I remember is your eyes."

~

Lo awoke to the sound of his parents talking quietly. He rolled over and sat up. They were in deep conversation and hadn't seen that he was awake. He tried to decide whether they were just talking or whether they were fighting again.

". . . all I'm saying is that they may not be *my* eyes. I can't be the only green-eyed girl you've spent the night with," his mom was saying.

"If it wasn't your eyes that I saw, why did the memory come back to me only when I was looking at you? I mean, do you have any idea how long I've been trying to remember anything from that year?"

"Probably since you found out that you had lost that time," she told his dad.

"Exactly! And no one, I mean *no one* was able to tell me anything that helped me remember!" he exclaimed. "But now, thirteen years after the fact, I'm able to remember green eyes! Why is that?"

"I've told you, Logan, I have absolutely no idea. All I know is what I wrote down in the journal, what I experienced and what you told me about—" his mom started to say, but she stopped and glanced in his direction. "Morning, Lo. Sorry we were kind of loud," she walked over and kissed his cheek.

"Hey," his dad waved a hand in Lo's direction. "I just can't understand why they would come back to me now," Logan continued the previous conversation before Lo could even speak. He waited to see if his mom would respond, but she gave his dad a sharp look and shook her head.

Lo knew that this meant she was done with the topic, but that didn't mean his dad did. *Please take the hint*, he held his breath. There was an uncomfortable pause, and then his mom saved them all when she asked, "Anyone ready for breakfast?"

When they were done and dressed, Lo wondered how he and his parents would spend the rest of Saturday, not that he minded playing some more *COD* with his dad, but his mom had a rule about too much video game exposure, so he was pretty sure she'd make them do something else.

He walked into the living area from his room and sat on the opposite end of the couch from his dad, since his mom was getting ready . . . still! Usually she was dressed and ready way before Lo even got out of his p.j. pants, but for some reason, this morning she was happy to sit around in her own pajamas until she and Lo had finished the breakfast dishes.

"So what do you want to do, today?" his dad asked. "Do y'all have a routine for Saturdays?"

"Not really," Lo shrugged. "I was just wondering about that . . ."

"Well, I had a little time to think while I was on the plane . . . Would you be interested in paintball?"

"Paintball???" Lo could see himself and his dad suited up and hiding from their enemies, just waiting to take the perfect shot. "Awesome!"

"I thought you might say that," Logan chuckled. "After all, it's a lot like a live action version of *Call of Duty*!"

Lillie humored her son and his father and tagged along when they went to the paintball field in Whitmore Lake. She knew they would enjoy themselves, but she was beyond leery about suiting up and shooting a paintball gun with the two of them. *I might still be agile enough to explore digs like a twenty-year-old, but I doubt that I can roll around on the ground and come up shooting the way that the boys will.*

"C'mon, Mom!" Lo begged, reminding her of when he was a little boy and said the same thing while tugging on her sleeve when he really wanted a certain toy. "We promise we'll be easy on you, won't we, Mr. Logan?" he turned to his father for confirmation.

"We promise," Logan echoed, but she remembered that gleam in his eye and knew that she had better cover herself well if she wanted to survive the game.

After a few moments of debate between the boys over which type of gun they wanted, Logan stepped up to the counter. It only took Lillie a second or two to realize that he was renting the guns and other paraphernalia for the three of them. "Wait, Logan! I'll cover myself and Lo," she moved beside him.

"I've got it, Lillie," he didn't even turn to look as he said it.

"No. If you want to pay for Lo, that's ok, but I'll pay for my own supplies," she repeated.

"You cooked my supper last night and my breakfast this morning. I've got it," Logan argued and paid the clerk before she could stop him. His stubbornness suddenly reminded her of all the times he'd bought her coffee when they were in college.

She shook her head and had to tell herself that he wasn't that guy anymore, even if he looked it. "Thanks."

By the end of the afternoon, Lille felt like she had been working a dig except that she hadn't had the thrill of finding any artifacts. She was tired, sore, thirsty, and ready to curl up with some coffee and a book, or even do school work if it got her out of these paint-stained coveralls and goggles.

Lo and Logan had kept their word for all of five minutes before they strategized together and decided to go out for blood. She liked to think that she had put up a valiant fight, but her clothes told a different story. After the last time Lo ambushed her, she held up her hands. "I surrender. Take me to your leader."

"Ha!" Lo cried. "We take no prisoners on this rock!" he yelled before he fired into her chest plate at point-blank range.

"Logan!" she screamed indignantly.

"Yes?" the original Logan asked, popping up from behind an old car.

"Not you! I was yelling at my son who didn't show his mother the mercy she asked for!" Lillie called hotly.

"My mistake," he shrugged and took the shot, hitting Lillie in almost the same location that their son had. She

133

felt the impact of the paintball and looked over at his wide grin.

"That's it! Forget the rules!" she aimed her gun and emptied it into the both of them. When the ammo was spent and both of them were staring at her in disbelief, she pulled her goggles up and tipped her rifle so that she could pretend to blow the smoke out of the end of the barrel.

~

By the end of the weekend, Lo decided that he had the coolest parents in the world. They had hung out, watched movies, and played paintball for the past two days. When he and his mom drove his dad to the airport after breakfast on Sunday, he was sad that it was over. *I wish that Dad could stay a while longer.* But his mom wanted to be sure they were back home in time for lunch so that she could still finish her grading and do a little studying before Mass at 5:00.

Though she normally went at 7:00 on Sunday mornings, she hadn't done so today because there wasn't time for that and breakfast too if she wanted to drive Logan. That was fine with Lo because it meant he didn't have to be up as early as he normally would. Still, because it was his dad's last day in Ann Arbor, he wound up not sleeping in.

"Well, Lo, it was a good few days," his dad told him as he patted Lo's back. They were standing in the terminal, and the flight to Raleigh had just been called.

"Yes, sir, it was," Lo agreed. "Thanks for coming."

"No problem, and I'll be looking forward to you coming to visit me in March," his dad reminded him.

Though Spring Break seemed to be eons away, Lo smiled and said, "I can't wait."

After a moment of looking at Lo, his dad turned to his mom. "It was nice seeing you again," he held out his hand, and she took it.

Lo was careful to watch his mom as his dad held her hand without shaking it. It took her a second to make eye contact and respond, but then she smiled slightly. "It was. Have a safe flight." She pulled her hand back.

"Will do," his father nodded "I'll call you in a few days, Lo," he said over his shoulder as he walked to his departure gate.

Lo nodded, since his dad wouldn't hear him anyway, and kept watching until he couldn't see his dad through the crowd any longer.

## Chapter 14

Logan thought that once he left Michigan, he would leave the awkwardness he'd felt too. It was only because she was angry with him that things felt the way they did, and eventually she'd accept his apologies or let go of her anger or both. In any case, *he* wasn't the one who had the problem. It was Lillie who kept things strained between them. All he wanted was to get to know his son. Why would he make that more difficult for both of them by antagonizing his son's mother? That was illogical. But when he touched down in Raleigh, Logan still didn't seem to be himself.

The eyes he had suddenly remembered while he was at Lillie's apartment were never far from his mind. Part of him was happy to have at least recalled something about that blank year after all this time, but the other part was annoyed that Lillie had something to do with the one thing he could recall. And when you coupled that with the inscription he had written in Lillie's book, it became pretty clear that Lillie wasn't exaggerating about their relationship. But sleeping with the same girl for three months straight just didn't seem like something he would do. *The last time I checked, commitment wasn't my thing. The problem is I only have her word to go on for this.*

And though he could tell that she loved Lo, he wasn't sure about her trustworthiness, especially when she seemed so freaking serious about the whole werewolf thing. *Aside from that, the woman has herself together, but that's a big exception. People have been locked away for a lot less.*

Not that he thought she was crazy, exactly. She was too organized and too good a mother to their son to be insane. But there was something that wasn't right where she was concerned. She was always wary of him. Always kept her distance. It was as if she was preparing herself for the fallout from some kind of nuclear explosion.

According to the journal, she had encountered him only once after he had lost that time, and though her description of the event was sparse, he could tell that it had nearly killed her when he didn't know who she was. And he could see how a loss like that might screw a person up, especially if he had been her first lover as her story seemed to indicate.

From what Logan saw, Lillie seemed to be a fairly devout person, and that she had even chosen to become his lover was something he couldn't figure out, even after reading the journal. The trouble with it was, the whole story focused on him and what he felt and saw. She gave him very little of her own feelings and observations.

And though she had lost her way for a little while, she seemed to be as committed to church now as she had been before he knocked her up. When he looked at the situation like that, it wasn't hard to see why she might be wary of him. He was a reminder of her fall from grace, and he hadn't been the charming prince she had dreamed about as a child.

*But that isn't my fault! If I had known . . . if she had just reminded me when she realized I didn't know about her—*

He had to force himself to stop that line of thinking. There was nothing he could do about any of that now. What he *could* do was make sure that Lo had what he needed and wanted, and that he knew that Logan would be there for him. *But what could he do about Lillie?* That was a question that he might have to consider a while. He wasn't at fault, he knew, but circumstances that he was a part of had caused life to be harder for her than it could have been, and he was sorry for that.

He knew all about collateral damage. The difference between him and his father was that he always tried to be aware of its victims and make amends, whereas Philip didn't give a crap about the incidental victims of his exploits as long as he got what he wanted.

~

Lo was hanging out with Alex, beating the crap out of him to be more precise, one chilly afternoon in February when his cell phone rang and interrupted their campaign.

When he saw that it wasn't his mom's number, Lo knew exactly who was on the other end of the line.

"Hey, Mr. Logan!" he cried before his dad could even get a word out.

"Hey, Lo," he heard the laughter on his father's end. "It sounds like you're doing pretty good up there in all that ice and snow!"

"I'd be doing better if they actually let us out of school for it here like they do at home. Are you good down there?" Lo wondered and couldn't help but remind himself that he and his mom would be back in North Carolina in a little over a month.

He knew they wouldn't be able to spend the whole week with Ma and Pa and his aunt and uncles this year, but it was totally worth missing out on their tradition, if it meant that he was going to be spending that time with his dad.

"I'm good, Lo. What are you up to today?"

Lo explained that he was in the middle of a game and had been killing Alex.

"Then, it sounds like you might be a little bit more competition than you were the last time you were here. Maybe I ought to get in a little practice time too!"

"Yeah, you'd better, if you plan on beating me now. Of course, you're a big-shot CEO dude, so I bet you can get by with playing Xbox at work!" Lo teased.

"Actually, I think my board might not look too kindly on it," his dad replied. "But maybe I can sneak in a game or two without getting caught."

"Sure you can! You can just say that playing *COD*'s a new company policy and fire anybody who has a problem with it!"

"I don't think that's quite the way things work, son," his dad laughed again, but things on Lo's end were suddenly quiet. "You there?"

"Yes, sir," Lo swallowed. "I'm here."

"If you're busy, then I can always call back after supper tonight," he suggested.

"Ok," Lo made himself answer.

"All right. You have fun with your friends, and I'll talk to you tonight," his dad still sounded pleasant.

"Yes, sir," Lo agreed. "Bye."

"Bye."

"Who was that, man?" Alex wanted to know.

"My dad," Lo whispered, having only said that word aloud a few times.

"For real, dude? I thought he wasn't around," Alex asked.

"He wasn't, but he is now," Lo answered and wished that they could talk about something else.

"What's he like? I'll bet, if you play your cards right, you can get all kinds of presents out of him, since he was gone for so long and probably wants to make it up to you." Lo could see the wheels turning in Alex's mind.

"I don't think it's like that with my dad. Ever since we found out about each other, he's made sure to call and talk every few days."

"That's just guilt, man. He's calling you because he knows he was a crappy dad for the first thirteen years of your life, and he'll probably try to make that up to you for the entire rest of his!"

Lo gave up trying to make Alex understand. He wouldn't be able to anyway, since both of Alex's parents had been with him his entire life. Maybe that was why Lo hadn't told anybody about finding his dad in the first place. No one would understand. And that was probably the reason that his mom hadn't told Ma and Pa about his dad either. Because she hadn't, he wasn't sure what part of Spring Break he would be spending in Manteo and what part he would be spending in Raleigh.

Usually, he and his mom went home for the entire break. This year was going to be different. *Especially since he called me "son" when we were on the phone earlier.* Lo knew that a ton of other people called boys "son," so it really wasn't anything special, but it hadn't been just anyone who had called him "son" today.

~

Logan made sure to call Lo again after he knew that they had eaten. He was still wrestling with what to do about the way things were between him and Lillie, and he definitely didn't want to antagonize her further by interrupting her supper.

He had to call on her cell now because he knew that when the two of them were together, Lo wasn't allowed to use his own. He geared himself up and dialed her number.

"Hey, Lillie," he said when she picked up.

"Hello," she answered.

"How are you?" he inquired politely.

"I'm fine, Logan. And you?" she asked just as politely. *When is she ever going to relax? I'm on the phone with her. There's no way I'm going to attack her from this distance.*

"I'm fine, too. I'm already planning for y'all's visit," he confessed.

"That's still several weeks ahead, Logan. I haven't even talked to my parents about it yet." *Why does that matter?*

"Do you think that your coming here to visit will cause some sort of problem?" he couldn't help but ask.

"I just meant that they don't know anything about you, and we stay with them during the break, so I want to let them know before we make any concrete plans," she told him.

"Ok. Is there a reason you haven't told them, if you're waiting on them to make a decision?" *This ought to be good.*

"I was waiting for an appropriate moment."

"Well, let me know when that moment arrives, but in the meantime, I'd like to talk to Lo." He needed to get off the phone with her before he said something Lo might not like.

~

Lo could tell that his dad wasn't especially happy when his mom was on the phone with his dad, but he didn't know if he really wanted to ask what was wrong. He had a hunch that whatever was bothering Logan probably had something to do with Lillie, and if that was the case, it might just be better if he didn't know. Otherwise, he might get really mad at his dad again, which would be kind of awkward since he was also still really stoked about actually having a dad. Instead, they talked about how his game with Alex had gone that afternoon and the fact that Logan had been practicing, but Lo knew there was no way his dad was going to be able to beat him at *COD*.

But when he hung up the phone, Lo took one look at his mom and asked, "What's dad mad about now?"

"He doesn't understand what family means," she sighed. "Not that I blame him. He hasn't really had a family that functions anywhere near the way ours does." She seemed more sad than frustrated with his father. *I guess that's better than* **both** *of them being mad at each other.*

"Well, even though it seems like he can be pretty cool, he hasn't made things easy for us," Lo shook his head.

"We haven't made life easy for him in the last few months, either, Lo. He never asked you to show up at his apartment, and he never expected to have a thirteen-year-old son. He never planned for that, and if you father is anything, he's someone with a reasonable plan, or at least a rough idea of what he wants to do.

"Now you're here, and he isn't sure how to react. He wants to do the right thing for you because his dad didn't do what was right for him, but wanting to do what's right and knowing how to go about it are two different things. Then there's me. If Logan wasn't planning for a son, he *certainly* wasn't planning what to do about the aforementioned son's mother. And when you look at it with all those factors in mind, his behavior isn't really that surprising, is it, Lo?"

"I guess I could see how he might be sorta overwhelmed," Lo agreed. "And he was really nice when he came to visit."

"Yes, he was," his mom nodded.

~

Lillie watched as the wolf loped away from her apartment on the night after Valentine's Day. Since she wasn't going to be locating its den during this Phase, she had decided to research an alternate way of curing Lo's condition. He had been a shape shifter for four months now, and during that time had had met his father. She couldn't make Lo go through the terrible confusion and sense of loss that Logan had, even though he would only lose a third of the time his father had. *Who knows what kind of adverse effects that type of amnesia could have on a teenager?* It wasn't something she was willing to risk, especially now that she would have to explain to Logan why Lo suddenly couldn't remember who he was. *On the other hand, if that did actually happen, I bet he wouldn't have any trouble believing that what happened to Lo happened to him too. It would be the logical conclusion, after all.*

She used her faculty access to search the University's databases for articles on Sarah Abbot, the girl whose lupine form had brought the curse down upon Logan and in turn Lo. Back in 2007, they hadn't found a body or any sign of the girl who disappeared from her cabin at the ski resort in Breckenridge on the same night that the rest of her youth group were murdered. *But maybe, just maybe someone has found something by now that might lead to an alternative cure.* If Lillie's working theory was right, then there had been a lycanthrope in the Abbot family in each generation, possibly since Colonial times, and if that was the case, the Abbots had to have some way of curing it or

143

at least repressing it, which was what she had effectively done with Logan. *And I bet whatever it is, the treatment doesn't have the same nasty side effects that mine had on Logan.* Otherwise, someone would have noticed that there was something strange about the Abbots, and in less tolerant times, strange families hadn't faired too well. *Case in point: the Salem Witch Trials.*

All of her digging turned up nothing suspicious about the Abbots of the past or present. Also, most inconveniently, there was no word of Sarah Abbot, other than one last article about a year after her disappearance that led Lillie to believe the girl had been relegated to a box somewhere in the cold case files.

The more she thought about it, the more she became positive that there had to be some way to get rid of the condition without the memory loss and without such great risk to the body. Without modern medical care, some of the previous Abbots could have very well died if they each had had to plunge through a mirror to end the phases. *And I'm not even sure that they could afford to buy a mirror large enough for a wolf to jump through in Colonial times, let alone afford to let that same mirror be destroyed.*

Lillie felt his arms around her and knew even before she opened her eyes. She almost didn't want to for fear that changing anything about the moment would ruin it. As it was, she could have spent the rest of her life in this dark, blissful place, secure in the comfort and strength of this familiar embrace. At length, she did though, and when she opened them, she saw that he was smiling in that soft, unguarded way that he did only when they were alone together. Here, where they were both vulnerable, he could risk dropping that ever-present freewheeling frat boy façade and show her that she wasn't another of his meaningless lays. He could be kind and press kisses into the hollow of her collarbone or brush the hair from her face. He could be gentle and run his hand up and down her arm while snuggling with her under the warm covers.

His lips moved in such a way that she knew he was about to speak, so she covered them with her own. Words would be too much, and if she wasn't careful—

But it was too late. Lillie rolled over and slapped at her alarm clock with much more force than was necessary to shut it off. She was awake, and she was alone in her bedroom. She had managed to sleep for all of thirty minutes after Lo came to in her arms, and in that short span, it felt as if she and Logan had spent hours together. She brushed tears away and reminded herself that the Logan who had just held her in his arms was the Logan of the past, not the Logan who had spent the weekend with her and Lo last month. She made the coffee as quickly as she could, but even with the cream and sugar that normally made that first sip so enjoyable, it didn't wash away the bitter taste in her mouth.

## Chapter 15

Lo could tell that his mom was nervous about making her weekly Sunday phone call to Ma and Pa. It was February 20th, which meant there were less than two weeks before they were supposed to go home for Spring Break. Most of the time they were both excited when it was this close to a long vacation, but at the moment, both of them were more worried than anything else.

Lo was worried about his Fifth Phase happening somewhere besides Ann Arbor. He was also worried that while he was a wolf he might do something terrible to Ma or Pa or someone else in Manteo. And if he and his mom were in Raleigh for the Phase, then he had to worry about his dad's reaction to finding out the truth. *Of course, he'll have to find out sooner or later, and the quicker he understands that Mom isn't a crazy liar, the better things will be.* But a part of Lo was afraid that if his dad was faced with having to accept that he and his son were lycanthropes, he might do a little more than hyperventilate the way he had when Lillie had finally convinced him of the truth. This time, since he really wasn't affected and didn't have to believe Lillie for his own well-being, Logan could very well choose to leave and never look back.

From what his mother had told Lo about his father, Lo could see where his dad might just decide that the two of them were too much trouble and walk away. He hoped it wasn't true, but he definitely couldn't deny his dad's commitment issues.

Lo tried not to think about his dad leaving anymore and listened to his mom's side of the conversation with her parents instead.

"Could you put me on speakerphone, Momma? . . . Because there's something I need to tell you and Daddy, and I don't want to have to do it twice. . . Yes, I know he hates the telephone, but I want you to put him on anyway." Lillie's lips were a hard line across her face, and Lo knew that she wasn't happy. *Then again, I don't imagine Pa will be too happy either.*

"Can you both hear me?" she drew a breath. "Good. I know we usually come home for the week of Spring Break, but we aren't going to be able to stay the whole time this year . . . because I'm taking Lo to Raleigh for part of the week to see his father."

To Lo's way of thinking, that was the last thing that his grandparents even heard his mom say. After that, they were too busy yelling at her to hear much more. He checked his watch. They had been on the phone for more than an hour, and she was telling them that she had known about his dad all along for what must have been the third or fourth time. *Thank goodness she's leaving out the werewolf part. If they have a problem with Dad now, who knows how freaked out they'd get if they knew he had been a wolf when I was conceived, and he passed it on to me?*

"Will you just please listen to me a minute?" his mom was asking. "I never meant to hurt you. I was only trying to do what I thought was best for Lo and me. I understand that, but at the time, I made what I thought was the best decision I could. I'm sorry! I was twenty-one years old! I wish I knew then what I know now, since none of this would have happened, but I didn't, and it

147

did. So, now the only thing I can do besides pray about it is to make sure that I don't stand in the way of Lo getting to know his father." She breathed raggedly for a moment when she had finished speaking, and Lo saw that she was blinking really quickly.

"I'm sorry I've disappointed you and Daddy. I only called to find out which part of the week would be better for us to spend with you . . ." Tears were falling now, and Lo couldn't stand it anymore, so he went to his room and picked up *The Zombie Survival Guide. If this isn't the beginning of the apocalypse, I won't know what is.*

~

Logan was sitting at his desk with the previous quarter's fiscal reports spread out in front of him. He had been reading them for a while now, and though he found that everything was still in the black, he didn't like the looks of the profit margin when compared to the two previous quarters. There was a recession, and slight losses were to be expected, but that didn't mean he could let himself off the hook. Sure, he had financial advisors who handled most of MCM's transactions, but at the end of the day, it was Logan Michaels who signed off on everything. It was his name that was on the line when the stockholders had questions, and that gave him the right to stew in his Jameson every once in a while.

He was up pouring another few fingers when his cell rang. It was eight thirty. No one from the office would bother him this time of night, and he doubted his mother would call again so soon. He reached for the phone. *Maybe I won't be stewing quite as much as I thought,* he grinned, thinking it might have been a lonely, yet lovely friend who was looking for company, but then he saw the number.

"Hello, Lillie," he said as he picked up and took a swig. He was going to need it.

"Hi, Logan."

"Do you have any idea when you'll be in town?" he asked, though he didn't expect her to know. *Why would she when she hadn't had a clue the last time he asked her?*

"Actually, that's precisely why I was calling. I was thinking that Lo and I would go to my parents' first and then come to Raleigh on Wednesday, if that works for you."

"And you'll be leaving on the following Saturday?" he calculated the number of hours she'd need for the return trip.

"We can wait until Sunday, if we leave about seven in the morning. Lo and I both have school on Monday the 21st."

Logan wasn't sure why Lillie and Lo had to spend any time in Manteo at all over the break, let alone the whole first half of it, but he had a feeling that if he asked Lillie about it, she might get aggravated, so he contented himself with, "I guess three days is better than nothing at all."

"Yes, I would say so," she agreed, and he felt the chill in her words. "We'll leave early enough that we get to your place in time for lunch, which will give us four full nights together," she said, as if that was some kind of gift.

"That's good to know," he told her and hoped she felt the chill on her end too. "Does that mean that you've talked to your parents?"

"Yes, of course," she sounded as if he had asked her the most ridiculous question in the world. He wanted to reach through the phone and ring her patronizing little neck. *So what if she has more college degrees than I do? I make more money in three months than she does in the whole year!*

"I take it they weren't too pleased," he continued the line of conversation before he actually vocalized his frustration and risked hacking her off so much that she might decide not to come.

"I've certainly seen them happier," she answered. "But their reaction to my decision is of no consequence to you, Logan."

"It is if it happens to affect my son," he reminded her.

"Why would their disappointment affect Lo? It isn't his fault they feel betrayed because I lied to them for the past thirteen years. If anything, *Lo* is the reason they're so angry with me."

"What?" *How the crap did I manage to stay with her for three months straight and not become as illogical and scatterbrained as she is? The woman makes no sense!*

"They agree with you, Logan. They think I selfishly deprived Lo of his father at a time when he needed a male role model the most. They think it wasn't my choice to make and that you had a right to know about Lo from the very beginning, but there isn't anything I can do about that now."

"No, there isn't." He was surprised to hear the resignation in her voice, but he worked to keep his own tone even.

"I won't apologize to you again, Logan. There's nothing more I can say on the subject. Besides, we both know that you will believe what you want, no matter what I do or say. I won't come between you and Lo anymore, but that doesn't mean I'll sacrifice his relationship with my family in favor of his relationship with you. He shouldn't have to trade one side of the family for the other. Asking him to do *that* isn't fair either."

"So you're saying this isn't about your parents' disapproval, but about being fair to Lo," he wondered.

"Yes. That's been the center of my whole life for nearly fourteen years. And if you have any plans of being a decent father to him, it'll be the center of yours too."

~

When Lo and his mom made it to Manteo on the first Saturday afternoon of Spring Break, he wasn't sure if he was more excited to finally be able to see Ma and Pa again or to finally talk to someone about his dad. Since the tense conversations his mom had had with both his dad and his grandparents, she hadn't really been keen to discuss the break or anything that it entailed.

He'd broken down and talked to Alex about it again because knew there was more to having a dad than playing Xbox and paintball. Sooner or later, he and his dad would have to talk about something more serious than the latest movie in the Marvel Comics franchise.

"I don't know, man. Me and my dad don't exactly hang out together like it sounds like you and your old man do. I mean, when I was a kid, he took me to the park and stuff, and he helped with my soccer team, but for the past couple of years, he hasn't said a lot to me if I wasn't getting grounded or being paid my allowance. It's like, now that I'm older, he doesn't have time for me anymore." Alex tossed Lo the hacky-sack he'd been kicking from foot to foot and finally looked at him. "But maybe it'll be different for you. My dad's had plenty of time to get bored of me. Yours doesn't even know you yet."

He was able to catch Pa alone on Saturday night after supper. Pa was on the front porch when Lo opened the screen door and took a seat beside him. As far back as Lo could remember, John Thomas Thackery had been the ultimate authority in his life. When he was small, Pa had seemed like the biggest, tallest man in the world. He had to have been the smartest too because everyone listened when he talked. Not that he talked a lot, or even very loudly, but there was something about him that made everyone pay attention. When he was a kid, there was no one Lo would have rather been with. They would spend hours playing with Pa's old Erector sets or baiting and setting crab traps, but for all of Pa's kindness, he could be frightening too. The one thing Lo dreaded more than anything was making Pa angry. That was why he was quiet for a moment after sitting down.

"What's on your mind, boy?" Pa asked in the gruff way that Lo had missed over the last several weeks since he had been here for Christmas.

"A lot of things," Lo told him.

"There are a lot of things to think about nowadays, that's for sure," Pa nodded. "I've been doing quite a bit of thinking myself." He paused long enough to light the pipe he kept tucked into his shirt pocket, and as he took a puff, Lo inhaled the familiar scent of cherry flavored Captain Black pipe tobacco. "I've been wondering why it is you thought you had to run off in the middle of the night and go clear to Raleigh without so much as a word to your momma or your Ma or anybody."

"I had to know, Pa," Lo whispered.

"What did you have to know?"

152

"I had to know who my father is." Lo avoided Pa's eyes.

"It isn't who he is that matters to me, Lo. It's who *you* are, and sneaking off behind your momma's back and disobeying her isn't something you'll think back on someday and be proud of. Is it?"

"No, sir." Lo still hadn't looked up.

"I know you're curious about him, and to tell you the truth, I think all of us are, but that doesn't mean that we can forget the things we've been taught all our lives just to find out who he is and how things might turn out in the future. You just remember who it was that took care of you your whole life and where it is you call home." Pa stuck the pipe back into his mouth and took several long pulls.

When Lo finally did bring his eyes back to his grandfather's face, he saw that the disappointment he had feared was there, but it wasn't the only thing, so he asked, "Do you think Mom was wrong to keep things a secret from us?"

"I don't know what I think about that, Lo. I don't like that she lied to us for thirteen years, that's for sure, but I can't say that I wouldn't do something just as bad or worse if I thought I was protecting the people I love." Pa shook his head. "And it isn't our place to judge her."

"*He* blames her," Lo said. "He stays mad at her all the time, and sometimes I'm mad too, but I don't know if I'm mad at her for making me miss out on knowing him all these years, or if I'm mad at him for being so mean to her."

"Well, I can see why you'd be mad at both of them, but as for your momma, you've gotta think about how things've been between the two of you for more than just these past few months. The woman's taken care of you all your life," Pa reminded him.

"I know it," Lo agreed. "That's why I'm not sure if I really am mad at her. She swears she only kept things a secret because she thought it was the best thing for me."

"Then that's what you have to believe, Lo." Pa put his arm around Lo's shoulders and finished his smoke.

Ma made a fuss about the smell of the tobacco that clung to their clothes when the two of them came back inside, but Lo knew that her threats to scrub them down with a Brillo pad before they stank up the whole house were empty. Pa might have thought he was the head of the family, and maybe that was true when things were hard and big decisions had to be made, but it was Ma who ran the household and kept them all in check.

Susanna Thackery had spent the better part of the last forty years running herd on her brood, and now that all of her babies were grown, she had the gift of grandchildren that she considered her heavenly reward for raising five children, three of whom were boys. She, even more than Pa sometimes, had been the person Lo could count on to listen when he needed someone to. Pa cared, he knew, but Pa had a tendency to go from listening to lecturing before their talk was over. When Lo came to Ma, he never felt like she was judging him or thinking of a moral that could be found in the situation. She was a shoulder he could lay his head on and a pair of warm arms to hug him, so he did just as Pa had taught him long ago. He smiled at her swatting hand and ducked his head when he said, "Yes ma'am" as she ordered him into the upstairs bathroom. He didn't have to look back to know that Pa was heading to the one down the hall.

154

~

Lillie had dreaded being alone with her mother since she and Lo had pulled into her parents' drive. She could tell by the look in her daddy's eyes that he was disappointed with her, and that was something she expected because it was inevitable. He would be aloof with her for the foreseeable future, but eventually he would forgive her for lying about Logan, and things between them would return to the way they had always been. *That's Daddy. But Momma may not forgive me until I make it out of Purgatory.*

She watched as her mother shooed "the boys" off to their baths and knew that the smoke was only pretense, so Lillie did the only thing she could: she sat down at the kitchen table and awaited her fate.

Susanna took the pot out of the coffee maker and poured two cups of decaf. Then she put one in front of Lillie and sat down directly across the table from her with her own.

"How much of what you told me thirteen years ago was true?"

It took Lillie a moment to answer, and in that time she saw her mother's eyes harden. "I was pregnant and on my own, Momma. That was the truth."

"But it didn't have to be, did it?" The narrower slant of Susanna's eyes served as a warning nearly equal to the tone of voice.

"I thought so then, and I still do now. I wasn't being selfish, Momma. I was actually being *selfless*," Lillie was already tired of defending her actions to people who would never understand.

"Tell that to Lo."

Lillie bit back a retort that might get her backhanded and took a sip of her coffee to buy some time, realizing too late that her mother hadn't doctored it. Much like Logan, Susanna tended to want to taste the actual flavor of the bean, and finding the unexpected similarity between them made Lillie smile. It disappeared quickly when she remembered that his taste in coffee was virtually all that had remained the same about him. "I'm sorry I wasn't honest with you and Daddy from the beginning, but I'm paying for it now in ways you can't even imagine."

"And I'm supposed to feel sorry for you?" Her mother took a drink.

"No, ma'am. I just want you to understand that my sins haven't gone unpunished."

Lillie's mother didn't speak again until they had finished their coffee. "What's he like?"

Lillie was glad they had finished because if they hadn't, she would have choked on hers. "Ma'am?"

"You heard me. The truth's out now, so I can hear more about him than 'he was just some guy at a party.' What's he like?" Susanna repeated when Lillie only stared at her.

It took Lillie a full thirty seconds to form any sort of comprehensible sentence in her mind, and when she was sure she wouldn't burst into hysterical laughter, she began her story with, "Logan was the most promiscuous man on campus."

"Well, I suppose I had to be there in order to understand exactly what it was about that boy that made you forget everything you were taught your whole life,"

156

Lillie's mother commented when she'd come to the end of her tale.

"To this day I don't even know why," Lillie shook her head. "One day, I was determined to snub him until he got tired of chasing after me, and then the next I was carrying Lo."

"But surely he didn't care anything about you if he could forget you so easily."

"We graduated, and I knew he wouldn't be the type to settle down. Asking him to would be like asking you to stop cleaning and organizing. It isn't possible. So I decided it would be easier for everyone if I let him go without telling him about Lo. And once graduation was over, he had no reason to think of a girl he'd gone out with for a few months that spring."

"And yet you named your son after a man who only thought of you as a temporary diversion." For the first time since she and her mother sat down at the table, Lillie thought she saw something more than anger and disappointment in Susanna's face.

## Chapter 16

Logan was debating whether he should tell his parents and Preston about Lo and Lillie. It wasn't like him to wait until the last minute to do anything, but it was Tuesday afternoon, and his son would be in Raleigh in twenty-four hours. If he were going to let them know, now would be the time.

*It shouldn't be this hard to do. I'm a grown man! What's Philip going to do, disinherit me?* He shook his head. He had three nights with his son. Three nights and then who knew how long it would be before he saw Lo again? That's why he was hesitant to tell anyone. The more people who knew about Lo, the more he would have to share Lo with those people, and the less time he would have to himself with Lo. *It's jealousy. I'm jealous of my time with Lo, and why shouldn't I be? I've got thirteen years to catch up on.*

And then he imagined what his mom would feel if she knew she had a grandson. *She would be thrilled beyond belief at having something to occupy her time other than those empty social functions she only attends so that she can avoid being at home with Dad.* He couldn't do to his mom what Lillie had done to him. Despite the fact that she never stood up for herself, his mom didn't deserve that. For her own part, she had loved and cared for him and Preston, even if she hadn't cared enough to put her foot down with her philandering husband. He shook his head again and dialed his mother's cell.

"Hey, sweetheart!" she exclaimed when she picked up after a couple rings.

"Hey, Mom."

"This is a surprise. It hasn't even been two weeks since I saw you." He'd been out of her house for almost twenty years, and Ginnie Michaels was still trying to guilt-trip him. *When was she ever going to learn?*

"Mom, I've got something to tell you, and you might want to sit down."

By the time Logan hung up the phone, he was sure his mother's entire housing staff had heard about his "irresponsible behavior," which was certainly nothing new for them, since his father signed their paychecks. They had also been aural witnesses to her histrionic mood swings, ranging from that of an embarrassed parent to an excited grandparent and back again.

When Philip called his cell minutes afterwards, Logan considered letting his voicemail pick it up, but that would only forestall the conversation, so he answered. That was why he was sitting across the desk from his father and trying not to say anything that might make Philip more upset. This conversation had been going on for the last half hour, and his dad didn't show any signs of coming to the end of his rant.

"Why you didn't call the lawyer the second that kid showed up is beyond me! Don't you realize that this girl could take you to court?"

"Like I've already told you, she isn't interested in money. I know that's difficult for you to wrap your mind around, since that's your primary means of communication, but not everyone operates the same way you do." Logan sighed, working not to roll his eyes.

"What the hell has she done to you, Logan? You think she doesn't know what your name is? You think she doesn't see how easy it could be for a judge to award her half of your estate? Not to mention a big chunk of the company? I might have expected Preston to do something like this, but you're not some untested employee with a degree so new that the ink hasn't dried on it yet. You are *the* 'Michaels' in Michaels Corporate Management, and if you think I'm going to spend any of the company's money to get you out of this mess, you don't deserve your title!" Philip had kept his voice low for the majority of this speech, but his face was getting pinker with every word.

"Don't you think that if she'd been interested in the money, she'd have come after me for child support as soon as she gave birth? As it is, she's waited nearly too long to do anything, and what kind of rebuttal could she give the court when she is questioned about that? It isn't logical. She doesn't want my money *or* yours. She just wants Lo to be happy, and that's what I want too, so I don't see how any of this is your problem. Besides, haven't you been on my back about getting married and having a kid since the day I graduated college? . . . Surprise!" Logan pasted on a grin. "Instant heir to the dynasty."

Logan really wasn't sure why he felt the need to defend Lillie's motives to his dad, but in doing so, he had just managed to land maybe the best blow he'd ever dealt the old man. *I'll have to remember to thank her for that.*

"That little urchin won't be the heir to any dynasty I'm a part of. If it—"

Before Logan was even aware of it, his fist had somehow slammed into Philip's face. "My *son* will be the heir to whatever I choose to leave him, and there isn't a lot you can have to say about it because *I'm* the head of MCM now, as you so conveniently reminded me, and I hate to tell you this, Dad, but your seat on the board is merely honorary. So when I step down as CEO, *I* will be the one naming my successor, and the only thing you'll be able to say about it is 'congratulations,' and that's only *if* you're even alive to see it."

Despite the bruise that was beginning to show on his jaw, Philip seemed to have no reaction to Logan's behavior. After a few seconds of silence, he picked up the tumbler of scotch that Logan had poured him earlier and emptied it. By the time he had set it down on the desk and pushed to his feet, Logan had called for Kim, his secretary, to bring Philip his coat.

When she came through the door, Logan and his father were walking in her direction. "Some days, I swear, it's like I'm looking in a mirror," Philip said with a smile as Kim passed him the suit coat, and he walked with her out the door.

Logan decided that it might be best to avoid taking any more personal calls until after work, so as he headed to his car, he checked his missed calls and found that his mother had tried to reach him twelve times, and Preston had called and texted too. There were no calls from Lo or Lillie's cell, so he shoved the phone into his pocket and headed home.

Half an hour later, he slid behind the wheel of his Camaro, and backed out of the space. He hadn't driven her in a while, but something about the day made him want to do something other than end it with half a bottle of Jameson, but he did have some Jäger in the passenger seat, in case he got the notion to pull over and camp out for the night.

Logan had a lot of memories riding around in this car with him. He had driven it since the day his dad had given it to him when he graduated from high school. It was a black '67, and they had seduced quite a few girls together. He laughed when he thought back to the day Andrew Stevenson had first seen it, and then even the 'Italian Stallion' was jealous of Logan Michaels's game. Girls might not have known the make or the model, but they knew a sexy classic car when they saw it, and nothing said sexy like a black paint job on a fast car.

He tapped his fingers on the steering wheel to the tune of "Back in Black" and wondered how many girls had ridden with him during that lost year, wondered if Lillie had.

For all that he questioned what had made him want her back then, when there had to have been easier girls at his beck and call, he questioned now what made *her* want *him*. If he had read the tone of her journal correctly, it seemed as if being with Logan was the last thing she'd wanted when their relationship began, but now they had a teenage son together, and she was once again keeping a safe distance. *But what had made her get that close in the first place? A momentary lapse of her usually good judgment? Then again, you couldn't exactly call spending three months as lovers momentary.* Still, it was clear that whatever weakness she'd had for him in her early twenties was shored up at this point.

Sure, she was polite, but there was aggression underneath that smooth veneer, and Logan would have no qualms wagering that the aggression was rooted in anger. *It would make my life a lot freaking easier if the woman would just come clean about why she's pissed,* but even with a girl like Lillie, he knew that just wasn't the way things worked. If he wanted to know what was eating her, he'd either have to deduce it himself or wheedle it out of her, and if the past few months were any indication, his powers of deduction (at least when it came to Lillie) were nonexistent. *And wheedling would be tons easier if she didn't keep treating me like some naughty kid to her indignant school principal.*

He thought back to the journal. At the end of it, she hadn't been angry with him. She'd been lonely, sure. She'd been sad that he was pushing her away, but she hadn't been angry. She hadn't blamed him for her having to raise Lo alone. That had been what she wanted. *But if it wasn't leaving her without any help, what had he done to make her so wary of and mad at him?* Yet she still felt safe enough with him to let him spend time with Lo. He shook his head, turned the music up, and pressed the accelerator. Logic was getting him nowhere, at least not tonight.

When he woke on Wednesday morning, Logan wondered if the Jäger last night had been such a good plan. It was six, and he felt like he had gotten all of ten minutes' sleep. His head was protesting consciousness vehemently, but he managed to stagger to the bathroom without it exploding. *At least that's a start.* He winced as he turned on the light, which reflected cruelly off the tile and mirror, and then turned it off again. *Who needs a light to brush their teeth anyway?*

By the time he stepped into the shower a couple minutes later, the water was warm, and he let it stream over him, washing away all the frustration and liquor that clung to him. Once he was dry and had shoved his mug into the coffee maker, he was alert enough to hear when the machine stopped running. He had the cup to his mouth and was sipping the Obsidian roast before he even took the time to cool it. A few more sips had him able to think clearly enough to grab a couple of pods so that he could have more coffee once he got to the office.

Logan only planned to work part of the day, and he was hoping to time it so that he could leave at about 11:30 and be at his place when Lo and Lillie got there. *Still, a man's gotta be prepared for the worst*, he thought, begrudgingly acknowledging the dull ache that persisted at his temples. He stowed the small plastic cups in his messenger bag and carried his fresh cup of coffee with him as he went to get dressed.

~

It was hard for Lillie to say goodbye to her parents when she and Lo left Manteo that morning. She had done it many times in the past, and this time felt at once familiar and strange. They would be back again for Mother's Day weekend, if she could swing her schedule to allow it, and yet she was reluctant to back out of the drive.

They knew where she was taking Lo this afternoon, and though they hadn't said anything about it after her talk with her mother, Lillie felt their disapproval as they watched and waved from the back door.

~

Lo was beyond stoked knowing that he would be eating lunch with his dad. He was still sort of nervous about phasing away from home, and while he was staying at his dad's, but his mom had promised that she would look out for him and make sure his dad saw the whole thing. *I just hope he doesn't think I'm a freak. Why should he,*

164

*though, if he went through the same thing when he was younger?* Lo tried not to concentrate on the part where his dad had no memory of being a wolf and thought his mom was crazy for writing about it and for believing it was true. *There'll be no way he can think she's crazy after he sees it happen to me.* Lo also tried not to think about what would happen if his mom wasn't able to track the wolf. *After all, she hasn't ever been able to keep up with it before.*

"What's the frown for?" his mom reached over and poked him. "I figured you'd be grinning all the way to Raleigh."

"Nothing," he shrugged. "Do you think he'll help you when I phase tomorrow night?"

"I don't know, baby, but I promise that I won't let anything bad happen to you. And if we're lucky, I might even be able to cure you before this phase is over," she smiled.

"I hope you do." he answered.

~

Logan didn't care how upset his parents were. He was sitting in his recliner, counting the minutes until noon and the time that Lo knocked on his door. He was even willing to put up with Lillie and her crazy for the rest of the week, anything almost if it meant he could hang out with his son.

He wasn't one to twiddle his thumbs and be content with it, but he was hardly suited for anything else at that point in time. He wanted some whiskey, but then he couldn't exactly have that on his breath when his teenage son walked in. If that happened, he'd never be able to enforce anything. He knew because he had felt the same way about his own dad once he was old enough to realize what the old man was really like.

He sighed and checked his watch. It was 11:50, and he wasn't exactly sure what time they would make it to town, so that information did him no good whatsoever. *Get a grip, man. You're as bad as a Kindergartener on the night before Christmas. They'll get here soon enough.*

Still, he pushed up out of his seat and walked over to the kitchen. It was clean; he'd made sure of that. He didn't know how the dynamics would work out over the next few days, but he did know that Lillie likely had a much bigger cooking repertoire than he did.

He caught himself drumming his fingers on the counter, and shook his head. *There's definitely something wrong with the world when I can't control myself enough to keep from fidgeting.* Giving up, he walked back to his recliner, sat, and turned on the Xbox. *Might as well get in a couple of practice rounds before the kid comes and humiliates me . . .*

~

Lillie put the car in park a block or so from Logan's building and tried not to say anything about Lo's inability to sit still. She hadn't had this much trouble with him in the car since he was little, but she couldn't blame him. *If I were going to spend several days with my father for the first time in my life, I'd probably be beside myself too.* "Can you get some of the luggage, my love? I just popped the trunk," she told him before he had a chance to bolt.

"Yes, ma'am," he answered as he unbuckled his seatbelt. Lo took both duffels without her prompting, leaving her to get her carry-on and the ice chest out of the backseat.

She let him lead the way to the building and press the button. "We're here, Mr. Logan," he said into the speaker, and the lock on the door slid open nearly immediately.

Logan met them on their way upstairs, and Lillie watched as Lo fought an internal war, evidenced by the slight changes in his expression. He was still enough of a boy to light up when he got excited, and he was just enough of a man to know he should tamp it down.

In the pause while Lo decided how to react, his father said, "Hey, Lo! You have anything else in the car?"

"No, sir," Lo shook his head. "Mom and I got it all on the first trip.

At this, Logan shifted his focus from his son and suddenly saw her. He moved past Lo, clapping a hand on his shoulder on the way. "Let me get those for you, Lille." He took the cooler and bag. He smiled as he did. It was the real, unguarded one, and for a moment, no more than a second or so, she froze. She had dreamed of that smile, seen it a hundred million times in dreams and memories in the last thirteen years, but now that she was actually looking at it, she was unprepared for its impact.

"Mom!" Lo called, "Mr. Logan!"

She found that Lo was already several steps above them.

~

Logan was so glad to have Lo back in close proximity that he caught himself appreciating the way Lillie's cheeks were slightly flushed, probably from carrying things in from the car. When he took them from her, he noticed that she stopped, like she was flinching away from him. He felt the smile slide off his face. *Oh, yeah. I've still gotta pay for whatever it is she's mad about.*

"Mom!" Lo called. He had moved a bit faster than Logan and Lillie had, and Logan's first thought was to catch up to the kid, but he looked back to find that Lillie was still standing in where she had been, and all the color was gone from her cheeks. *It's almost like she's seen a ghost. What—*

"Mr. Logan?" Lo called again, and Lille jumped at his words. He was smart enough to pretend he hadn't noticed anything as they moved forward.

They wound up eating barbeque for lunch because as Lillie said, she hadn't had the real thing since who knew when. There was a small argument when it came time to pay the bill, but Logan won out of sheer determination, that or the fact that the waiter was still traditional enough to pass the bill to the man at the table.

Lillie was boiling when the waiter left discreetly to give Logan time to determine method of payment. He could have sworn he heard her mutter "chauvinist" under her breath. "Would you feel better if you handled the tip?" he chuckled.

Her eyes narrowed, and her mouth thinned. "I'd feel better if you 'good ole boys' would stop congratulating each other on being members of the club and let people pay their own way," she told him.

"Come on, Lillie. It isn't chauvinistic to have manners, the last time I checked. Or have you been up North too long, and those Yankees have made you forget all about what it means to be polite?" he raised a brow.

"I can assure you that I have *not* forgotten what it means to be polite, nor have I forgotten what it means to have manners," she told him coolly. "So I thank you for the meal."

"Just chalk it up to Southern hospitality. You two are my guests for the rest of the week, after all." Logan sent Lo a wink.

"Yeah, thanks for lunch, Mr. Logan," Lo nodded.

"The both of you are welcome," he grinned at the way Lo had remembered his manners so quickly.

"I know the two of you just got here, but I was thinking about the rest of the week and was wondering if you might want to meet your grandparents tomorrow or the next day." Logan addressed his son, but he was also watching Lillie out of the corner of his eye. Her lips and eyes narrowed again. *Out of the frying pan and into the fire.*

"That sounds pretty awesome," Lo admitted. "Can I meet your brother too?"

"Well, I'm not exactly sure what Preston's schedule's like for the week, but I'll text him and see if we can set something up."

Lille cleared her throat. "Are you sure that's the best idea?"

"Why wouldn't it be?" Lo wondered just as Logan was about to ask the same thing.

"Because from what your father told me about your grandfather, he might not take the news of your existence in stride," Lille answered.

"I told them yesterday, so they're over the initial shock, and if the old man's still pi—upset about it, then he doesn't have to meet Lo," Logan said. The situation was clear-cut from where he was sitting. He calculated the tip, added it to the subtotal, and closed the book.

~

She remembered now, in the car on the way back to Logan's apartment, why it was that she hesitated to let Lo come to Raleigh. She was outnumbered, and she didn't care for it. Not that her son would consciously defy her, but the novelty of being a father and his desire to get along with Lo made Logan a bit careless to her way of thinking, and Lo was still so awestruck that he'd agree

169

with his father even if that meant agreeing to jumping off a cliff. It wasn't hard to be the adult and the voice of reason when you were the sole caregiver, since there was no one around to contradict you, but now that she was merely *primary* caregiver, things were sticky.

## Chapter 17

Lillie woke up on Thursday morning in Logan's bed, or rather the bed in Logan's guest room. She had dreamt of the days before she had lured the wolf to the mirror, and it was always a shock to wake and remember how long gone those days actually were. The dreams had been more of a problem for her since Lo had tracked his father down than they had been in nearly ten years. She supposed it was hearing Logan's voice every few days or seeing him very occasionally that brought them back, but at the moment, she didn't care what it was that had reopened the gaping tear in her insides, it was what she was going to do about that vulnerability that she was concerned with.

*I can't let him suck me in again*, she thought and cursed her stupid sentimentality. And the sad thing was, this time he wasn't even trying to seduce her. *Somehow, it's as if I **want** him to want me, but I don't even want him, or at least not this version of him who's nothing but an older version of the self-absorbed frat boy I first met in the stacks.*

She took a deep breath, banished the thought that the sheets she was wrapped in smelled like him, dried her eyes, and got up in search of the coffee maker she knew he would have at the ready.

~

Logan awoke to the sound of someone moving around in his kitchen and the smell of coffee. For a moment, he tried to remember who he'd had over last night and why she was already awake. *Lillie.* Her name appeared in his mind and had him sitting up and throwing back the covers. He pulled on a t-shirt and shorts and padded quietly into the living area, remembering that Lo was on the couch.

She was in the recliner that was opposite his, and she was reading a book. She looked up at him and pointed to the pot of coffee she had made instead of using the single-cup brewer. She had managed to find the coffee cups and had set one out for him on the counter next to the pot. *I could get used to this . . .* he thought before he could stop himself.

He filled his cup and drank, hoping that the caffeine would clear whatever crazy, delusional dream-haze he was walking around in before he found himself thinking anything else that was frightening enough to make him want to throw up.

~

When they had all eaten breakfast and were dressed, Logan called his mom and made sure that it was okay for them to come over for a visit. Lo got the feeling that neither of his parents was very happy about going to see his grandparents, but he didn't care. He was just happy that now he was going to have more than one side of the family.

He hadn't really thought much about having any other family when he decided to sneak off to Raleigh to find his dad. After all, that was all he had wanted for as long as he could remember. But now the really cool part was that not only did he have a father who was pretty freaking cool, if he did say so himself, but he also apparently had a grandmother, grandfather, and an uncle to boot.

The three of them took his dad's Lincoln, which happened to be the coolest Lincoln he'd ever seen. It was nothing like the Towncar that Pa and Ma drove. His dad's car was sleek and black and just plain fast-looking. Still it was no Camaro.

"Mr. Logan," Lo said when they were headed out of the city.

"Hmm?" Logan glanced at him in the rearview mirror.

"Do you still have the car you drove when you were in college?"

"Sure," Logan grinned. "Why?"

"I-I was wondering if I could ride in it with you sometime, please, sir," Lo ducked his head even though he was in the back seat.

"Sure, kid. I just didn't think she'd be the most comfortable thing for us to ride in for four hours. Did we ever take the Camaro?" Logan asked Lillie.

"Once or twice," Lo heard her answer, and it sounded like she might have been smiling.

~

As they pulled onto the private drive that led to Logan's parents' house, the reality of his background finally began to sink in for Lillie. In the back of her mind, she had always known that Logan was rich, which was why he fit in so well with the collegiates who were more concerned with their social calendars than with the academic one, but the glamour of Asheville reminded her that there was rich and there was *rich*.

She looked back at Lo, saw that his eyes were as round and wide as globes, and suppressed a chuckle. "Make sure you're polite to Mr. and Mrs. Michaels, Lo. Their home is going to be a lot nicer than what you're used to, so try not to stare, and remember to say please and thank you when they talk to you."

"Yes, ma'am," Lo nodded.

"When we come around this curve that's ahead, you'll see the house," Logan announced.

Despite herself, Lillie had to release the breath she caught when it came into view. If she had been expecting extravagant, she got it. The house was three stories, at least, with turrets on either end, and there was even a tiny one in the center of the front roof. She wasn't much for modern architecture, but it had a distinctly old European feel with its grey stone, cream-colored paint and darkly stained trim that matched the textured shingles on the roofs. Save the porch that spread across the entirety of the house front, it could be mistaken for a castle from the Alps. She was admiring the picture windows that looked out on each side of the front door when Logan pulled around to the side of the house, and the feeling of going back in time several hundred years passed.

On the back, nestled out of sight from the main drive, was what looked to be a four-car garage, and beyond that there was a privacy fence, which seemed to be hiding a large pool and perhaps even an outdoor kitchen. Logan stopped at the edge of the concrete pad that had been poured for parking, well away from the garage door and any cars that might be inside.

He got out without a word and waited for her and Lo to do the same. Then he entered a code into the keypad and raised the garage door. Just as they reached the back door, a woman, whom she took to be Logan's mother, opened it.

"Hello, sweetheart," she said to Logan, and he dutifully stepped into her open arms.

"Hi, Mom."

"You must be Lillie," she said with her head still perched on Logan's shoulder.

"Yes, ma'am, and this is Lo," Lillie answered and felt Lo tense beside her.

The second that Logan stepped away from her, she came forward a few feet and gave them both a warm smile. "I'm Ginnie, Logan's mother. I'm so glad you came. You all must be tired. Won't you come in?" Though she was dressed modernly enough in tailored gray slacks, a dark blue blouse and had pearls at her throat and ears, her accent made Lillie think of cotillions and hoop skirts.

On their way to a sitting area, Lillie caught glimpses of a large chandelier that was dripping crystals and paintings and rugs that she was sure predated the 20th century, and she was nearly positive that she saw a Ming vase in her periphery.

Ginnie showed them into a spacious room that was probably referred to in the family as a den, and almost immediately a girl who couldn't have been more than twenty appeared with a tray of cobalt glass goblets and a large pitcher of iced tea.

"Thanks, Rachel," Logan took the tray and poured a glass for Lillie, his mother, Lo and himself. Then he took a seat next to Lo on the sprawling couch.

"Well, Lillie, when Logan was telling us about you, he forgot to mention how lovely you are," Ginnie said after a sip of tea.

"Thank you, ma'am," Lille answered, and felt that though politeness called for such a compliment, Ginnie meant it as more than perfunctory.

"And my stars," she exclaimed, putting a hand to her chest as she glanced at the boys. "I do believe you are the very image of your father," she told Lo. "How old are you now?"

"Thirteen," Lo said shyly but managed to meet her eyes. Ginnie merely nodded, and Lillie had to wonder if she was calculating to make sure the timetable was plausible.

"Logan tells me you're in graduate school getting a . . . PhD, isn't it?" she asked Lillie before an awkward silence could fall between them

"Yes, ma'am. In archeology."

"Where did you go for your master's, if you don't mind me asking?"

"NCSU."

"And now you're in Ann Arbor? Don't you find that awfully far from your family, dear?" Ginnie raised a brow.

"Mom, it's Lillie's business where she lives and goes to school," Logan spoke for the first time in several minutes.

"It's all right," Lillie said, looking his way and immediately wishing she hadn't done so. He was so relaxed here that he seemed even more like the man she'd woken up with on those oft remembered mornings. "My parents think that too, Mrs. Michaels, but I'm nearly done with my coursework, and after that, I plan to come back to the South," she punctuated her sentence with the pleasant smile she used with her colleagues.

"Please. Call me Ginnie," Logan's mother told her as soon as she'd finished. "And I apologize if I seemed to pry. I was just wondering how large a part we are going to be playing in each other's lives."

Lillie felt three sets of eyes on her as she responded. "That all depends on Logan, Mrs. Ginnie."

176

~

*Way to go there, Lillie. Throw me under the bus, why don't you? And after I just tried to save you from any future guilt trips from my mother!*

"I expect we'll be seeing as much of Lo as his mother's schedule allows," Logan added. *At least that's a bit of damage control.*

"I've got summer coming up at the end of May, so maybe I can spend some of it with Mr. Logan," Lo suggested, finding his voice at last.

"That would be fine with me, kid," Logan smiled at the eagerness in the kid's voice, but he wasn't a fool. Lillie was still playing some kind of tacit chess match, and he didn't want Lo to be disappointed. "Summer's still a long while away, so let's just play things by ear, and if you don't come to Raleigh, then I'll come to you."

Lo wasn't quick enough to hide his disappointment, but Logan saw that Lillie relaxed fractionally at his words.

"I have no intention of standing in the way of Lo's relationship with Logan," Lillie assured his mom.

Something in her tone suggested that she also didn't plan to let her son visit him without supervision, but she was shrewd enough not to say as much. Before Logan had time to formulate a response, there was a sound at the back of the house and his little brother appeared.

"Pres, this is your nephew, Lo, and his mother, Lillie. Lillie and Lo, this is Logan's brother, Preston," his mother made the formal introductions.

"Hello," mother and son responded simultaneously.

"My Lord, you're right, big brother. That kid's face is just like looking in a mirror. I'm surprised you even waited for DNA," a younger, more jovial copy of Logan took a seat across from his mother.

"Pres," Logan spat.

"What? If I'm your mini-me, then he's mine. How ya doin', kiddo?"

"I'm fine, thank you, sir. How are you?" Lo smiled at what he appeared to take as a new ally.

"I'm pretty good, seeing as how I woke up a couple mornings back and suddenly had a new nephew to hang out with," Preston answered. "You wouldn't be interested in seeing the theatre room, would you?"

"Theatre room?" Lo took the bait instantly.

"Yeah. It's like our own personal movie theatre, complete with blackout curtains, a digital projector and Surround Sound," Preston explained.

Lo looked pleadingly at his mom and asked, "May I be excused?"

"Yes," Lillie nodded, "but remember your manners, and mind your uncle."

"Yes, ma'am," Lo's grinned.

"It's upstairs. Follow me," Preston barely hid his laughter.

"Thank you, Mr. Preston, sir," Lo said as he disappeared behind Logan's brother.

"You can call me uncle if you want to," Preston's voice chuckled.

"Really? Thank you, Uncle Preston, sir." Lo repeated reverently.

~

Lillie was getting nervous when she hadn't seen or heard from Lo in more than an hour. It wasn't that she didn't trust Preston. It was more that she was afraid of what Lo might do or say while she wasn't around that could be misinterpreted and, therefore, recalled and used against her sometime in the near future.

After the initial standoff, Ginnie had remained warm, and Lillie hoped that it wasn't just good breeding. *Life would be much easier if we got along,* At the moment, she and Lillie were discussing their mutual love of black and white movies.

"I just don't think there's anyone in Hollywood today who's as striking as Greer Garson," Ginnie said.

"Oh, then you must adore *Random Harvest!*" Lillie replied, naming her favorite Greer Garson film on instinct.

"Not as much now as I once did." There was a flash of something like pain on the older woman's face.

Belatedly Lillie recalled that a major plot point in the movie involved the hero being wounded and developing a serious case of amnesia. *Why, why couldn't I have mentioned Mrs. Miniver? So much for getting along!* She could have bitten off her own tongue. Lillie looked at Logan, expecting to see that all-too-familiar anger, but he seemed merely bored.

"I'm sorry," Lillie forced herself to meet Ginnie's eyes as she said it. "I wasn't thinking." But if Ginnie was upset by the reference, there was no trace of it in her face now.

"It's all right, dear. No harm done. That was thirteen years ago, and even Logan has stopped trying to puzzle all that out." Her smile was as pleasant as ever.

When Logan looked from one woman to the other in confusion, his mother said, "Sweetheart, I think Lillie might be ready to check up on Lo. Would you show her the way?"

"Yes, ma'am." He rose immediately, but the confused expression hadn't quite left his face. He waited until she set her tea glass on a coaster and then headed for the stairs in silence.

When they emerged onto what she took to be the third floor, he paused. "What were you apologizing for down there?"

"I misspoke and probably offended your mother."

"Over a movie? She has thicker skin than that! She's a socialite *and* a Michaels. Besides, the sooner you show her that you make your own choices, the better off you'll be."

~

Lo had had a really awesome day at his dad's mom and dad's house. It was still very hard to believe that Mrs. Ginnie was his very own grandmother, but she did seem really nice. He and Uncle Preston had watched one of the old *Transformers* movies that his uncle had grown up with on the big screen in the theatre room, and just when he thought that things couldn't get any cooler, Uncle Preston revealed an Xbox in the theatre. Lo and Preston were happily causing a zombie blood bath when his parents found them.

"I never want to leave this room!" he shouted when he saw his mom. "Are you seeing this? The zombies are practically the same size as me!"

"I see that, my love," she answered and winced when he landed a particularly well placed shot, and blood covered the entirety of Lo's portion of the screen.

Lo grinned, pleased with his score and then pressed pause.

"Hey! What's your problem, pal? We're in the middle of a game here!" Preston demanded.

"Mr. Logan, do you want to play?" Lo turned to his dad.

"I'm good, kid. You'd just massacre me again, and I can't have my baby brother seeing that. I'd never live it down."

"Are you sure? It's almost like you're right there in the game with the other players since the screen's so big. . . I promise to go easy on you!" A moment's inspiration had him throwing in that bit.

"Ouch," Preston laughed. "He's got you there, *Mr. Logan!*"

"Like he hasn't been schooling *you* this whole time," Logan grumbled as he picked up a controller.

~

He was very surprised to see how well things were going today. He hadn't been sure exactly how his family would take to Lo and Lillie, but his mom had seemed truly excited, and Pres and the kid had gotten closer in the span of a few hours than he and his brother had ever been in all of their childhoods.

But now came the real barometer–dinner with Philip. Because they had four hours to drive later, it really wasn't dinner at all, more like what the Brits called Tea, seeing as it was a light meal at five in the afternoon. When his mother had brought up the idea a few moments ago, Logan had wondered if it was the wisest thing to do, and Lillie looked positively horrified, but if his mom had seen that, she didn't let on. "It would be a shame to have come all this way and not let Lo meet . . . Philip," Ginnie persisted, despite having stumbled a bit at the appropriate terminology to indicate her husband's relationship to Lo.

"Oh, Mrs. Michaels! That's such a kind offer, but we couldn't possibly impose upon you like that. I'm sure your husband's very busy, and I'd hate to interrupt his schedule just so we can have an early supper," Lillie protested, and though her reasons for doing so were perfectly acceptable, Logan thought he heard an urgency in her voice that went beyond concern for politeness.

"There is no imposition, my dear." Ginnie smiled beautifully, and all Logan could think was, *Watch out, Lillie. You're playing with the big girls now.* "Logan has the run of the company now, so the only pressing appointments my husband has are those with his golfing buddies at the club, and Lo is certainly much more important than a few holes that can be played on any number of other days. No, I *insist* that you stay for dinner. I would be very upset, were you to refuse."

A lifetime of living according to society's standards had left Ginnie a master at the game. She may not have been clever enough to gain the upper hand with her husband, but she made up for that by ruling over everyone else within her sphere of influence with the absolute confidence of a queen, which was why the true state of Logan's parents' marriage was known only to the family. None of the servants would dare to be anything less than discreet about the happenings in the Michaels's household. If any of them were, those unfortunates would have to move clear out of North Carolina if they wanted to do more than flip burgers or check groceries for the rest of their lives.

Because it was Lillie's first time to experience his mother's powers of persuasion, Logan found this an entertaining show to watch. It had taken him years to figure out how to escape the snares she set to keep him under her thumb, but he had perfected his technique by the time he had left for NCSU. *And thankfully, I haven't relinquished much of any of it to her over the last twenty years.*

182

He glanced at Lillie to see how her rebuttal was coming along, futile as it would be. She was pale, and though her expression remained friendly, Logan could see the strain in her eyes. *Something's wrong.* He moved from his seat on the couch with his mother to where Lillie and Lo were seated across from them and crouched in front of her.

"My word!" his mother exclaimed at his unexpected action.

"Are you all right?" he peered into her face and wondered yet again, what on Earth could be going on in that head of hers.

~

Lillie was having the worst case of dèja vu in her life, and now was *not* the time for it. She needed to do battle with Ginnie Michaels, not only do battle, but also win against her. She couldn't afford to lose, not while the stakes were Lo's life. And instead of planning a way to call Ginnie's bluff without losing everything, all she could think of was the unabashed concern for her in the steel gray eyes that were watching her so intently.

"Are you all right?" his words echoed in her ears, and somehow she was both present and past. She was in the living room of Logan's parents' lavish mansion, staring at him as he crouched in front of her, and yet she was in her own bed in her on-campus apartment at NCSU, and Logan was brushing the tears out of her eyes during their first time together. "Are you all right?"

She swallowed and tried to make her voice work, but she didn't know whether she meant to say yes or no, so the only thing that came out was a sort of confused whimper.

"Lillie, what's wrong?" he laid a hand on hers, and then she knew.

"No. No, I-I'm sorry, Mrs. Michaels. I'm suddenly very dizzy. Could you tell me where I might wash my face?" She directed her response at his mother.

"Yes, of course. Logan, why don't you show her the way, in case she isn't steady on her feet?" Lillie was dimly aware of Ginnie's voice in the background, but Logan was speaking again, and then he was helping her up and leading her out of the great room.

Suddenly, he took his arm from her and nudged her companionably. "Great job out there! I've gotta hand it to you. For a minute there, I thought you had met your match, but this, *this* was pure genius. Malady, feigned or otherwise, always trumps politeness, especially when it comes to the desires of the hostess." He gave her a congratulatory smile.

"I don't—I don't know what you mean," she shook her head. She had stopped walking when he released her arm, and he turned back at her words, steel eyes narrowed sharply, considering.

He came the forward the few steps that separated them. "What are you afraid of?"

## Chapter 18

"We can't stay here," she told him.

"What?"

"We have to go. Now."

"Look, I know you've heard a lot about my dad, but he wouldn't dare to say or do anything as bad as all that to you or Lo. He doesn't have a guarantee of your silence the way he does with us." He pointed to the door they had come to. "It's this one. There are towels next to the sink. But, I promise you have nothing to worry about."

"It's not that, Logan. It's not that at all. We just can't stay here. We shouldn't have even come. We have to go," she turned around to head back to the others. "I know it's rude, but I'll make whatever apologies I need to, if you'll only take us back to Raleigh. Please." She was shaking slightly, and she knew she sounded desperate, but she didn't care. Not about what his parents thought. Not about what his brother thought, and not even about what Logan thought. Lo was the only person who mattered.

"Wait!" Logan's hand closed around her wrist. "If it isn't my father, what's the matter?"

"We have to go. We need be somewhere, *anywhere* else, and we *have* to get there before sundown," she answered.

~

Lillie wasn't making a bit of sense. It was clear that something was wrong, but he had no idea what. And if he'd had any doubts about the sincerity of her emotion, they all disappeared the moment he grabbed her wrist and felt the shivers beneath his fingers. "All right," he nodded to her wide eyes. "All right," he pulled her forward and opened the bathroom door. *In a million years, I never thought I'd have to use force to get a chick to follow me in here,* he would have laughed at the irony of the situation and the fact that it was Lillie who he was dragging into the bathroom if she hadn't had that look on her face.

He closed the lid of the toilet and gave her a light shove so that she sat down on it. "Everything'll be okay. Just tell me what's wrong," he wet a washcloth with cold water and put it in her hands. Logan watched as she mechanically bathed her face with it, but she didn't look any calmer when she was done.

"Lillie. What's wrong?" he crouched in front of her again and repeated his question in as gentle a tone as he could manage.

"We have to take Lo home," she whispered, green eyes locking on his face. "Please. We have to go home."

"Yes, I know. I'm asking why. Why do we have to go home so quickly?" Logan clarified.

"Because we'll barely make it before dark if we leave now."

"That's okay. I don't mind driving in the dark," he smiled, hoping to reassure her.

"You don't understand!" she shook her head. "We can't be in the car when the sun goes down!"

"Why? Is he afraid of the dark? He's a little old for that kind—" Logan had started to say, but she spoke again, louder than before.

"Please, please, Logan. I know this doesn't make sense to you and that you think I'm hysterical, but I assure you, I'm as calm as I can possibly be in light of the situation."

"WHAT situation?" Logan shouted. "I'd be more apt to think you were calm and take you seriously if I knew what was going on," he added, managing to lower his voice to an almost conversational tone.

"No you wouldn't," she drew a steadying breath, stood, and laid the washcloth on the edge of the sink. "Please, just take our son and me home. I'll try explaining everything to you again, but there isn't a lot of time, and we need to be back in Raleigh before nightfall."

Logan surveyed the woman before him. It was true that she seemed to be scared to death, and he supposed his mother would describe her as "looking slightly disheveled," but one thing the woman didn't look was incoherent. Her face was set, lips thin and eyes serious. He shook his head, knowing he had about as much of a chance at getting any more information from her as the waves did of moving the rocks they crashed against on the shore.

He didn't care that he was speeding as he pulled off his parents' drive and onto the highway. He'd made excuses for Lillie to his mom and ushered her and Lo to the car in less than fifteen minutes. His mom had been gracious, but he knew she was angry, and he couldn't blame her. Pres looked a little concerned and more than a little confused, and Lo just looked embarrassed. Logan couldn't decide which one he identified with more, so he just kept quiet.

They had been on the road about ten minutes when he heard Lo speak from the back seat. "I'm sorry, Mom. I didn't think about what time it was. If I hadn't stayed upstairs with Uncle Preston so long, then maybe we would be home already."

"How is any of this *your* fault, Lo?" Logan snarled.

"Who else's would it be?" Lo answered, "Unless it's yours."

"LO!" Lillie cried beside him, breaking her silence. In the rearview, Logan could see Lo hang his head.

"What does he mean, Lillie?" Logan took his eyes off the road long enough to glare at her.

"I mean that you passed this stupid condition on to me, and I'm tired of you being mad at her for it or thinking she's crazy! She's not! Everything she's ever said to you was true! You really were a werewolf when she met you, and because of that, so am I!" he had never heard Lo raise his voice, and Logan couldn't decide whether he was more shocked by his son's volume or his words.

"Logan Thackery, you apologize this instant for speaking to your father that way!" The force behind Lillie's words made him jump. *She has the whole mom/teacher voice down pat!*

"No, ma'am," Lo said, and Logan saw in the mirror that Lo had inherited the stubborn set of his mother's mouth.

"*What* did you say to me?" Logan saw Lille raise an eyebrow with the pitch of her voice.

"I said 'no, ma'am' because I'm not sorry for what I said *or* the way I said it," Lo's voice was quiet but steady, and Logan had to admire it.

"I don't care if he told you the Earth is as flat as a pancake! That doesn't give you the right to yell at him. You are thirteen years old. You may not like or agree with what he said, but he's an adult and your own father, and I *will not* have such a disrespectful child living under my roof. You apologize for being rude right this minute, or we'll leave Raleigh just as soon as you come back to yourself, and you can spend the rest of Spring Break thinking about what you've done."

Lo still hadn't looked up, but Logan thought he heard a small sigh from the backseat, and then, "I'm sorry I was rude and disrespectful to you, Mr. Logan."

Logan had to bite his lip to keep from laughing, since the whole situation was bizarre, and the kid had been exactly right in accusing him of thinking Lillie was a lying lunatic. And unlike his son, he just didn't have the guts to cross her at the moment, especially since she was doing an awesome job of scaring the crap out of the kid. *I'll bet he thinks twice before he raises his voice to a grownup any time soon!*

"Apology accepted," Logan told Lo as gravely as he could. "There have been times when I was just as disrespectful to my ol—father. Besides, we're both sorta new at the father/son thing, aren't we?"

"Yes, sir," Lo met his eyes and actually seemed to be contrite.

~

As they drove, the car was quiet, and Lillie attributed that to the enormous elephant that was riding with them. She knew that Lo was justified when he lashed out at his father, and Logan knew it too, but she figured there really wasn't any way for him to broach the subject without insulting her or Lo or compromising his almighty logic.

She was still afraid that they weren't going to make it back to Raleigh before the moon dominated the sky, but a part of her wondered if this wasn't the best way to convince Logan of the truth. *I'd just rather not be trapped in a car with a crazed wolf when he finally believes me.*

The traffic that afternoon was atrocious, and the longer she stared at the clock, watching the minutes tick by, the more nervous she became that they weren't going to be parked in time.

Lillie glanced at Lo, sleeping in the backseat, still as human as she was. It wouldn't be long now. The sun was already hanging low in the sky and was turning a pinkish orange. They'd be safe, she knew, so long as it was visible. By her calculations, they had about two hours left on the road, and only thirty minutes of daylight.

She closed her eyes and concentrated on breathing in through her nose and out through her mouth. *I'm nearly thirty-five years old, and I will **not** be guilty of fainting, not now. Especially not if the first time is in Logan's car! I'm not some simpering southern belle!*

But "mind over matter" was working about as well as her ingenious plan never to reveal the truth about Lo's father had. She cracked one eyelid wide enough to see to direct the air vent on her face and promptly closed it again, before she was able to catch a glimpse of the clock.

Still, it was only a few more seconds before she gave in to curiosity and looked. Barely five minutes had passed. *Five precious minutes we could have spent making sure he could find his way back to the car in the morning.*

"Logan," she swallowed hard.

"Hm?" he flicked his eyes toward her.

"Can you pull over?"

"I thought you were in a hurry to get home," he smirked, obviously still refusing to accept what would soon be evident to him, counterintuitive or not.

"We aren't going to make it to Raleigh in time, Logan, so I need you to pull over because we have to make finding the car easy for it. Otherwise, we might spend half the morning searching in the woods while Lo wanders around stark naked, looking for us."

She saw him check the rearview before he responded. "Really? Really. You seriously expect me to believe that you've acted like a crazy person all afternoon because my son is going to magically transform into a wolf at any minute, and you wanted him to do it in my apartment?"

"I do because that is exactly what is about to happen to *our* son, and without a familiar scent to lead the wolf in our direction, there'll be no telling where Lo'll wake come sun up," she told him. "So pull over, and we'll try to make sure Lo's scent will lead it back to the car."

"Wait! Am I given to understand that you expect the two of us to spend the night in the car while we wait for him to become human again?" he sounded even more incredulous.

"Did you think I was going to leave him here without clothing or food or a way back to civilization?" she shot him the most hateful look she could. "You're already gunning for Father of the Year, aren't you?"

"No, but if I was, I might consider having your mental stability tested," the barb was well placed, though she knew the threat was empty.

Lillie struggled against herself as she watched the trees and mile markers continue to pass. Logan seemed determined to keep driving, and she wasn't sure how much longer she could allow him to do that before her mother's instinct took over, and she did something extreme, like knocking him in the head and taking the wheel. But Logan was right; doing something like that would look terrible if he ever did try to get vindictive. *Then there's the money and clout that comes along with being a Michaels in North Carolina*, she reminded herself. *There would be no end to the line of "good ole boys" he has in his pocket, just waiting to speak for him in court. But then none of that would matter if Lo were to be—*

She stopped before she could think anything that horrible. "Lo, how are you, my love?" she called loudly enough to wake him if he really was merely sleeping. He remained quiet. "LO!" she called even louder. Still nothing. "Please, Logan! Please! You've *got* to stop the car!"

"I can't stop the car right now, Lillie. We're on the interstate, and we haven't gotten to our exit yet," he countered with his infuriatingly ever-present logic.

"Then pull over on the shoulder! I'm not kidding, Logan! If you don't pull over right now, we're going to die!" Lillie screamed.

~

Logan really did consider pulling the car over, but it wasn't because he was afraid they were going to be killed. It was because he wanted to get this raving woman to shut up. *But Lo might not like it too much if I threw his mom out on the side of the road.*

"Don't you see, Logan? He's already lost consciousness. It's only a matter of time before the moonlight overpowers the sun, and then he'll phase. He's got to be out of the car before then or who knows what the wolf will do when it comes to!" her shrill shouts broke through his thoughts.

"For the last time, Lillie! I'm tired of all this werewolf crap! You're a smart woman, and Lord knows what it is you're trying to pull, but I'm not that stupid! I'm not a werewolf, and neither is my son, so you can just—"

An odd sound from the back seat suddenly caught his attention, and he thought Lillie gasped. He looked in the mirror. Lo's body was convulsing, and the boy did appear to be unconscious. A strange feeling began to grow inside of him, chilling and simultaneously burning with urgency.

"Why the h—why didn't you tell me he was epileptic? We could have been at the freaking hospital by now!" Logan checked that no cars were close behind them and slid into the right lane, then over the warning strip and well onto the shoulder. He had his cell phone out, ready to dial 911, when Lillie jerked it away.

"Listen to me, Logan. For goodness' sake, just *listen*. We can't call 911 or take him to the hospital because by the time any help gets here, Lo won't be Lo anymore. We've got to get him out of the car and into the trees without anyone noticing. Can you help me with that?"

Logan couldn't take his eyes off Lo's limbs and torso, which were thrashing violently. "We've got to help him!" he shouted and got out of the car.

By the time he reached the other side, Lillie was blocking the back door. "We *will* help him. The only way we can. Now, swear to me that you'll do what I say and won't interfere with what's about to happen. You won't be doing Lo any good if you get yourself hurt. He'll only blame himself, and you don't want that."

"What are you talking about???" he tried to shove her out of the way, but she was stronger than she looked.

"Logan. Listen. I'm his mother. Think about it logically. Why would I lie about this? Why would I put my own son in danger over some elaborate ruse? That doesn't make sense, does it?" she paused. "If Lo had epilepsy and was suddenly seizing and nonresponsive, wouldn't I be the first one to call an ambulance? But I'm *not* calling an ambulance, am I? I'm not calling an ambulance because Lo *doesn't* have epilepsy, and calling for human medical attention won't do him any good."

## Chapter 19

"Lo is about to begin the first night of his Fifth Phase, which means that he *will* change into a wolf any second now, and there's nothing we can do to stop it. The best thing that we can do for our son right now is to get him out of this car and into the woods before the wolf gains consciousness. Otherwise neither you nor I, nor your car will be of any use to him when he comes back to himself in the morning," Lillie explained as calmly as she could, given that her worst fear was becoming a reality. She watched unblinkingly as Logan seemed to attempt to process her words.

"So you actually believe in lycanthropy," he whispered, and she almost laughed at the fact that he was still avoiding the word werewolf.

"Yes, I do," she nodded, relieved that it finally seemed to be sinking in for him. "Now, I'm going to need you to help me get his clothes off and get him into the woods fairly quickly. Can you do that?" she raised a brow.

When he nodded, she opened the door and crawled in with Lo. He was still himself, but he was thrashing more violently than he had been. "It won't be long now," she said as she pulled his shoes and socks off. "Logan, can you get his shirt off?" Lillie began to struggle with Lo's jeans.

She looked up after a moment and saw that Logan hadn't moved. "Logan, I need you to help me. *Lo* needs

194

you to help me. Can. You. Get. His. Shirt?" She touched Logan's hand.

Logan blinked and then said, "No, you get his shirt, and I'll handle the jeans."

She finished wrestling Lo's shirt off and found that Logan had managed to get him down to his zombie-covered boxers. He was staring at the ghoulish cartoon figures as they jerked along with Lo's body. "There is no shared consciousness between Lo and the wolf, so it might be easier for you if you just tell yourself that it isn't Lo you're seeing right now," she said quietly.

"If it isn't Lo I'm seeing, then who is it?" Logan shoved a hand over his face and up into his hair.

"Don't think, Logan. Don't think. Just help me get him into the woods before he gets claws or teeth. He'd never forgive himself if he hurt one of us."

"How do you know?"

"You never did," she whispered.

~

Logan and Lillie watched from just inside the trees as the body of their son ceased to exist. They were about two hundred yards away, but they could still see that the thrashing lump was now covered in fur, and the limbs that kicked out were undoubtedly lupine.

"There's no way he can possibly survive this," Logan breathed.

"I think the same thing every time I watch this," Lillie said into his ear. "But I tell myself that you did this thirteen times, so I know that Lo can live through this one."

Her words had him freezing, not that he had been moving very much since they'd first crouched here a few minutes before. The only thing he'd had time to do since he'd come to the conclusion that this really was happening and was not some Jäger-induced hallucination left over from his *Animal House* days at NCSU was do what Lillie asked of him and worry about the kid.

There was nothing left to do but watch, and now Lillie had forced him to think of something more than Lo's survival or his own self-preservation, which could be dangerous. "If Lo really is a lycanthrope, does that mean all the things in your journal are true?" he asked before he was aware he had vocalized the thought.

Beside him, he heard her chuckle softly. "I knew you'd get there eventually."

"And that means to cure Lo, we have to get the wolf to jump through a mirror?" This time he knew he was asking under his breath. The wolf had stopped twitching.

"I'm hoping to find another method that's a bit less dangerous for all the parties involved. And I'd rather Lo not lose the last six months of his life. Who knows what something like that would do to a child's psyche? You were grown when you lost that year, and look what it did to you! You're everything you never wanted to be."

He kept a wary eye on the still unmoving wolf, but made it clear that he was insulted. "How do—I must have told you," he began but answered his own question.

"We were very close at one time. There were a great many things we shared in our brief time together," she smiled darkly, and for a moment he thought he could see why he had gone after such a hard sell.

"And those things that you shared with me . . . have you shared them with anyone else?" he teased.

She broke eye contact.

"No one? There's been no one else in nearly fourteen years?" he marveled. *What is she, a nun?*

But she didn't have time to respond. There was movement in front of them, and he looked over to see the wolf standing on all fours, shaking its head groggily. It took a few hesitant steps, sniffing the air, and when it was seemingly sure of itself and its surroundings, it loped off into the darkness of the trees.

~

Lillie clapped a hand on his shoulder to make sure he knew to be quiet and still. Chances were that the wolf wouldn't hear them anyway in its rush to find food, but she didn't like to think about what might happen if its keen hearing did detect them. She had misjudged a wolf once fourteen years ago, and she didn't mean to be guilty of that again.

When they could no longer see its figure glide smoothly through the trees, not stirring so much as a leaf, she took her hand away.

"What now?" he asked in a whisper.

"Now we wait . . . and pray that when the sun begins to rise, the wolf's instincts lead it back in this direction," she stood and walked carefully back to the car.

She had taken what precautions she could in those few moments after they had hefted the body out of the backseat and into the woods. She grabbed Lo's shirt and pants and brushed them near the roots of several trunks, taking care not to touch the bark with her skin.

The Lincoln was ink black in the dusk of the evening, and she wondered what it was about Logan and black cars. She tried the handle of the passenger door and found it open.

"How do you do it?" he wanted to know when both doors were closed and the two of them were locked inside.

"It's simple. I don't have a choice," she shrugged at his disbelief. "Every night since I first suspected I was pregnant, I prayed that the baby would be normal. And every night for the first six months of his life, I watched him sleep, waiting for some kind of sign that he wasn't. For a time, I fooled myself into believing that he really was fine, that the curse really had been cured. But in the end, on that first morning four months ago, when he woke me with his cries, I went to him without hesitation. It made no difference to me. Curse or no curse, he's my son, and I love him."

She must have slept briefly. When she woke, she found that Logan was still sitting in the driver's seat, staring straight ahead.

"I've been on the phone."

Lillie swallowed the fright she felt curling into a large ball in her throat. "Have you?"

"I called Andrew."

"Did you ask him to schedule you for a brain scan?" she sighed. *How many times am I going to have to explain this to you?*

"I seriously considered it." The half-smile he wore made her relax a smidge. *Maybe he's beginning to figure out that there's more to life than logic.*

"But I decided to ask him about you instead."

"You would've been better off asking him to check for a brain tumor. I never met Andrew, or Mark, remember? And I'm sure they told you that the first time you called to check my story." She wanted to be relieved that he hadn't called the cops or animal control, but she couldn't be. Not yet.

"They did, but that's not what I asked him. Andrew did say that I was MIA for several weeks just before I woke up in the woods, and he reminded me of Mark's suspicion that I had been consistently dating the same chick on the DL. Apparently, I hooked a girl from the library up with Mark, and one night, she let it slip to him during pillow talk that I was asking about another one of the girls who worked the circulation desk with her. The guys never got her name, but they claim that it was along about that same time that I stopped bringing girls home for the night and became strangely obsessed with actually studying for my classes."

Lillie couldn't keep the smile of satisfaction off her lips, but she had the decency to look at her lap.

"There's something that's been bothering me, something I want to know," he continued. "Ever since I remembered your eyes when I came for the weekend back in January, I've been trying to figure it out." Logan leaned across the console, tucked his finger under her chin, and lifted it so that they were eye to eye.

She wasn't prepared for the sudden shock of that familiar touch or the frank way he was looking at her, and she flinched. If he hesitated because of that, it was only for a moment, and then his lips were a breath away from hers. Lillie lost the ability to do more than fear.

A second passed, the beat of her heart, pounding in triple time, and another, and then another. With something like caution, he took that small leap, and she was tumbling down with him, powerless against the current.

~

Logan was dizzy. He pulled away, chalking it up to a lack of oxygen, but when he'd filled his lungs and expelled the air in them, his head wasn't any clearer. It also didn't help that there was a sudden white-hot force searing his left cheek. It took a moment, but her anger was obvious to him at once, as he resisted the urge to cover the place where her hand had been with his own.

"What was that for?" he questioned through clenched teeth.

"I'm not some brainless blonde that you can seduce with smooth moves and a sleek car! *Our son* is out there roaming the woods as a wolf, and all you can think about is getting laid!"

"It was a kiss, Lillie, not a proposition. Or has it been so long that you can't tell the difference?" he smirked. The hurt on her face should have made him feel like a jerk, but his face still stung, so it didn't. "Besides, weren't you the one making innuendos a little while ago?"

"Everything you hear becomes an innuendo, and I can see that, like every typical male on the planet, you need things spelled out for you, so I'm telling you plainly. I'm not interested."

"What do you mean, 'not interested'?" *Does she even hear herself? Wasn't she the one who was so desperate for me to believe what she wrote in that idiotic journal?*

"I hope that we can be friends, for Lo's sake, but I'm not interested in anything more," she explained in a proper tone.

Logan couldn't keep in his laugh. "I think it's a bit late for the Friend Zone at this point."

"This isn't a joke, Logan!" She turned to look out her window, but not before he thought he saw a tear.

*Smooth, Logan.* "Lillie," he put a hand on her shoulder.

200

"*Don't* touch me," she jerked away with a violence he wasn't expecting.

"There it is again, that latent hostility I was talking about the last time we saw each other. Would you kindly tell me why your problem is, so we can get past it?"

"*I* don't have a problem. *You're* the one who can't keep his fly zipped!" When she finally faced him again, anger had erased any trace of whatever might have made her cry.

"Finally, we get to it! You're upset because I had sex with you fourteen years ago!" He felt like he'd just solved a complex calculus problem. "I hate to tell you this, but it takes two."

"It's not about the sex," she shook her head.

"Okay, what, then?"

"I can't do this again, Logan. I don't think I can survive it this time," she was looking at her lap.

"What can't you survive? Typical male, remember? Spell it out," he was careful to speak softly.

Lillie looked at him. "You. I can't survive you."

## Chapter 20

Lo had a headache that was worse than the one he gave himself the time that he accidentally played video games for an entire day straight without eating. He tried to sit up and found that he was on the ground. He opened one eye. Not only was he on the ground, but he was also in the middle of the woods, and he was butt naked.

*Where am I?* He stood up and opened both eyes this time. *Where's Mom?* he took a few steps, but he had no idea where he should go. *Nothing looks familiar. Why am I not in my bedroom?*

Every other time he'd phased, when he'd come to, he'd been on his bedroom floor, and his mom had been close by. *It looks like the wolf didn't make it back from wherever he went last night. What was different about last night?*

*Raleigh. We were in the car with Dad, heading back to Raleigh* . . . but he couldn't remember anything else. When he gave up trying to, a terrible thought had him running, though he still didn't know where he was going. *What if I phased in the car?*

Lo forgot about being naked and embarrassed about it. Who had time to be embarrassed if you'd torn your parents to pieces? "Mom! Mom! Where are you? Can you hear me?" he yelled, and the only sound other than the insects and small animals was the echo of his fear.

~

As soon as the sun was up, Lillie got out of the car. She didn't think she'd ever been so thankful to be out of a vehicle in her life, even after a flight to South America or a road trip with Lo when he was a toddler. She knew Logan thought she was being unreasonable, but she couldn't help the way she felt.

"I'm going to look for Lo," she said without looking back.

"Wait up!" he called from behind her, but she kept walking. Nothing he said would change anything.

She had crossed into the trees when she heard him beside her. "He may want these," Logan handed her the shirt and jeans Lo had been wearing.

They searched in silence, as they had been sitting since she answered his question. Truthfully, Lillie didn't care if her admission had made Logan feel awkward. *At least now he won't keep asking me what I'm upset about. Maybe he's learned his lesson and won't ever ask me anything again,* but even as she thought it, she knew it wouldn't happen. *The crazy thing is, I wouldn't want it to.*

She had been having to fight herself since December, when she'd first heard Logan's voice on Lo's end of the call, and she would probably have to keep on fighting herself until one or both of them was dead. It wasn't pleasant, but at least now she didn't have to rely solely on dreams.

Lillie kept her eyes on the ground and looked for any sign that the wolf had been there. She pushed away thoughts that Lo might be wandering in an opposing direction, that he was scared and alone.

To Logan's credit, he was doing his part. They had taken different paths, and using the compasses on their cell phones, were hoping to find him by covering a large amount of ground. They texted every few minutes, since they could no longer see each other, and she only hoped that his irrepressible logic would serve him well.

~

Logan tried to concentrate on the task before him: finding his son. He tried *not* to think about what the poor kid was thinking right about now, lost and alone in these woods. He tried not to think about what might happen if he or Lillie didn't manage to find Lo before someone, or some*thing* else did. And most of all, he tried not to think about what Lillie had told him in the car.

*It isn't like I should be surprised*, he reminded himself. He had actually suspected as much when he came to the end of the journal. It really wasn't hard to see why she didn't want to get too close. The poor girl had actually fallen for him when they were in school, despite his warnings against it, and he imagined that it had taken her a while to get over it. It was only logical that she'd want to avoid making the same mistake again. *Maybe she makes more sense than I thought.*

He checked his phone when it vibrated in his pocket, and saw that she had gone several hundred yards since the last text with no luck.

"Lo!" He hadn't seen anything either, but he figured calling for the kid couldn't hurt. "Lo!"

It was pretty chilly, even in his fleece pullover. *The kid's probably freezing to death!* He picked up his pace. "Lo!" His voice bounced off the trees and came back to him, seemingly faintly distorted. "Lo!" he repeated, but this time the resonance definitely didn't match.

He stopped walking and tried again. "Lo, can you hear me?"

"Mo—" came the sound; he was certain this time.

"Lo, where are you? I can hear you!" he shouted.

"Mom!" The kid seemed to be somewhere on Logan's left.

"Don't move, Lo!" he called, heading toward the sound. I'm coming! Just keep yelling so I can follow your voice!"

It took him about fifteen minutes. He was running by the time he caught sight of Lo, standing stock-still with his dirty hands cupped around his mouth and his head tilted toward the sky.

"Lo," he called out once more. The boy looked at him and wore nothing but relief on his face.

Logan meant to slow to a jog as he approached, but he saw that Lo was reaching for him, and then he was moving faster than before, needing to reach Lo. Lo was moving too, and at last, Logan was holding his son in his arms, pressing the boy tightly to his chest. "I've got you, Lo. I've got you," he said as he felt Lo shaking. "I'm here now. It's all right now, son. It's all right."

Lo's response was muffled in his shoulder. "Thanks, Dad."

~

When Lo had been younger, he had hated it when Lillie had to leave him for the summer to go on a dig. One of the hardest things she had ever thought she would have to do was leaving him in tears at her parents' house. She told herself then that it wouldn't be so bad for him because he was in his own home, with people he'd lived with every day of his life.

That paled in comparison. Walking through the woods, searching for her lost child was officially worse than leaving him with his grandparents for the summer. All night she had been calm and attempted not to dwell on how she would locate Lo when the sun was up. And she was calm still, had to be. Melting down wouldn't help her find Lo, and Logan wouldn't know what to do if she lost it. *Who knows, he might even lose it himself!* No. Panicking was a luxury she could not afford. Logan was another.

To pass the time as she went, she sang to herself. "As I was going over the Cork and Kerry Mountains, I saw Captain Farrell, and his money he was counting." "Whiskey in the Jar" had been covered countless times, but in her mind, she always heard Thin Lizzy's version of the old Irish folksong. "I first produced my pistol, and I then produced my rapier. I said 'Stand and deliver or the devil, he may take ya!'" She stopped for a moment to listen and then make sure she hadn't veered off course. "Whack for my daddy-o! Whack for my daddy-o! There's whiskey in the jar-o!"

Lillie walked a little farther and had started the verse about Molly, the traitorous lover, when she got a text.

FOUND HIM. HEADED BACK 2 CAR. MEET U THERE.

~

"We can't just let it happen to him again!" Lo heard his dad's voice when he stepped out of the shower, grateful to finally be clean after the long ride back to Raleigh.

"I'm not happy about this either, Logan, but we don't know where the wolf's den is, and we certainly have no way of knowing where it'll go hunting tonight, since this will be its first time to do so in Raleigh. I think it'll just be better for everyone if we wait to try anything until we can have some way of predicting what the wolf will do." His mom's voice was even and reasonable, and her words made sense to him, though that meant two more nights of being a wolf and waking with the mother of all headaches.

"You didn't find him in the woods, naked and shivering and calling for his mom. If you had, you wouldn't be wasting time arguing with me. You'd be on the Internet, researching the migration patterns of North American wolves right now! Or at least looking for a mirror!"

"I *have* researched," she paused, and Lo imagined that she was shaking her head. "You just don't remember it, but it's all in the file folder. The species of wolf that you're talking about is commonly called the gray wolf, and because this wolf has no pack and no female, its movements will be harder to predict.

"It isn't easy for me to sit idly by! He's phased four other times, and I dealt with it by myself. *You* haven't watched it happen twice in one night and then had him wake in your arms frightened and in pain, knowing that the whole thing will happen twice more, and there's nothing you can do!"

As Lo walked into the living area, he saw his mom wipe away a tear. Because he didn't like it when that happened, he went to her and gave her a hug. "It's not your fault, Momma."

"I'm still sorry for it, baby. I know it must have been terrifying for you to wake up like that this morning," she told him as she kissed the top of his head, and after all that had happened, he didn't mind.

"I was scared for a while," Lo admitted, "and my head hurt pretty bad, and it was freezing cold with no clothes on, but then Dad found me, and when he promised that everything would be okay and he would bring me back to you, I believed him."

"You don't have to do this alone anymore," Logan spoke, and Lo wondered why his dad felt the need to stand all the way over there at the bar, when he and his mom were on the couch. "I mean it."

"Thanks, but I think Mom's right. There isn't anything we can do until we find the den," Lo looked at him expectantly, hoping he'd agree so that they wouldn't argue anymore. "But I don't really want to spend anymore of the day talking about this, okay? We only have two more nights in Raleigh, and I don't want to waste them."

## Chapter 21

And waste them he wouldn't. Logan decided that if he couldn't do something to ensure that Lo was cured before nightfall, then the absolute least he could do for his son was to help him have a good time during the last few hours of vacation he had left to be himself. If nothing else, Lo's immediate happiness was something he had control over.

*When did the entire world spin out of control?* He wondered again. Common sense, science, and history all told him that what he had lived through during the past twelve hours was impossible. Reason was no longer governing anything that was happening around him, and it hadn't been since the moment Lillie's panic attack began at his parents' the afternoon before.

She had been right all along, and he had been wrong. There was no way that could be the case, and yet it was. There could be no denying that Lo was a lycanthrope; there could be no denying that Lillie's journal entries were true; ergo, there could be no denying that this whole illogical nightmare was his own fault, and it would keep happening over and over until the wolf maimed or killed someone, or they found a mirror and put an end to things.

*But would a mirror really end it all or just suppress the curse until Lo has his own son?* And could he really be a party to causing Lo the same sense of loss and confusion that had screwed him up so badly fourteen years ago that he was still paying the price for a sense of normalcy? *You're everything you never wanted to be,* Lillie had told him as they waited in the woods, and it was true.

It was strange for Logan waking up on Monday morning without a boy on his couch and a green-eyed woman waiting to complicate his life. He was glad to be by himself again, but somehow not as glad as he'd imagined he would be while they were still there and he was using that thought to keep himself from saying something inappropriate.

But the world had to get back to normal eventually, right? Time didn't stop just because he had been attacked by a werewolf on his twenty-first birthday, or just because he had gotten a chick pregnant, or just because his kid was a freaking werewolf now too. No matter how screwed up life seemed to get, time kept going, and it didn't matter that it would be at least two months before he could see Lo for any amount of time. It was Monday morning, and he had a job to do.

~

Lillie was teaching her second Intro to Anthropology class of the morning when her phone's screen flashed to life. It was on silent, but she still had it in plain sight so that she could keep an eye on the time. She glanced at the notification and saw Logan's name as she finished the thought she was in the middle of expressing.

By this point, he texted her periodically, and she had become accustomed to the jolt she always experienced when he did so, though she was always careful not to let the sudden surge of emotion have any outward reflection. Thus, despite the excitement that now hummed just beneath the surface of her skin, Lillie continued her lesson on Political Systems without more than a momentary pause.

When she was in her office, trading one book for another, she could wait no longer to open the message.

NEED TO TALK. WORKING ON THE CURE.

I'M TEACHING TODAY, BUT I MAY HAVE TIME TO CALL AT LUNCH, she replied, and only afterwards wondered if she shouldn't have waited a bit longer before doing so.

~

"Did you have a good spring break, bro?" Alex asked Lo when they saw each other outside the cafeteria after they were finished eating.

"It was too short," Lo replied, "but it was cool hanging out with my dad."

"See, I told you you had nothing to worry about! Your dad's only known you for three months. You've got at least ten more years before he gets bored of you!" Alex grinned. "What did you guilt him into letting you do while you were there?"

"Well, we just kinda hung out and played Xbox, but I did get to meet my Uncle Preston, and he let me play *Left 4 Dead* on his mom and dad's in-home theatre screen!"

"What?!?" Alex looked skeptical.

"Yeah! It's an eight-foot screen! The freaking zombies were bigger than *me*!" It was Lo's turn to grin. "And then we played *Call of Duty*, and I slaughtered him and Dad both! It was awesome!"

"You don't think you could talk your dad into letting you bring your best friend with you the next time you visit, do you?" Alex wondered, and Lo had to laugh.

"My dad might not care, but my mom would, and I'm not sure how Dad's parents would act."

"You're worried about your *grandparents*? Don't you know grandparents give their grandkids whatever the crap they ask for? It's practically their job! Like, if they didn't do it, I'm pretty sure it would be considered a form of child abuse, and the state department would have to get involved! Seriously, Lo. You're weird." Alex looked at him like he was a psycho.

"Ma and Pa aren't like that, dude, and you should hear what my dad told my mom about his dad before I was born. It sounds like the guy's a dictator or something. Nobody crosses him because they're afraid of all the crazy-bad stuff that might happen to them if they did." Lo explained.

"Who's a dictator?" J.J. wanted to know. Lo jumped at his voice. *What are you, some kind of ninja?*

"Lo's grandpa. Or at least he *thinks* he is," Alex answered, somehow unaffected by J.J.'s sudden appearance.

"I thought you liked your grandpa," J.J. looked confused.

"That's my mom's dad, Pa. I do like him, but I haven't met my dad's dad, and everything I've heard about him makes him sound kinda scary!" Lo tried to clarify.

"Tell Thackery that grandparents are supposed to spoil you and let you do whatever the crap you want," Alex demanded.

"He's right," J.J nodded solemnly. "But if we had to tell you that, then it pretty much sucks to be you."

Lo thought about the conversation that he and his friends had had for the rest of the day. *I think it's pretty freaking awesome that I have a whole other side of my family that I'm getting to know.* And truthfully, he wasn't even looking forward to going back to Raleigh this summer just because he would get to see his dad.

His mom had been sure that meeting his dad and then his dad's side of the family would be a big disappointment for him, and now he had met all of them except for Mr. Michaels, and he wasn't disappointed at all. *If it hadn't been for that stupid phase, I might have gotten to meet the whole family,* Lo shook his head. Mrs. Ginnie wasn't anything like Ma, but he hadn't expected she would be. And Uncle Preston wasn't anything like his mother's brothers and sisters, but he wasn't surprised at that either. Next time he went home to North Carolina, he was going to meet his grandfather one way or the other, and even if Philip Michaels really was the biggest jerk-wad on the entire planet, Lo was pretty sure that he wasn't getting the short end of the stick.

~

He hung up the phone. *A few fingers of Jameson sure would feel good right about now,* he thought as he went back to his computer, but he was at the office and on the clock, so to speak, even though he had cleared his calendar for the day. When your name was on the door, it was amazing what you could do with your workday. Even so, he figured it would be better not to indulge, since whiskey might hamper his ability to follow any leads he might happen upon.

Logan wished for the three hundredth time that day that he had thought to ask Lillie if he could make copies of the research she had complied in that battered old file folder of hers. *It would really help if I knew which stuff she's already eliminated.* But when it came to anything to do with

Lillie Thackery, it seemed like nothing would be simple. When he was with her, the only thing he wanted to do was to get away before he said the wrong thing. *Because it's obvious that I'm going to say the wrong thing if I'm around her for more than five minutes at a time, the only thing that's unclear is* **what** *I'm going to say and how I'm going to have to pay for it later.* But when he had space enough to think straight, more often than not, he found himself wondering what she was doing, and what she might think about whatever it was he was doing at the time.

For all the woman's faults, and she had plenty, he had to give her credit for being so methodical about everything. For a female, she seemed exceptionally rational, especially when she was in the midst of a crisis or a crucial decision. *Any other woman probably would have had the poor kid shipped off to a mental institution or some kind of scientific lab like in the <u>X-Men</u> movies when she found out he was a lycanthrope. Come to that, any other college girl would have run screaming to the campus PD when she saw a frat guy phase into a wolf.*

But Lillie hadn't flipped out on either one of them, and when he looked at it that way, instead of looking at her like she was some kooky new ageist who believed in spirit animals or whatever, he knew that what she had done over and over, first for him and then for Lo, had taken a kind of determination he only wished he possessed. If he had, maybe he wouldn't have spent the last fourteen years in another man's shadow.

When Lo answered Lillie's phone that night, Logan was expecting to hear his voice, so he wasn't sure why the mere sound of it made him so happy. It was true he already missed the kid, though they had been gone only a day, but missing him didn't explain the excitement.

"Hey, Dad!" Apparently, Logan wasn't the only one who was excited.

"Hey, kid. How was your first day back?"

"Is it summer yet?" Lo deadpanned and had Logan chuckling. "I'm already colder than you've been since January."

"May'll be here soon enough," Logan smiled, absurdly pleased that Lo was already anticipating spending more time in town. "How's your head?"

"Oh, it's fine. The headaches only last a few hours, so it was gone by the time we stopped for gas and got lunch yesterday," Lo told him.

"That's good. And the good thing is that we don't have to worry about it again until the middle of April, right?"

"Yeah . . ." Lo said.

"Listen, kid. Don't worry about it. We've got plenty of time between now and then to figure out how to stop it. And remember what I told you before you left yesterday. I'm going to do whatever I can to help you and your mom." Logan was very serious about his promise to his son, but something about the uncertainty in Lo's voice made him even more vehement than he had been on the first morning after he'd seen the phase for himself

"Yes, sir."

"I've been thinking," he began when Lo put Lillie on the phone several minutes later.

"Okay." He could hear the hesitation in her voice and wondered what it meant.

"I really think we ought to try and end this thing when Lo phases again in April," Logan told her bluntly.

"Really? The thought hadn't even crossed my mind." The scorn stung him from seven hundred miles away. "What do you think I've been doing since November, Logan? Sitting around, doing nothing and hoping the problem would go away?"

"That's not what I meant, Lillie."

"Then what did you mean?"

"I'm trying to say that we should do something as quickly as we possibly can."

"Again, why do you feel compelled to tell me something I'm well aware of? If I knew where the wolf's den was, I'd already have a plan in place for the third weekend in April! I've had a lot longer to think about this than you have."

"Then why haven't you—" Logan bit his lip and stopped before he made things worse. "I'm trying to help here, Lillie."

"You could've fooled me." The tone of her words had him biting his lip again.

"I just don't want it to be as hard for him as it was for me," he heard himself confess before he even knew he'd said it.

There was silence on her end for a second or so before she answered. "Then we won't let it."

~

Cooperating on a dig came naturally to Lillie. It was the only way to retrieve what time had tried so hard to swallow up. One archeologist might discover a site, which takes so long to excavate that he never lives to see the last artifact being unearthed. The unknowing was an accepted, although unpleasant, fact of life for those lived at the mercy of the past because it was generally outweighed by the thrill of discovery. At least, that's how Lillie was able to console herself when her patience with something puzzling was running thin.

But cooperating with Logan Michaels on a research project took a near supernatural strength that she wasn't entirely sure she possessed. *He has **got** to be the most stubborn, bull-headed male to have ever walked the Earth!* It wasn't the first time in the last week or so that she had thought it, and judging from their past, it wasn't likely to be the last.

He was just sure that if they went over the same documents once more, something "new" would pop out at them, and they would miraculously find a cure for Lo that didn't involve massive memory loss. Never mind the fact that Lillie had done so herself at least three times since Lo had begun to phase. *How did I stay with him long enough to even get pregnant?* she wondered.

"Listen, Logan. I appreciate how dedicated you are to helping us, but you can't rush science, as much as you'd like to. If we want to ensure that April is Lo's last phase, our best bet is to locate the den on the first night and set a trap that is similar to the one I used last time on the subsequent day. That way, if something goes wrong on the second night, we always have the third for backup," she told his end of the phone.

"I still think there's a better way. We just haven't found it yet. How else do you think the Abbots have been able to keep this thing under wraps? I mean, I don't know about you, but I think I would notice if multiple people in the same family kept developing amnesia!" His frustration was evident, and she tried not to laugh.

"I've searched and traced Sarah Abbot's family back at least a hundred years, and there aren't any reports of disappearances, strange events or mental illness, so maybe the only thing they had going for them was sheer luck," she told him calmly enough.

"You don't believe in luck any more than I do, Lillie. We both know you were the only thing that kept both of us alive." He was right, but that didn't mean she had to acknowledge it.

"If you're trying to say thank you, it's a bit late. Don't you think?"

"I'm serious, Lillie! You don't know what it's like losing a year of your life with no logical explanation. You don't know what it's like to wonder whether you're sane or not. To question everything you once knew about the world and how it works! It nearly killed me, like you said, and you really want to put Lo through that?"

"And you'd rather we look for alternative methods? What will we do when Lo kills someone in the meantime? Neither of our options are very good, but I'd much rather have a son with amnesia than one who's been convicted of manslaughter or murder."

"I'm not going to let that happen."

"I hate to tell you this, but you're not Superman. If the wolf gets a taste for humans and decides that it wants more, there'll be precious little you or I could do to stop it."

"I'll die trying, then," he argued. "I'm not saying that we have to wait forever. I'm just saying that we should try other methods first and save the mirror as a last resort. Are you going to sit there and tell me that if we erase the past four months of Lo's life and later come to find a less traumatic cure, you wouldn't feel like crap for causing him who knows how much psychological damage?"

"Is this really about preventing what happened to you, Logan, or is this about Lo forgetting that you even exist?" She was almost certain that the latter was the case, and from her experience, she could hardly believe she would have acted otherwise, had she known then what she knew now.

"You'd like that wouldn't you? Lo forgets all about me, and you can go on with your life in Michigan without a fuss. No more travelling from one place to another or worrying about how to share him.

"Yes, I'm afraid of what might happen when he can't remember who I am, but it's more than that. It's that I don't want him to ever be in a place where he has to question his entire belief system." Something in his voice as he admitted that made her wish she was near him.

"Why not? Doing so is a normal part of becoming an adult, and you've done it," she hoped that moment of softness hadn't come through in her voice.

"And like you said, look where that got me!" He had a valid point, and it didn't help her pride any that he had used her own words against her.

"I'll see what I can do," Lillie sighed, "but there's only so much digging I can do with the Internet and a database. Actually going to New England would be more productive."

"Why didn't you say so in the first place?"

## Chapter 22

Lo couldn't believe what was happening. He and his mom were about to board a plane to Boston, and that wasn't even the most unbelievable part of it. The crazy thing was that his mom had actually taken *two* days off work for this. It might not have sounded weird to anyone else, but for as long as he had known her, his mom had been a workaholic.

If she wasn't teaching undergrad courses, she was studying for her own, and even though studying wasn't the same as going to work, Lo figured it counted anyway. But at that moment, he didn't care that his mom was doing something she wouldn't have ordinarily done.

"I'm really surprised that you're not grumpier," his mom teased as they stood in line to check their duffels. She'd gotten him up a little before 4:00 that morning, and then they'd driven nearly an hour from their apartment to the airport.

"Why would I be? I'm gonna fly for the first time, and then, when we land, I'll get to spend the weekend with Dad!" he answered, but he was yawning almost immediately.

"Remember what we talked about, though, Lo. We aren't going there as vacation," she warned.

"I know, I know. We're going so you and Dad can do research and see the records, but the buildings have to close sometime, and we have all night to hang out and do stuff!"

"Well, I'm not sure how much 'stuff' your dad's going to be up for. He's already paying for our plane tickets, and those aren't cheap."

Lo shook his head. *And you almost had a cow when he told you he was doing that.* It was kinda cool that his mom was able to do whatever she wanted without any help from Ma and Pa. He got that. *I mean, it'll be seriously awesome when I can get an after-school job and buy whatever video game I want, whenever I want.* But it confused him that she got into a fight with his dad over who was paying almost every time they did stuff together. Paying for stuff was the dude's job, as far as Lo could tell. Hadn't Pa always told him that good manners meant treating girls better than you treated other guys? Wasn't that why he was always supposed to open doors for them and pull out their chairs? *Heck, I'll bet Ma hasn't ever gotten gas for her car! Pa always does that.*

Yet for some reason, every time his dad tried to do anything nice for Lo and his mom, *she* got really upset. Still, he knew better than to point that out.

"Come on, Lo," she said, taking her purse from the counter. "We've still got to go through security before they'll let us board."

Lo shifted his backpack on his shoulder and followed his mom to the line of people who were going through metal detectors. *Who cares if she makes no sense? **I'm** about to fly in a plane!*

~

Lillie couldn't believe what she was doing as she placed her pocket change, keys and purse into the plastic bin. Once they landed again, after their layover in D.C., they'd be in New England. The historian in her was as jittery at the mere thought of being in the Colonies as Lo might be if she let him have a Double Shot. The realist in her was skeptical that she'd be able to find enough information about the Abbot ancestor and the reason behind the curse to stop the Phase that would happen in two weeks, if she didn't. The cynic in her was positive that spending three days with Logan in Massachusetts was going to tear her apart.

She read to pass the time during the flight, having lost the wonder at seeing the tops of the soft, cottony clouds, made all the more striking against the crisp cerulean, that kept Lo's eyes locked on the view from his window. There was no need to make him aware of the uneasiness swirling inside her, and reading always calmed her, especially when it was research related. She had picked up *The history of the colony and province of Massachusetts-bay* at the UM library yesterday. It was out of print, since it had been published in the '30s and actually penned in 1767, but it seemed to be a good source, since it was written by Thomas Hutchinson, the then lieutenant governor of the province, and it encompassed a good span of the Massachusetts Bay Colony's early years.

The pages were damp and yellowed with time, and the words were written in Early Modern English, so her reading speed was a good deal slower than it might have been with a more modern work, but being a lover of history, she was used to these conditions. Lillie dived into the Puritanical world in front of her and scoured the pages for any mention of the surname Abbot until she was startled back into the present by the pilot's voice announcing that they were about to land in D.C.

By the time they touched down in Boston, Lillie had put down and picked up at least three other books, and in the process, she had discovered that a man named Edmund Abbot had been born in the Massachusetts Bay

Colony county of Essex in 1692 or thereabouts. He was the son of a Jacob Abbot who seemed to have come to the Colony some time shortly before 1690. She couldn't find the name of Jacob's wife, or whether the woman had been born in the Colony or emigrated from England as her husband had, so it appeared that this Jacob and his son Edmund were the end (or rather the beginning) of the Abbot line in North America.

~

He met Lo and Lillie at Logan International at 10:15, and he had been waiting since nine. Not that he planned to tell her. He had been keeping watch for them, and felt an unexplained relief when they appeared in the crowd of people searching for their luggage at the baggage claim.

Lo was the first to see him, and Logan knew the moment it happened. The kid's expression transformed from slight concern to elation. *I have never in my life managed to make anyone that happy*, he thought with a start, his mind going at once to the myriad of possibilities he'd had to do so. Then Lo was waving frantically at him, and all those nameless women he'd recalled slipped away.

"There he is, Mom!" Lo's lips said, and Lillie turned from her search, momentarily confused. "There's Dad," Lo pointed, and Logan's hand instinctually went up. He knew when Lillie had spotted him too. Her face blanched, as if she'd gone all-in on the last hand and realized too late that she'd bet everything on a 2-3. *There it is again*, he sighed and felt the smile he hadn't known he was wearing fade a bit as he made his way to them. *What is it that scares the crap out of her every time she looks at me?*

By the time he reached them, she had found their two duffels and was shouldering hers as she passed the other to Lo. "What did you think of flying, kid?" Logan asked, sliding his arm around Lo's shoulders.

"It was *amazing*, Dad! I never knew how tiny people really are compared to the world! We look like ants from up there! And the cars! The cars and buildings look like dolls could live in them!" he answered rapidly.

"It is pretty cool, seeing things from the air for the first time," Logan grinned. "Did you have a nice flight?" he looked at Lillie.

She managed a polite smile. "It was fine. Between the time in the air and the layover in Washington, I was able to find what I hope to be the key to figuring out what we need to do."

There was a brief pause when she'd finished her sentence, while she seemed to question whether to continue. "I was thinking we could get settled into the hotel and then get lunch before we start the research," he suggested at last.

"That's a good plan," she agreed. "I'd really love a shower and maybe latte, if we can find one. The cup I had in the car at a quarter to five this morning's long gone."

Logan booked a room in the Hotel Commonwealth, which was only about fifteen minutes from the airport. He made sure that there were two queen sized beds and a sleeper sofa in the "sitting area" for the kid. *No need in anyone feeling any more awkward,* he'd reasoned.

Once they'd left the rented MKZ with the valet and picked up the room keys at the front desk, he could tell that whatever had been bothering Lillie was about to cause an explosion. He only hoped that when it did, he'd actually be able to understand what it was he was doing that was upsetting her. The elevator ride was a silent one, and Logan watched Lo from the corner of his eye to make sure he wasn't upset. The kid's eyes were stretched wide, and he appeared to be taking in every detail. Logan coughed to hide his chuckle.

He used his keycard to unlock the door and followed Lillie and Lo inside. He hung back and let Lillie put her satchel and duffel down on the bed next to the window, and then he took the other.

"Lo, you'll be sleeping there," he pointed to the sofa. "It folds out into your own bed."

"Wow, Dad! This is a pretty fancy hotel!" Lo said, a bit breathless.

"Look out the window, there, kid. That's Fenway Park."

"Isn't that where the Red Sox play?" Lo wondered.

"Yup," Logan smiled. *What teenaged boy wouldn't think that was cool?* It was part of the reason he had chosen that particular type of room.

Lillie's eyebrow went up. "You're shameless," she shook her head and headed for the bathroom.

"So I've been told," he called after her.

~

By the time she was finished with her shower, Lillie was seething. *First, it was the plane tickets, and now look at this bathroom!* She admired the gleam of the marble surrounding her. It was a very lovely room in a very lovely hotel that she was positive she couldn't pay for a third of, let alone two. She had been calculating how much wiggle room her budget allowed and how much she was going to owe Logan, and the discrepancy made her nauseous.

225

She dried herself and dressed as quickly as she could. *There's no need to put it off any longer.* She looked at her reflection and the way her damp hair fell, the way her lips and eyes seemed to blend into her skin if they weren't colored and lined. *On second thought, making my case and being presentable while I do it isn't a bad idea at all.*

When she emerged half an hour later, the boys were absorbed in watching ESPN on the flat screen. Logan's head turned slightly at the sound of the bathroom door opening, and she couldn't help the smile his surprise had dancing on her lips. "Can we talk a minute before we go for lunch?" she asked quietly, since Lo had yet to tear his eyes from the commentators onscreen.

Logan got up just as quietly and followed her to the sofa. "Is everything all right?"

"Yes, I just think we need to discuss the money before we do anything else."

"What money?"

"The cost of the trip," she clarified. "You insisted on covering the plane tickets, and I still say they cost too much—"

"Lillie, we've—"

"They cost too much, but I don't want to talk about that anymore, since we aren't going to agree on that," she continued when he would have interrupted. "But the hotel room's a different story. How much is the bill?"

"It doesn't matter how much the bill is. I'm happy to pay, if it means I get to see Lo, and we might be able to cure him weekend after next."

"I appreciate that, Logan, I really do, but it isn't right that you cover everything. I want to pay our part," she persisted.

"And *I* was taught that in situations like this, the man should cover the expenses, something which I am glad to do," he countered stubbornly.

"I'm not your wife, nor am I your girlfriend. If you want to get technical, we aren't anything more than acquaintances, and I don't think that rule applies to paying for three-night stays in luxury hotel suites for mere acquaintances." Lillie had to work to keep her voice even.

"The hell you are!" he shouted, causing Lo to jump and look anxiously in their direction. "Sorry, Lo," Logan put his hands up. "You're the mother of my son!" he cried, although more quietly. "I'd say that's a smidge more than a 'mere acquaintance,' wouldn't you?"

She wanted to break down, had since she'd voiced the raw truth of their relationship a few moments before, and that, coupled with his biting retort, had her lip threatening to quiver, something she absolutely could not allow.

"Oh, I see!" he said suddenly. "That's the problem, isn't it? You're still angry that I forgot about you, and that left you raising Lo on your own." His eyes had gone flat and cold.

She sighed. "Sure. If that's what you need to tell yourself, then, yes. Yes, I'm angry, angry that you forgot me, angry that I had to be a single parent, angry that you were right . . ." She risked a look in his direction, but she couldn't see things clearly.

~

*Crap!* was all he had time to think as he saw the single tear roll down her cheek. That one was immediately mirrored by one on the other cheek, and then he stopped thinking, stopped calculating the odds of winning, just stopped, and took her in his arms.

She was trembling, so he pulled her closer, pressed her head into the hollow of his shoulder, and held on. Logan was rubbing her back when he felt it, a shift inside himself that he couldn't recall happening before, except maybe earlier today in the airport, but even that wasn't the same thing. "It's okay," he whispered, but he didn't know which of them he was talking to. "It's okay," he said again. "I'll fix it, Lillie."

"You can't," she said into his shoulder.

"You'd be surprised," he told her softly. "Look at me." He waited until she'd picked her head up and met his eyes. Her mascara had rimmed her eyes, and her cheeks were damp. "I'm sorry, Lillie. I wish I hadn't forgotten you, and I wish I could remember more of that girl right now than just your eyes. I'm sorry you had to carry Lo alone, go into labor alone, have him alone, raise him alone. I know that doesn't change anything, but it's true. I wish you hadn't had to go through those things by yourself."

She looked at him with those glass-bottle green eyes, the ones that had somehow managed to survive in his memory, and they filled again. "That's the point, Logan. So do I."

## Chapter 23

He was way out of his depth, and he knew it. He'd apologized and meant it, and she knew he meant it, but she was still crying, and he had no freaking clue what to do next. He looked over at the kid, who was still pretending to watch TV, but as someone who had spent many an hour of his childhood pretending to do something else in order to hear what he wasn't supposed to, Logan knew better. Lo had heard every word of their conversation, at least since the moment he'd been startled by Logan's tone of voice and choice of language. *Great! As if it wasn't hard enough to deal with a weeping woman, I've gotta resolve the situation fairly successfully or risk looking like the bad guy in front of the kid!*

It wasn't as if he had no experience with the female mind. It was just that emotions were an area he hadn't exactly paid much attention to. Why would he? That was the beauty of "no strings attached." And that was the reason he fastidiously stuck with the women who played by that rule. *So what possessed me to break it with Lillie?* But it didn't matter why he'd done it. He had, and now he had to pay the piper.

He studied her face again. Beneath the redness and tears, there was something, if he could only figure out what. *It doesn't seem like anger. She goes frosty when she's pissed. It isn't guilt either; else I wouldn't be the one having to apologize in the first place. And those sure the crap aren't tears of happiness!* He made a mental list of the possibilities and reasoned them

229

away one by one. *Well, that was helpful!* He was out of ideas, but he couldn't just sit there and stare at her, so he went with his gut.

~

She would have laughed if she hadn't been so terrified, as she watched Logan's face while he tried to work out what to do. *Men never know how to handle tears.* But then he wasn't thinking anymore. He was leaning in, and, at first she thought, hoped, that he was aiming for her forehead . . . all right, then maybe her cheek—

The nanosecond she had to steel herself wasn't enough, and the shock of his lips touching hers had her sinking in. They were soft, open, warm. Not hot or demanding, just warm and familiar. She let go.

The ache that she had long since learned to lock away flooded in and covered everything: the want, the need, the joy. She gasped involuntarily, and he pulled back, eyes that soft, unguarded gray she had only seen in her dreams for the last fourteen years. They pierced her through.

"No," she sobbed, shaking her head. She pushed at him with her hands.

"Lillie. . ."

"No," she repeated. Then his arms were around her again, and she wanted so much, so very much to melt into them, but the pain was there, a searing throb, stronger with each wave that washed over her.

"Noooo," she wailed. "No. No. No. No. No," she cried each time it swelled and beat against her.

"Lillie," the wind called, and she thrashed, defenseless against its burning whips. "Lillie," she heard faintly over the thunderous roar, and she knew at last that there was no hope. Nothing left to do but relax into the sea of warmth. The hurt met her kindly, smiling as it pulled her into its depths.

~

"What's wrong with her?" Lo demanded. He had rushed over to the couch when he heard his mom start to cry again and had seen from the corner of his eye that his dad had tried to kiss her. Part of him thought, *This is seriously gross!* But a different part of him was happy about it. After all, other moms and dads did that kind of thing on TV, especially when they'd had a fight and were making up. It was just something they were supposed to do, unless Alex was right. He said that parents only kissed and had sex and stuff when they were trying to have another kid, and otherwise they pretty much stayed away from each other.

But Lo didn't have time to figure out why, if that was true, Alex or even Lo himself had been born in the first place because now she was pushing away from his dad and saying no over and over again. *That isn't the way girls usually react when they like the guy who's trying to kiss them . . . Something isn't right!*

"I *said*, what's wrong with her?" Lo repeated as he watched his mom's fists pound into his dad's chest.

"I have no idea, son," Logan shook his head, but he held on tight to her. Lo couldn't decide if he should be mad at his dad or not. For one thing, it was his job to make sure his mom was okay, *And this is definitely not okay*. But his dad wasn't being mean to her or anything. And for another, it looked more like she was being mean to him, and all he was trying to do was keep her from hurting him or her own self. It was like she didn't know what she was doing, like she was having a dream or hallucinating even. *Sure, she may not have wanted Dad to kiss*

231

*her, but she isn't hitting him because she's mad, at least not anymore.* She wasn't even looking at him or responding when he called her name.

"Lillie," he heard his dad say for what must have been the third or fourth time, and then he watched her go limp.

~

Logan felt it the moment Lillie fainted, and it wasn't anything like they made it look in the movies. Her previously taut body wilted as he held it, and as he loosed his hold, she curled into herself like a petal deprived of light and water. All color left her face. He put a hand to her cheek and hoped fervently that she would come round. "Lo, go to the bathroom, and get a damp washcloth, please." *C'mon, Lillie. Don't do this to me again,* he thought of the afternoon last month in one of his parents' guest bathrooms.

The kid appeared with a wet cloth, and he took it, pressing it first to her brow and then each cheek. "Lillie, can you hear me?"

"Mom?" Lo added.

She stirred at that, and Logan watched as her eyelids fluttered tentatively, and then popped open all at once. "No," she said again. "If we're to be spending any time at all together . . . No!" She seemed to understand that she wasn't making much sense. *Maybe it was the expressions on our faces that tipped her off.* So she shook her head, took a breath, and began again.

"Logan, you told me once long ago that you didn't want the same things I wanted, couldn't give them to me— I know you don't remember it, but you did. That's why you needn't have apologized for anything that has happened between us. I told you back then that I would take whatever you could give me and be happy with it, and I did, and I was, or at least I thought so until recently.

"You were right, Logan. You were right all along, and I wish to heaven that you hadn't been. That the memories and the son you gave me had stayed enough. But they didn't." She had kept those jadeite eyes on his all the while she was speaking. They never faltered.

"What's this about, Lillie? Are you sure you're all right?" he examined her complexion skeptically. *She's still white as a sheet.*

"If you and I are going to continue to spend time together, we have to come to an agreement. You cannot have any physical contact with me that couldn't take place in polite company," she answered in an even tone.

"What exactly does that have to do with you bursting into tears, dissolving into hysterics, and finally fainting in my arms, all within the span of half an hour?" *I think I really was right the first time. This woman's out of her mind!*

"It has everything to do with what must have appeared to you as some hormone-induced melt down," she told him, using what he imagined was her professor voice. "If you don't want something similar happening in the future, I need your word. As much as it pains me to admit, this agreement is the only way I can be sure to remain in control of my actions."

"You're blaming this emotional roller coaster on a *kiss*? Seriously?" he nearly laughed. He hadn't even meant to do it, not after the last time he had, and she slapped him hard enough to have him regretting it the next day. Even now, he wasn't sure what had possessed him to think that kissing her would "fix" anything.

*It had to be the tears. Had to be.* He never quite knew what to do when chicks went all blubbery. In fact, he was usually doing pretty freaking good if he managed to ignore the instinct to run away at the sight of them. Despite what she seemed to think, kissing her wasn't the worst reaction he could have had, although it was close.

He nearly smiled at the absurdity, but her expression hadn't changed. "Fine," he answered with a straight face, "but if I'm keeping my hands and lips to myself, you can't give me a reason to use them."

~

Logan took Lo with him on the pretext of finding coffee for Lillie. She knew perfectly well that room service was just a phone call away, but it was nice of him to give her the space and attempt to distract Lo from what she was sure had been a horrifying experience.

In hindsight, *she* was horrified for Lo and his father. Despite the gaping hole that he had just ripped into her, she didn't blame Logan. *He's a good man, and he's proved it more than once today alone.* It was why she had wanted him in the first place, why she wanted him still, and more importantly, why she could never let him kiss her again.

## Chapter 24

As soon as they'd left the hotel room, Lo's dad decided it would be an awesome idea to ask, "Are you all right?"

Lo had never in his life been forced to work so hard not to say something like "Ya think?" He settled for shrugging his shoulders. A silent response was the safest. It was harder to detect attitude in one, especially if the adult was new at handling interactions with kids.

"I think she'll be okay if we just give her a few minutes," his dad said, as if Lo had asked for his opinion.

They walked down to the patio where they found a Starbucks. "Do you know what she'll want?"

"It'll be simpler if I just do it," Lo said and stepped up to the counter. "I'll have a Ristretto Grande, two pumps Dark Caramel Sauce, Caramel Drizzle with Whip Caffé Latte; a Tall Chocolate Powder stirred Vanilla Powder with Whip Cappuccino; and whatever he wants."

He stepped back so his dad could order, and saw that the dude was clearly confused. Logan blinked, shook his head, and then told the barista, "I want a Venti in your coffee of the day, and I want it black."

~

By the time he and the kid came back with coffee for three, her hair was combed and glossy. Her makeup was nothing short of flawless, and her smile was nearly natural.

235

"Mom," Lo's obvious relief gave her what she needed to take it up one more notch, and the curve deepened into believability.

"I'm all right, my love," she answered the question he didn't ask and took the cup he passed her. "Thanks," she nodded at Logan.

"It's nice to see you've decided to let me cover what I want to without putting up a fight," he braved a joke, hoping that the calm she was presenting wasn't purely for appearances' sake.

"I figure letting you pay's the least I can do," she answered and left him to come to whatever conclusion he might like.

~

Over New England clam chowder, as cliché as it was to order while in Boston, Lillie outlined what she had discovered on the flight. "It just makes sense to check public records here and in Essex. It looks like the Abbots settled in the county of the same name, but it's hard to tell where exactly."

"How far is Essex?" Logan asked from across the table.

"About twenty-five or thirty miles, according to my phone," she told him. "We could easily drive up there this afternoon and take a look around."

"What are we even looking for, Mom?"

"I'm not sure yet, Lo. I'm hoping we can find living relatives of Jacob Abbot, who are still in the area."

"I thought you said you knew that Sarah girl was one of his descendants."

"I did, baby, but after looking at that branch of the tree, I couldn't find anything that might indicate past cases of lycanthropy, which makes me even more suspicious that over the years, the Abbots found some way to cope with the effects of the curse. Otherwise, they wouldn't be able to live in the same place for very long without arousing suspicion and leaving a trail of written evidence behind them. Then there's the problem of young Sarah Abbot herself. When she killed the members of her youth group and escaped, she was never found."

"Where would a little girl who woke up in some strange woods go?" Lo wondered.

"Who knows," Logan shrugged. "Maybe she tried to head home, wherever that was, and just never made it. I mean, it was March at the time, and there was plenty of snow on the ground even when the guys and I were there."

"But, if she killed those people two weeks before y'all came to Breckenridge, how could she have still been phasing by the time you took your ill-fated walk for firewood? The phases are triggered by the moon, and, as far as we know, they only occur on the nights surrounding the full moon, meaning a three-day phase," Lillie pointed out.

Logan pressed his fingers to his temples. "Could there have been a blue moon that month? Maybe a lunar anomaly happened, and that's how she was able to do it."

She reached for her file folder and thumbed through its contents for a minute before retrieving a computer printout. "According to NASA's records, there wasn't a blue moon in March of '07, but there was one in May of that year."

"Good try, Dad," Lo said consolingly.

"Now what?" Logan threw up his hands. "Every freaking time we think we've made some sort of progress, we hit a snag and somehow end up right back where we started fourteen years ago!"

Lillie tried to cover laughter with a cough and hastily took a drink of her water. "I hate to keep telling you things like this, but that's exactly what you told me when we were trying to find a solution the last time."

He scowled.

"The problem is," she continued, as if he wasn't trying to kill her with his eyes alone, "that when we're dealing with something that potentially goes back more than three hundred years, there are gonna be a lot of dead ends. We may have to travel down a wrong path or two to find the right one." She wanted to pat his hand, which was resting only a few inches away beside his glass, but she refrained. *There's no need in a repeat of this morning. I'm not sure either of us could survive that.*

"We don't have time to go down a few wrong paths, Lillie! This isn't some sightseeing trip! This is Lo' life, and the longer we take to find a cure, the more likely he is to get hurt or hurt someone else, so I'm sorry if I happen to be impatient. But the last time I checked the calendar, it said that we have just under two weeks until his Sixth Phase, and I, for one, would really like it if we could find a cure before that happens." The frustration boiled out with Logan's words, and she couldn't blame him for the fury.

"I know. I'm working as fast as I possibly can," Lillie deliberately spoke in an even tone. "We aren't sitting on our thumbs here, Logan, and if worse comes to worst, we do know one way to solve the problem."

"That's unacceptable! I refuse to allow him to lose the last six months of his life! Do you have any idea what that kind of memory loss does to a person? It took me *years* to feel like I wasn't at least partially crazy. But besides that, it means that he'll forget—"

"He'll forget he ever knew you," Lillie finished Logan's thought when he hesitated to voice it.

~

"I'm sorry." The words were quiet and empty, inadequate, as he'd uttered them too many times already. The thought of losing Lo now, now that the kid had somehow managed to become central to his thoughts, didn't really compute. *What would I do without the texts or phone calls?* They had become a daily thing, and he wasn't sure when or how it had happened, but he knew for a fact that he'd miss them if he didn't get them.

"I know you are, and I am too. Now do you see why I thought it might be better for all three of us if we just stayed out of your life?" The expression on her face really did seem contrite, and it made him wonder just how she had been able to live with the hole his absence must have carved, knowing that he was living and breathing but was, for all intents, dead to her. It would be that way for him and Lo if they couldn't find a different cure, and he wondered if he could make the same decision now that Lillie had back then, especially knowing exactly what they were going to lose.

"You did what was right at the time, and I see that now," he made sure to look her in the eye as he said it.

"I forgive you," she whispered, and Logan knew it was finally true.

## Chapter 25

Drive to Essex, they did. One of the former county seats, and thereby the place where Lillie expected to find the courthouse and its public records was Salem, *the* Salem of infamy, much to Lo's delight.

"Can we see some of the touristy stuff while we're there?" he asked politely.

"I suppose by 'touristy' you mean 'things related to the Witch Trials?'" She had been his mother too long to take the innocent expression in those gray eyes at face value.

"Don't you even want to see all that historical stuff just a little? Think of all the Pilgrims and settlers who lived and died there hundreds of years ago. Don't you even wanna know what their lives were like?" Lo smiled sweetly at her.

She cuffed him in the shoulder. "Of course I do! The archeologist in me is positively *dying* to see those places and artifacts, to touch the names and dates carved into those headstones . . ." she trailed off momentarily. "But we *aren't* here for a dig or even to sightsee," she caught herself. "We're here to find new information about the Abbots and how they handled our problem."

"I know, I know," he sighed, "but I had to try. We're in the city most famous for witchcraft probably in the entire world. Did you expect me not to be interested? I *have* seen that old movie *Hocus Pocus*, you know, and if there's a Black Flame Candle anywhere around here, you can bet I'll be trying to light the sucker." The grin on his face made him look so much like Logan that she had to glance over and make sure that Logan was actually still sitting in the driver's seat next to her.

"I can't believe you'd be so stupid! I thought you said you'd seen the movie!" Logan joined the conversation with a grin of his own.

"I know you're new at this, but I'm not sure you're actually supposed to call your own kid 'stupid,' Dad," Lo's voice came from the back seat and sounded mildly insulted.

"Well, what other word do you want me to use? If you did find a candle in some creepy old house-turned-museum and it woke three witches from the dead, wouldn't that be a pretty stupid thing to do, considering you already know what happens to the kid in the movie?" Logan asked, winking at Lillie.

"You have to admit it, my love. That *wouldn't* be the smartest thing you've ever done," she agreed, and was somehow able to maintain a straight face.

"Dang, Mom! What happened to the good cop/bad cop thing? Isn't at least one of you supposed to pretend to be on my side?"

"That is a good point. But that routine takes two, and I'm just so used to playing bad cop all by myself that I forgot all about the good one!" The end of Lillie's sentence was nearly lost in her laughter.

"Tell me about it," Lo murmured.

The first place they stopped in Salem was the Registry of Deeds for the southern half of Essex County, in Shetland Park.

"I still don't see why you couldn't have looked all this stuff up online," Logan said.

"Like I told you before, I'm not sure what I'm looking for, and it's much easier to find information in older records like these by looking at the actual words on the paper," Lillie answered, carefully turning the pages of microfiche as she viewed the copies of old records page by page and strip by strip in the reader, like looking through a huge, boxy View-Master. "Besides, online records only go back so far, and I've a feeling that anything we'll find useful won't have been considered important enough to be digitized."

She became absorbed in her work, and the boys were left to their own devices, seeing as how there was only one microfilm reader, and all the records that predated the '50s were only available on film. Lo had his iPod in, but Logan was determined not to waste time. *After all, there are only a limited number of hours we can spend in Essex County, and who knows how deep the right info's buried, or what exactly the "right info" is.*

He had his cell out and had accessed his data to use the Internet. *Thank goodness for unlimited plans,* he'd thought when he saw there was no Wi-Fi in the office complex where the Registry was housed. According to the stupid journal, Lillie was an ace at research, and he didn't have to have some notebook to remind him that he was crap at finding stuff. *That's what Google and secretaries are for,* he told himself before he had a chance to feel inadequate. *Plus, there's something to be said for beginner's luck.*

Half an hour later, Logan stumbled across a genealogical site that mentioned an "Edmund Abbot"—a name he was pretty sure he'd heard Lillie mention in the car—who was born in Essex County circa 1692. He was the only son of a "Jacob Abbot," who'd happened to survive into adulthood, but there was no mother listed.

Luckily, this Edmund dude had married in his early 20s, and he and his wife Patience had produced a dozen children, most of which seemed to have been named from the Bible and half of which succumbed to Indian attacks or disease before they reached double digits. The oldest surviving son was apparently one "Jonathan Abbot," born in 1720 or so.

"Hey, Lillie," he tapped her on the shoulder when he felt he had enough of a hand to play one round. "Are you still in the 1700s?"

"Yes," she jumped at his touch and looked away from the viewer long enough to scowl. "Why?"

"Because I need you to look around 1750 or so, and see if you can find evidence of a Jonathan Abbot being deeded some land at the death of Edmund Abbot." He didn't even try to suppress the smirk. Logan glanced in the Lo's direction; he was sound asleep, but even his snoring didn't drown out the faint thud of the music coming from his ear buds. *Too freaking bad the kid's asleep. It would've been awesome to have a witness to her face right now!*

The thin line of Lillie's lips somehow became even thinner. "Nice work," she said, but she'd already turned back to the films.

~

Not much seemed to have been known about the "venerable Jacob Abbot" before he came to the town of Ipswich sometime before the birth of his son Edmund. He apparently brought a wife with him, since there was no mention of a marriage between himself and any of the local women, but Edmund's birth was mentioned. Still, Lillie found the records to be fairly well kept, probably since the town had been incorporated some thirty years before the Abbots settled there. She couldn't find a

243

record of his passage to the Colony on any ship from England, but then she couldn't confirm where or exactly when it was he had come from before living there, be it England or some other coastal city in the Colony.

Jacob had been a farmer and a member of the Puritan congregation, but he didn't seem to have taken any leadership roles in the church or even in the skirmishes with the "Savage natives" that happened occasionally. When he died in 1728, he left all his property to his "beloved Son Edmund."

Edmund seemed to be a totally different sort than his father, or at least history painted him as such. Where his father's name was pointedly absent, Edmund's was scrawled all across the pages of record books.

After Edmund and Patience had married in 1718, there were plenty of birth records for their children and evidence that Edmund had expanded his landholdings substantially, due to his success as a corn and tobacco farmer, and had become a church elder, and most surprisingly, that he had been involved in the 1787 tax protests responsible for coining the phrase "no taxation without representation" while in middle age. He had even been jailed briefly because of his part in them.

After a bit more research, Lillie also discovered that Edmund had been very vocal against those same "Savage natives" his father had managed to live peacefully with and had actually led several raids after local soldiers and fishermen had been captured.

"Well, our pal Edmund wasn't political at all, was he?" Logan said pointedly after they finished compiling notes. "Protesting the Crown's taxes and killing Indians to boot."

"He wasn't the only one to think the taxes unfair, thank goodness, and I'd venture to guess that his attitude toward the Native Americans stemmed from the fact that some of his own small children were killed when raiding parties attacked Ipswich during what appears to be battles of the French and Indian Wars," she was quick to explain. Nothing irked her more than modern society looking down on the people of the past without bothering to broaden its lens.

"When you put it that way. . ." he agreed.

"Do you think this guy might be the beginning of the curse?" Lo piped in, surprising them both.

"Looks like you got your nap out," Lillie teased. "But yes, because of his aggressive behavior, the chances are good that it originated with Edmund," she answered seriously. "Unfortunately, we have no way of proving that theory, since, according to the records we have, he isn't associated with any abnormal behavior. That's what I meant when I warned y'all that finding what we need might not be as simple as identifying a name on a land deed."

"So let's look at this guy, Jonathan. *He* might have gotten the curse from his dad just like I did!" Lo's excitement was undeterred.

~

By the time they returned to the Hotel after driving back to Boston for supper that night, Lo was sick of Abbots. He had long before stopped caring whether the name was spelled with one T or two. He felt like he had spent the entire afternoon reading First Chronicles. *With so many names and dates one right after the other and a ton of people sharing the exact same name, it's no wonder the people back in the day kept crappy records. They were confused as heck, and who could blame them?*

He was yawning as they stepped into the elevator. "Don't fall asleep standing up," Lillie poked him in the shoulder. "You're a little bit big for me to pick up and carry, don't you think?"

"I'm good, Mom," he frowned. *Did she really have to make such a big deal about it in front of Dad?*

"Wake up, kid. I thought we were going to make use of the Xbox and flat screen TV!" his dad slapped him on the back.

"We are," he agreed around another yawn.

~

Logan pulled out the bed for Lo while Lillie shoved the kid's toothbrush and pajamas in his hands and pointed his sluggish feet in the direction of the bathroom. Once the door shut, she turned to him. "Most of the time I forget he's only thirteen." She turned down the sofa bed and fluffed the pillows, but Logan figured she didn't realize she was doing it. "But then he stays up too late or has too much caffeine or sugar or throws a rare fit, and I remember just how young he really is."

"He's a good kid," Lo told her, unsure of where the conversation could be going from here. Instinct told him that though the topic seemed innocuous enough, with Lillie, there was no telling. *I'd hate to have to call her bluff.* But that was exactly what he was doing.

"He really is," she agreed, clicking on the lamp on her nightstand. "I just hope he's still that way when this is all over."

"It isn't that bad, Lillie. We think we've found the beginning of Sarah Abbot's line, so somewhere in there's gotta be the guy responsible for all this crap. We'll narrow

246

it down, and when we do, we'll find a better way to cure Lo, and then our lives will go back to normal." He hoped his words were a comfort, since he'd agreed to be hands-off.

"Oh, I've no doubt we'll find the person who's responsible. I'm just not sure we've found the right branch of the Abbot tree, and I hate to think of Lo phasing again or what effect phasing will have on him later on in life." He wasn't positive, but he though he saw her blink a tear or two away as the bathroom door opened, and Lo emerged wearing Transformers pants and a shirt that said "Keep staring. I might do a trick." and looking more like Preston than he had a right to. He shuffled to the bed and crawled beneath the covers.

"Good night, my love. Sleep tight," Lillie called as she turned off the overhead light.

Lo mumbled a reply before rolling over. In less than fifteen minutes, Logan heard him snoring softly.

~

Lillie was nervous. She had been since she got on the plane this morning. Lo was asleep, and she and Logan were basically alone. The last time that had happened had been in Logan's mother's guest bathroom, and she'd had other concerns on her mind. Now, in the dimness of the hotel room, she could think about what she hadn't had time to then, what she'd almost gotten lost in that morning.

"I'm going to wash my face and get ready for bed," she announced quietly and headed for the bathroom before she could start trying to discern his silhouette from the other shadows as he bent over his suitcase.

When she'd shut the door and turned on the light, she changed into her pajamas, pulled her hair up into a clip and put her old sweatband on to keep the wisps of hair on the sides of her face out of the way. She wet a washcloth and watched herself in the mirror as she rubbed the cleanser in circles over her skin. It was the same cleansing routine she'd had since college, and the mindlessness of completing the familiar steps allowed her thoughts to wander to another night when she'd stared at her own reflection in a mirror, but that night hers hadn't been the only eyes that were watching.

She blinked away the few tears that the astringency of the toner brought about and hastily applied her moisturizer. *It isn't vain to be proud of the way I've taken care of my skin,* she told herself again as she did most nights when what she saw in the glass pleased her—the same face that most people guessed to be mid-twenties, not a couple months shy of thirty-five—but tonight wasn't one of them.

Tonight, all she could think of was how she'd looked at twenty-one, the last time Logan had seen her and known who she was. He had wanted her then, so badly that he'd broken his own rule and agreed to be only with her.

*Would he have been able to stay faithful if I hadn't killed the wolf?* she couldn't help wondering as she examined the few tiny wrinkles that had settled faintly beneath her eyes and at their corners, the ones she was sure hadn't been there fourteen years ago. Judging from the kiss he'd given her this afternoon, he didn't mind them.

Shoving her toothbrush in her mouth, she worked not to remember the way his lips had made her feel today before the panic and pain took over. *Don't do this to yourself,* she ordered. *He sees the world in black and white, and he's already given you his word. He'd see any ungentlemanly behavior as unacceptable because to behave that way would be*

248

*breaking that word, something Philip would do and, therefore, certainly **not** something Logan would. So there's no use. He wouldn't kiss you now, even if he wanted to.*

~

*Why?* he wondered as Lillie came out of the bathroom. She was wearing white pants with cursive writing in pastel colors covering them and a pale gray V-neck t-shirt that fit tightly enough to make him ask that question. Her hair was pulled up into a loose ponytail, and he couldn't remember if he'd ever seen it like that before. With it out of the way, he could see how small and delicate her ears were and the slight glint that rode on each lobe. He looked away from her face before she could catch him, and his eyes landed on her bare feet. He thought her toenails were polished, but he couldn't be sure because of the lighting. Not that he was complaining. That frigid professor he was used to seeing was nowhere in sight. She'd been replaced by a woman who was soft as she had been cold and as mysterious as she had been hard. *Why???* He stood up and fisted his hands by his sides instead of touching her with them. Suddenly, a thought occurred to him, *Maybe **that's** why I started seeing her!*

"Ahem," he cleared his throat. "I'll take my turn now," he nodded toward the bathroom. At the door, he stopped and looked at her once more and shook his head. "Good night, Lillie."

"Good night, Logan," he thought he heard her whisper.

## Chapter 26

She sat up in bed in the darkness of their hotel suite. Her eyes quickly found the shape that was Lo across the room in his little alcove. *He's fine,* she sighed and nearly turned over and went back to sleep, but then Lillie's eyes fell on Logan's form. If she scooted to the edge of her bed and stretched her arm out a few feet, she could cover the span of the nightstand and touch him on the shoulder.

*But what would happen then?* Could she even survive the loss if he couldn't commit to her as was likely to happen? If she was honest with herself, she doubted it, but there he was, mere feet away from her, the secret dream she had wished for in every private moment she'd had since that terrible night in 2008.

*It's wrong. Just as wrong now as it was back then.* She'd thought her guilt complex would provide adequate enough punishment for the fornication, but it hadn't been the guilt that had tormented her the most in those days since she killed the wolf and along with it her chance for happiness. No, it had been the grief; the gnawing ache of the hole he'd left throbbed endlessly. She could never be positive of course, but she thought it quite likely that she knew exactly what Katherine de Roet felt when she was separated from her beloved John of Gaunt. It was that pain, and the desire to prevent it from reoccurring, that made Katherine willing to disregard public opinion as well as religious teachings, appear in court as the Duke's mistress, and even bear his bastards. *Essentially I've done the same thing, except that I live in a more tolerant time period than the Middle Ages, so I don't have to depend on Logan to provide for me and Lo the way Katherine and her children had to depend on John.* And if she were comparing herself to Katherine, then maybe she would have to take whatever opportunity fate presented to her in order to be with the man she loved. *The man I love,* she corrected. *The feeling is present tense.* Why should she lie to herself now?

The question was, did Logan have any interest in anything other than sex? *In all these years, it doesn't seem like he's had even one steady girlfriend, the way his family talks. He cared for me once, but he was a different person then, one who'd learned that relationships could be more than just business arrangements without resulting in hurt and disappointment. He's back at square one, with no faith in anyone but himself, lost and alone.*

The answer was no, and now she had to decide what she was willing to do with that. The wanting hadn't gone away with her consciousness. She knew because it had woken her from sleep only moments ago. That was clear. It was her ability to withstand the brutal consequences she would definitely face if she did give into the wanting again that worried her.

*Is the pleasure worth the pain?* At one time, her answer had been yes, but that was before she'd spent Lo's whole life trying to staunch the wound. And what about Lo, for that matter? Could she really live with herself if she made things more difficult for Lo by increasing the strain on his parents' already awkward relationship? Masochism was one thing, but hurting Lo for her own momentary gain wasn't something she was prepared to do. *His life is hard enough as it is. I'll just have to make due somehow until we cure his lycanthropy, and then I'll be careful to keep my distance from his father. I owe him at least that much.* Resolved, she lay back down and adjusted her covers for warmth, though Lillie was under no illusions that she would be getting anymore sleep that night.

~

Lo woke to his mom's voice. Though he hadn't yet opened his eyes, somehow he knew it was Saturday and that it was way too early to be awake on that day of the week. And since he hadn't moved, there was a good chance that his mom didn't know he was awake, which meant he could sneak a few more minutes in before she made him get up and do whatever it was she had on the list for him to do. It was a good plan, and he was nearly asleep again when he remembered that he wasn't in his own bed, and there was a very cool reason for that.

In his enthusiasm, he got up quickly. As he sat on the side of the bed and rubbed the sleep from his eyes, he saw that she was turning the pages of one of her notebooks. The thrill he had just experienced was extinguished as fast as it had formed. *The only thing I have ahead of me today is more research in another boring municipal building or library. Why didn't I think of that **before** I got up?*

He calculated his chances of going back to bed before getting caught. *After all, Mom hasn't seen that I'm awake yet.* Her eyes were still focused on what she was reading. *If I move very slowly, so I don't attract any attention to myself—*

"Don't even think about it, kid," his dad's voice was right next to his ear. "She woke me up at five forty-five this morning, running water in the bathroom. If I don't get to sleep in, neither do you."

Lo was right about the day being filled with research. What he hadn't counted on was that they were conducting what his mom called "field research," which meant that they were going to actual places to find clues and not just searching through old records. It took her until noon on Saturday to find what she had been looking for.

They had been in the Johnson Building of the Boston Public library since it opened at nine that morning, and as usual, his mom had her nose in the dusty public records. He knew he should be working with her and his dad, since they were only trying to help him stop phasing into a wolf, but neither of them could describe to him what was important information and what wasn't, so yesterday he had stopped looking at all the dead people's names and who owned what piece of land for what period of time. Now he was watching old episodes of *The Walking Dead* on his phone and wishing that he were back at the hotel room so he could watch on the flat screen instead.

Lo had just seen zombified Merle Dixon get killed by his own brother, Daryl, and was taken by surprise when his mom gasped and suddenly shoved her chair away from her table. As fast as that motion was, she was slow to do more than put her hands to her mouth. He watched as she stood unmoving and wondered just what it was she had stumbled across.

"Mom?" he ventured, knowing that if she was still thinking, interrupting her before she was finished was a bad idea.

"You find something, Lillie?" his dad asked, looking up from one of the oversized record books.

"Maybe," she breathed and lowered her hands, as if she was afraid to jinx what she had found.

~

"It's possible that the Abbots, *if* these are the same Abbots that Sarah came from, discovered a connection between abating the curse and water." Lillie couldn't believe what she was saying any more than the looks on Lo's and Logan's faces told her they could.

"What do you mean, *water*?" Logan spoke his words carefully.

"I mean that I've found four instances of death by drowning, and all of them in the same body of water," her answer was steady, so unlike her insides, quaking as they were now.

"And? I'm sure any number of my own ancestors has drowned over the centuries. What's your point?" Logan raised a skeptical brow and confirmed that it wasn't merely the prospect of a clue that unsteadied her.

"There's a pattern," she assured him. "The deaths occur every third generation, each creating an interval of about twenty-five years."

"But wouldn't the deaths need to occur *every* generation? There definitely isn't a twenty-five year interval between me and Lo," Logan countered logically.

"Yes, I know. There's only about fourteen years, but maybe the timespan gradually decreased. Or maybe there are other deaths in between that we aren't aware of. The important thing to consider is that there's some sort of connection between the Abbots' deaths and this particular place, Clark Pond," she explained.

"Just because four people from the same family died in the same pond doesn't mean it had anything to do with the curse," Logan insisted.

"Why don't we go check it out anyway? The pond is public, so there wouldn't be any questions asked," she tried again. "The worst that could happen is that we find nothing and move on."

"No. The worst that can happen is that we waste a lot of time, find nothing, and then Lo has to phase in May and possibly even June." His anger was uncontradictable.

"It's the best lead we've got, Logan," she sighed.

~

*At least the kid is happy to be here*, Logan consoled himself, glancing over at Lo's expression of contentment. And he had to admit that the atmosphere at Clark Pond was refreshing, if brisk, after the hours spent beneath fluorescent lighting, breathing in dust along with the heated air, but as he looked out over the water, he doubted very much that she would find anything here that had anything to do with ancient curses. There were lots of houses behind them, and a little way away, he could see the Sound and the small boats that floated there—all signs of modern times. If anything had been left here hundreds of years ago by an Abbot, it was long gone. He shivered as he stood and watched the other people on the shore and wondered what possessed them to be out here in temperatures just above freezing. *A fall in right now would be seriously tempting fate.*

"Do you see anything?" he asked Lillie. She was crouched down, staring off into the wild blue. *Lord knows, I don't!*

~

Motionless, she closed her eyes and waited for the past to whisper its stories, for the voices that had long ago faded into silent shadows and stirrings of leaves to finally reach her hearing. There were ghosts here, so Lillie listened.

~

"It's probably a good idea not to bother her right now, Dad," Lo said beside him. "She doesn't like a lot of questions when she's trying to think."

"I'll try and remember that," Logan answered.

~

She stood slowly, picturing, as she did, the pond as it would have looked to the Native Americans who'd inhabited the land more than three hundred years before. The water was good, fresh, a source of life along with what their nets captured. She imagined there had been a line of trees, handy as much for the shade they provided from the glare of the waves as the break they made in the frigid wind, which must have howled here then just as it did now. It had been a good place to gather people, water, fish, but was there something else that drew them here? Something sacred? Something sinister?

~

After a moment or so she blinked, shook her head, and said, "I think we'd do better checking out the former topography of the Pond. We also need to know exactly how long it's been public property and whether the Abbots would have had easy access to it when it wasn't. It could be that there's something significant about this particular pond, or it could be that this was just the most convenient body of water they could use at the time."

"Or it could be that those deaths had absolutely nothing to do with the curse," Logan reminded her.

She made no attempt to acknowledge him. "Lo, my love, do you feel any differently?"

"Not really, Mom." Lo shrugged.

Logan had to work hard to bite his tongue and keep from pointing out that he had told her this was a waste of time before they even drove out here. "All right, then. It sounds to me like we'd better head back to the stacks once we've had lunch." His watch told him it was already a quarter 'til one.

~

Despite Logan's apparent victory, she couldn't shake the feeling that there was something going on at Clark Pond. Granted, it looked just like an ordinary pond, filled with lily pads and murky water, but there had to be a reason why four Abbots had met their ends there. *Or maybe they were just unfortunate victims of circumstance, as Logan would have me believe.* . . But she had seen enough episodes of the BBC series *Sherlock* to know that when it came to coincidences, "The universe is rarely so lazy."

Lillie had little trouble locating the maps in the library's cartography section. With them, she found that there had been no permanent structures constructed near Clark Pond. A bit more digging taught them that the Native Americans had indeed used the area as a place to fish and hunt, but since it had been sold to colonists in the 1600s, no one had actually settled there. It looked to have remained communal, if not public, property ever since.

To her way of thinking, this made the location a perfect one for the Abbots to use. There was and had been plenty of forest around the pond, and a wolf would be likely to bed down near a secluded source of water and food, such as the pond must be. Also, should family members want to lure the wolf there and kill it, drowning would probably raise the least suspicion. And best of all, drowning was a fairly quiet affair when compared to other means of killing the wolf, like shooting it.

But now they had come to a dead end, as she had no way of proving her theory other than speaking with a living relative of the men who'd drowned, and getting someone to discuss the family secret with perfect strangers would be just as difficult as convincing Logan to believe her had been, or maybe even more so.

By the time dusk fell, Lillie had found a possible trail at her supposed dead end. The youngest Abbots, and thereby the ones most likely to cooperate, living in the area were Sam and Jessica.

Somewhere in his early forties, Sam was the younger brother of Dean Abbot, who was the father of one Sarah Abbot, their own personal Lycanthrope Mary. Lillie logged off the genealogy database she had been accessing and wondered how disheveled she looked. *It doesn't matter anyway, since it's nearly six, and too late to drop in on people we haven't met,* she sighed, checking her watch. Still, they had one more day in the Boston area, and she had to hope that Sunday afternoon visitors would seem harmless enough.

~

She told Logan her plan over dinner. Lo watched his parents look at each other across the table. They'd been polite in the face of the waiter who came to ask for their drink order, but the moment he had gone, the politeness had too. "This is a bad idea," his dad had announced without even waiting to hear what she wanted them to do after they got to the Abbots' house and asked the guy to tell them whether he remembered any of his family members acting strangely or drowning in Clark Pond.

"Then, what, *exactly* do you propose we do next?" she demanded. "You were right that there weren't any clues at the pond itself."

"I don't know, Lillie, but what I do know is that they aren't gonna come clean about family secrets to us! They're gonna take one look at us and think we're some kind of scammers or serial killers, and then they'll slam the door in our faces and dial nine-one-one . . . or at least that's what *I'd* do!"

"They won't if we have some kind of angle," she paused as the waiter returned with Lo's Dr. Pepper and his parents' icky unsweetened iced tea. "We could say that we're conducting research on the original settlers of the area (which is true) for some of my anthropology courses. If they Google me, like any intelligent person would, then they'll be happy to find my faculty bio, photo and electronic CV right on the university's website!"

Lo could tell by the look on his mom's face that she was pretty pleased with herself. "My mom's a freaking secret agent! Just how many of those 'digs' you did back in the day were actually covert operations for some secret division of the government?" he teased. "Have you even *been* to the rain forest, or was that code for a black ops mission in North Korea?"

"You've been playing *way* too many video games, Lo," Lillie shook her head as she began to read her menu, but he noticed that she hadn't actually denied anything he'd accused her of, so he grinned over his plate.

As awesomely crazy as their lives had been recently, he could totally see somebody in Hollywood making the story into another *Indiana Jones* sequel, but this time they wouldn't have to depend on Spielberg's imagination, only to have it crap out again like it had halfway through the fourth movie. *How else could you explain the total cop out that was the ending to that travesty?* They could just pretend that *The Kingdom of the Crystal Skull* had never happened and

259

totally rewrite the long-lost kid angle so that instead of some greasy jerk-wad son, an aging Indy discovers he has a daughter who's just as awesome in archeology as he ever was, with the added bonus that she's not afraid of snakes. Then she could help him save some unsuspecting government from incurring the wrath of yet another ancient evil–say, the curse of the moon, for example–and in the process of their epic adventure, they could all learn to get along, so that by the end of the movie, she, Indy, and her mom could ride off into the sunset in an old-timey car with a grown-up Short Round in the driver's seat, one big, happy family.

*She'd love that!* he thought, and glanced over at his mom, half expecting her to have that look of glee on her face that she got when she was in the midst of figuring something out. But she didn't look excited at all. She just looked annoyed at something his dad had said, like she'd had all through dinner.

Lo sighed. *One big, happy family.*

## Chapter 27

She had thought it best to leave Lo in the room with the flat screen and his beloved zombie games for company while they went to talk with the Abbots, and Logan hadn't argued, which was why they were alone in the car. It hadn't happened since they'd spent that anxious night sitting in his car on the side of the interstate, waiting for the sun to come up and Lo to come back to them.

It was quiet, the unsettling kind, and he was fairly sure he knew why she hadn't said anything since he'd pulled out of the space in the Hotel's parking lot. He was fairly sure he knew because he was nearly positive that he was thinking about the same thing she was.

But he'd given her his word that he wouldn't do anything even remotely romantic unless she made the first move, and she hadn't so much as glanced in his vicinity since her melt down. He gripped the steering wheel tighter to keep from tapping his fingers. *Just because she's let her emotions make things weird, doesn't mean I have to acknowledge it.* And yet he found himself thinking of starting a conversation with her not a full minute later. He turned up the radio instead.

~

Lillie stared out the windshield at the road in front of her, telling herself that they'd be out of the car in less than half an hour. It didn't help that she didn't even have to turn her head. She could see him in her periphery. *You knew this would happen when you decided to leave Lo*, she reminded herself, which also didn't help. She could smell his cologne, only slightly different from what he'd worn in college, not quite as "young," but still she found the familiar notes of something spicy and dark, laced with hints of danger and pleasure. In defense, she took small breaths between nearly closed lips and prayed the taste of him wouldn't somehow find its way to her tongue.

~

When they were only few blocks from where the GPS put the Abbots' house, she apparently decided she couldn't wait any longer. "Relax, Logan."

His face snapped to hers momentarily at the words. "What?" His eyes were back on the street by the time he spoke.

"Relax," she said again. "If there's tension between us, they'll feel it, even if they don't recognize it, and it'll make for a harder sell."

"*If* there's tension? '*If* there's tension,' she says! Like either one of us has been able to breathe easily since we left Boston!" he all but exploded.

"We can't let them see it, though. We're two coworkers who are conducting graduate research. Why would there be anything but rapport between us?"

"Do you honestly think we can pretend to be work acquaintances? Come on, Lillie! Our teenage son can look at us and tell there's more going on than that, and *he* spends most of his time observing creatures that happen to make a normal workplace friendship look like it's emotionally charged! And your plan is to tell two married adults that our relationship is purely platonic? Seriously???" He parked the car on the street and glared at her.

"Fine. How do you want to play it?" she used her teacher stare on him without a qualm.

"We play it as close to the truth as we can. You're doing your research, like you said, but instead of bringing a coworker into the field, I say you've brought your . . . long-time boyfriend," he stumbled a bit at the terminology. *No point in making this any* **more** *uncomfortable!* "And he isn't exactly happy to be here, for whatever reason they choose to imagine."

"It could work," she nodded and surprised him with her quickness. "Especially since it isn't much of a stretch for you to seem disgruntled." The flash of her smirk had him itching to say something in return, but they'd already been parked a minute or two, and the longer they sat in the car, the more suspicious they would become to anyone who happened to be looking out the windows. Plus, he was getting his way now, and like any successful gambler, he knew how to quit while he was ahead.

~

He was out of the car and opening her door before Lillie had time to question the wisdom of his idea. From the moment she stood, Lo's life depended on her ability to stay in character, so she smiled at Logan and took the hand he offered.

As they approached the house, he kept his hand on the small of her back. She was careful to lean in so that there was almost no space between them. He took her hand in his again as they stepped up to the door and squeezed briefly before knocking.

Like any disinterested boyfriend, he stepped back and let her do the talking when a blonde woman answered the door, which Lillie appreciated. "Hello," she used her first-day-of-class smile, the one that had a reputation for calming antsy freshmen. "I was wondering if a Mr. and Mrs. Samuel Abbot live here."

"I'm Mrs. Abbot . . ." the woman answered not unkindly.

"Oh, good! I'm Lillie Thackery, and this is my boyfriend Logan." The thought struck her that she had never before been able to use that sentence out loud, and she bit her cheek to keep from giggling.

Logan, who still had her hand, seemed to sense something of the sort and squeezed again. She swallowed. "I'm a PhD candidate at the University of Michigan, and I'm doing part of my dissertation research on the founding families of the Massachusetts Bay Colony. I was wondering if I could ask you and your husband some questions about his ancestors."

"You don't sound like you're from Michigan," Mrs. Abbot told her bluntly.

"No, ma'am. We wouldn't. You see, we're from North Carolina, originally," Logan clarified. "We only moved to Michigan because Lillie insisted on getting her doctorate at Ann Arbor."

"Do you think we could come in and talk for a little while?" Lillie reminded the woman.

"Well, Sam's busy in his home-office right now . . ." she hesitated.

When Lillie glanced at Logan and saw that he was using the smile that got results, she had to bite her cheek again, but it only took a few more seconds for them to be invited in. *That's the first hurdle cleared! Too bad this is a triathlon.*

Jessica Abbot, as it turned out, was more open to their questions than Lillie and Logan had planned. Though she wasn't what Lillie would call a "primary source," she was as close to one as a secondary source could ever hope to get. Once she'd decided to trust them and let them in the door, she'd shown them to the den, offered them something warm to drink, and then skipped right past the small talk that Lillie had been dreading. *The trouble with lies always comes with sticking to the same details.* And she and Logan hadn't had time to agree on anything, so when Mrs. Abbot sat in the armchair across from them and asked, "What do you want to know about the Abbots?" she let out a breath and felt her shoulders sink. *Too Much,* she thought belatedly.

Logan caught her eye from the corner of his. "Well, I'm here mainly for moral support," he filled the silence and put his hand on her knee in what must have appeared to be a gesture of comfort. *My word!!! Breathe. Just breathe.* "She gets a little nervous, don't you, doll?"

Her first instinct was indignation, but then she heard him call her "doll" just as he looked her directly in the eyes, and she had no room for anger or even the worry that she'd felt only seconds earlier as she'd tried to figure out how to cover her silence.

Not once in their time together had Logan ever used a term of endearment. She'd chalked it up to his rule forbidding romantic attachments to the girls he slept with, and by the time she began to suspect that she'd become exactly that, he'd forgotten her altogether.

"I'm better with artifacts," she finally said to Mrs. Abbot, who looked like she was starting to question Lillie's intelligence. *Get a grip on yourself!* ***You*** *aren't the teenager; Lo is!* "In the South, it would be considered rude or presumptuous to ask someone I've just met the kind of personal questions I'm hoping to ask you." Lillie reached into her purse and pulled out the micro recorder she'd brought along.

"This isn't for some newspaper or website is it?" Mrs. Abbot's delicate brow arched fractionally.

"No. It's for my own research. I assure you. I even have a confidentiality agreement that you and your husband can sign, in which I agree not to publish my final product in a public market without first taking great pains to protect the identities of all living family members."

"Then why would I mind any of the questions you ask?"

*Why indeed. . .* Lillie thought as she clicked the recorder on.

~

Logan had listened to the "casual" conversation that Lillie and the beautifully built Mrs. Abbot were having for nearly half an hour without contributing much more than nods of agreement at the appropriate times. He was, he thought, doing a good job of seeming bored.

"So as far as you know, no one has seen or heard from your niece since 2007?" Lillie confirmed.

"That's right. The poor little thing went off on that ski trip with some of her friends from school or some place, and the whole group was killed. Six or seven of them, including adults." Jessica's sadness was evident in her voice and eyes.

"It must've been a terrible time for your family," Lillie nodded. "I can't imagine how it must have felt to lose her and not have the closure that you would have had she died a natural death."

"Some have said that it would have been easier on us if she'd died in a car wreck or gotten sick, but when it comes to losing someone as young as she was, I'm not sure if more details would've made a difference," Jessica was looking at her lap, and Logan bet it was to mask tears.

"Did anything else of the kind happen to the Abbots before Sarah was killed?" Lillie's question was soft, but it seemed to startle Jessica.

"What do you mean? You think someone might have a problem with my family?"

"Not necessarily. My job is to trace patterns over time, so if anyone else has died prematurely or of unnatural causes, that would be something I need to make note of. I document deaths from natural causes as well, but unless there's a family history of heart disease, I'm not likely to find many correlations there." *She covered that one pretty smoothly*, Logan thought and remembered not to show approval. *At least one of us has to stay cool.*

"Well, no one else has been murdered . . . or kidnapped that I'm aware of, but Sam could be more positive about that, maybe."

And he was. When Mr. Abbot finally emerged from the depths of the house, Logan was beyond relieved. It was clear the wife's knowledge had been tapped out, and she hadn't known anything more than what Lillie had already uncovered.

"Sam, this is Lillie, a PhD student who's doing research on the Abbots," Jessica announced as her husband took a seat and sized-up the newcomers. The man's eye lingered a bit longer on Lillie than needed for a casual glance, and Logan pretended not to notice.

"We've been chatting about the more recent branches, since I don't know all the ins and outs of the family as well as you do," Jessica smiled up at Sam who was head and shoulders taller than his wife even now that they were both seated.

Logan pegged him as a lawyer on his looks alone. Add to the suit and haircut the fact that Jessica was about five years Sam's junior, give or take, and she was wearing Cartier, and Logan would've bet Ivy League at that.

"I'm Logan," he cleared his throat, since it was clear that he wasn't going to get an introduction. Lillie looked his way and blushed a bit.

Sam stuck out his hand, and Logan leaned forward to take it. "Nice to meet you. What was it you wanted to know?"

~

Lo was playing one of his favorite worlds in *Zombies: Dead Men Rising 4* (the one that allowed the player to steamroll all the zombies around if he was lucky enough to find a piece of equipment that would actually run) on the hotel flat screen, and he watched his kill points shoot up by the tens and hundreds as he continued to move toward his next check point, accompanied by the sound of the roller squashing bodies as he went. When he was in between missions, he would check his watch, maybe wonder for a few seconds whether his parents had been able to find out anything from the people they had gone to visit.

Part of him was worried about what would happen in the car when just the two of them were in it. From the way they had been acting since Saturday morning, he figured the ride wouldn't be any fun. *If I know Mom, she's liable to go off on him!* He felt sort of sorry for his dad, now that he thought about it. As long as he'd known the guy, his dad had at least been polite to his mom. And even though Lo wasn't exactly a player, he had seen enough to know that something had changed between the two of them, at least for his dad.

When Logan first came to visit Lo and his mom, he had been nice to her, but things still weren't quite friendly between them. Then, when Lo and his mom had gone to Raleigh, his dad had been super-friendly. This weekend, his dad looked at his mom like he wanted her in his bed, the same way some of the junior and senior guys at school looked at the blonde girls in short skirts.

Lo had to admit that he'd seen a few chicks that made him want to ask them out just because of the way they walked as they passed him on the way to class, but he never had because he knew they'd only laugh at him. Lo had even had some dreams he was glad his mom didn't know anything about, and that's exactly the way his dad had started looking at his mom, like he had dreamed about her that way. *But he'd better look somewhere else.* If Lo knew anybody in the world, it was his mom, and she was about as close to letting his dad sleep with her as she was to letting Lo move back to North Carolina without her.

He knew for a fact that his mom had loved his dad when they were together in college, otherwise he would have never been born. For whatever reason, his mom took her religion even more seriously than her PhD, and she would have never had sex with Logan if it hadn't meant something to her because she would have been risking all sorts of punishment for her sins. *I'm sure J.J. and Alex would say I'm being stupid about things because she's my mom, and it's gross to think about her naked, let alone doing it with anybody, and that grownups do it all the time, but if that's true, why hasn't she had a single boyfriend since she and Dad broke up?*

*But if Mom loved Dad enough to lose her freaking virginity to him*, he shuddered, *why does she treat him like crap now?* Lo understood that she had been mad at his dad for not believing her when she said that Lo was his son and a werewolf, but he had gotten on board with all that now, so what was there to be mad about? *There's only so many times a guy can apologize for calling a girl a crazy liar, and he'd pretty much taken care of anything she or Lo could possibly need since then, anyway.*

Lo shook his head. There was no way to tell what his mom was thinking other than that she was P.O.ed, but it seemed like his dad was doing his best to make up for not being there for the past thirteen years. *And it **would** be kinda awesome if Mom weren't single anymore.*

He thought about how touchy she was when other adults mentioned that she hadn't dated in a while or was the only single person they knew. About how her face sort of closed up like a drawer when one of her brothers teased her about being an "old maid" when the family got together. About the girl who wrote that journal when she was in college and how much she wished she hadn't had to do what she did. Then he turned off the Xbox and reached for his cell phone, thankful his dad had picked a place with Wi-Fi access.

Lo looked up from the website he had been surfing when he heard a hand on the door handle. He barely had time to click out of his browser and onto one of his games before his mom appeared and asked, "How'd your afternoon go, my love? Has the threat of the undead been neutralized?"

"It was fine. I got a few more areas unlocked at least," Lo told her as his dad came in and shut the door behind him. "Hey, Dad! Did y'all find out anything?"

Lo watched his parents look at each other for a second. Then his mom sat next to him, and his dad sat directly across from them on the other bed.

"Oh no! . . . Just tell me the bad news already." he bit the inside of his cheek to keep from doing the same to his lip as he waited for their answer.

"Well," his mom looked him in the eye. "The bad news is that we still have no idea why Sarah Abbot turned all those years ago, since she's the only case of a female lycanthrope we've found evidence of in her family history. And we still don't know what happened to her or why she was never found."

"I knew it was too good to be true," Lo stared at his lap and tried not to blink. Blinking would make the frustrated tears fall that had sprung up at the thought of having to phase again and again, and his dad just couldn't see that.

"Don't you want to hear the *good* news?" he heard his dad ask. He couldn't help jerking his head up at that, so he wiped his nose quickly once he realized what he'd done.

"According to Abbot family legend," Logan began on a chuckle, "to cure certain 'wild' tendencies in a young boy, in the height of his 'misbehavior,' he must be made to see the man he can become."

"And just what the heck is that supposed to mean?" Lo threw his hands in the air.

"We think it means your mom was right," his dad said, still smiling.

271

"Does that mean it has to be here at Clark Pond?" Lo shivered. Just *thinking* of jumping into that freezing water in a couple of weeks made him feel like he was catching a cold.

"According to Sam, there's nothing in the family lore concerning location," his mom answered, "but that doesn't really mean much. I'm almost positive that he never took the curse seriously. What legalistic, rational person would? And since we couldn't appear to either, some of the stranger parts of the story may have been left out when he told it to us. He did say that he had never known anyone in the family who'd gone any wilder than teenagers are apt to."

"That means either his brother didn't phase; he was unaware of it, if it happened; or he was lying," Lo decided.

"Here's hoping he was being truthful, at least as far as the geography goes. I'd rather not have to fly the three of us back to Boston during the weekend after next," his dad said lightly.

"But you'll come to Ann Arbor, right?" He didn't like the idea of his mom dealing with the wolf by herself, especially since she didn't have to anymore.

Logan reached across the space between them and laid a hand on Lo's shoulder. "I couldn't be anywhere else."

## Chapter 28

Lillie was nervous, had been since she and Lo left Boston on Monday morning. *Why?* she wondered again. But asking that question again did her about as much good as it had the first few thousand times she'd done so.

It didn't matter. Logan's plane was landing in a little while, which meant he would be arriving at her apartment in less than two hours. He was flying in this afternoon because he'd wanted one night with Lo before his Sixth Phase started tomorrow night, and she couldn't blame him for that. The moments he had left to spend with his son could be rapidly depleting.

Still, knowing Logan's motives for spending the next three nights with her and Lo did not explain why the nerves that had been bubbling within her almost constantly for the past ten days had now reached a rolling boil. Understanding that once they had done whatever they had to do this weekend, she could have her space and hopefully never have to get this close again did not help her as she struggled to catch her breath, keep her cool in front of both of them, maintain the barrier she had worked so hard to shore up. She felt it all eroding, slowly weakening, and she tensed reflexively.

~

Logan got behind the wheel of his rental car and finally let a maniacal grin spread across his face. He had been itching to do so since his plane had taken off, but he didn't want the people near him to think he was a lunatic with a concealed weapon, so he'd worn his poker face, hiding all evidence of the full house he was about to play, and no one was the wiser.

He still couldn't believe the kid had actually called him the night before. It had been a pretty gutsy move for a thirteen-year-old. *But Lo isn't just any old thirteen-year-old*, he reminded himself. *He's **my** thirteen-year-old!* His mouth curved even more at the pride he felt with the thought.

He let himself belly laugh for a minute, as he'd wanted to last night while he thought about their phone conversation.

"Dad, are you alone?" the kid had asked soberly once Lillie had handed him the phone.

"Yeah. . ." Logan had told him. He wasn't sure he liked the sound of the question, so he was careful about his tone.

"Good. Because I just went to my room and shut the door, so I'm alone too, which means we can talk about our problem."

"What problem?" Now Logan *knew* the kid was up to something.

"Look. You gotta be straight with me. Do you wanna have sex with Mom?"

"What the—" Luckily, Logan caught himself before he said something even a novice father knew not to say in front of his son. "*What* did you just ask me?"

"You heard me, Dad. Do you want to have sex with Mom?" It didn't sound any better coming out of Lo's mouth the second time.

"I don't see how that's any of your—"

"Dad! Can you just stop trying to say what you think a dad's supposed to say for two seconds and *listen*? It isn't like we've got a lotta time here. I'm only allowed to talk with my door shut for fifteen minutes at a time. Apparently, planning dangerous teenage stunts takes more time than that."

Despite himself, Logan agreed with Lo's sarcasm and sighed. "I'm listening."

"Right. Besides the fact that we're like twenty years apart, we're both dudes, and I'm gonna need you to remember that. Now, I'm asking you one last time: do you want to have sex with Mom?"

Logan would've collapsed in hysterical laughter if he hadn't been afraid of hurting the kid. "I don't see how the answer matters, Lo. We both know your mom doesn't want to have sex with me," he said evenly, and to reward himself for that, he took a swig of Jameson. *Who knows, I might need a little help digesting whatever it is that comes outta his mouth next.*

"Are you or are you not Philip Logan Michaels, the same guy who could have any sorority chick he wanted on the entire NCSU campus?" Lo demanded.

"Kid, that dude graduated a long freaking time ago." He shook his head and set down the bottle. *Disappointing your kid is something best done sober.*

"That's a cop-out. Uncle Preston said you're up to your armpits in chicks any time you want 'em."

"So? That doesn't mean I go after the ones who aren't interested!" *Why am I getting defensive? I'm the adult!*

"I'm not asking you to! I know my mom, and I say she's so interested, she hasn't slept since we got back to Ann Arbor!" The challenge in Lo's voice rang clearly in his father's ear.

"Just how the heck do you know that?" Logan was proud of himself for not tacking the phrase "young man" onto the end of that sentence, but it was a close one.

275

"Like I said, I know the woman. Just trust me, okay? I've never seen her treat anybody the way she does you, and it got me to thinking: what if the reason Mom's so mean to you is the same reason most of the chicks at my school are mean to people? They're afraid of something. And what could an adult like Mom be afraid of? Not that someone's more popular or hotter than she is. Not of crushing on some dude who doesn't like her back. Been there; done that. And that's when it hit me. *That's* why she's afraid of you, why she acts like she can't stand to be close to you. She's done all that before, and she knows what'll happen if the two of you get together because of what happened the last time, but because she *has* done all that before, she knows what it feels like to be with you, which makes her want to do it again, even though she's scared of what'll happen after it's over."

"Now wait—" he started to argue, but realized he couldn't. *The kid's actually making sense!* "Okay, Lo. Let's just say, hypothetically, that I believe you, and I think that maybe your mom *would* be . . . interested in me. None of that does us any good." *Thank God for Lillie and her sense of propriety.*

"Why?" the kid demanded before Logan could even appreciate his sense of relief.

"Because she made me promise to be hands-off. Remember when she freaked out at the hotel in Boston? And that was just a kiss. Imagine what kind of fit she would throw if I tried to feel her up!" *I'm officially a terrible father! I just talked to my son about feeling a chick up!* He eyed the Jameson and wondered how taking another slug would make this conversation any worse.

"Don't sell yourself short, Dad! Are you gonna sit there and tell me you'd give up that easy?" The kid was having none of that.

"I'm not The Fonz! I *have* been rejected a time or two, hard as it is to believe." Logan laughed sardonically.

"By a girl you really wanted?"

"Who says I want her in the first place?" They had circled back to the beginning, and Logan was starting to smell victory.

"You did. Every time you looked at her when we were in Boston. Every time you checked her out when you thought I wasn't looking. We've already established that we're both dudes. I know what it means when a guy looks at a girl the way you look at Mom. You want her! It's true, isn't it? Admit it." The kid had a good eye; Logan had to admit it.

"You have absolutely no proof. I admit nothing." *Take that, you little schemer! I don't pay a corporate lawyer for nothing.*

"How long has it been since you went out with someone?" Lo countered.

"It's hard to say, offhand. . ." *I shouldn't have to think about this.* But he did.

"Then, if everything I've heard about you is true, that's *way* too long, and I'm pretty sure the reason it's been so long is that you can't stop thinking about Mom long enough to go to bed with anybody else."

"Look, Lo. I don't know what your plan is, but I've already pointed out that it ain't gonna fly with Lillie."

"Let me take care of that angle, then. Now, answer my question, please, Dad!"

"Isn't that fifteen minutes up yet?" Logan stalled.

"I broke down and told her I was talking to you about guy stuff. She gave me an extra ten."

"I bet she did," Logan shook his head. *How in the crap did I get defeated by a teenager?*

"What's it gonna be, Dad? Are you gonna lie to your kid, or are you gonna man up and tell the truth?"

"Fine! I wouldn't mind it . . . *if* the opportunity arose. Are you happy now?"

"Almost. Just one more thing . . . You need to be ready for that opportunity to arise when you come to Ann Arbor tomorrow."

So he was prepared all right. He just wondered how well prepared the kid was. Lo was about to incur all sorts of wrath from his mother with this little plot of his, if Logan's gut was anywhere close to right, and it was going to be quite entertaining to watch it all play out.

~

Lo was too freaking excited for words. He had a lot of trouble sitting still in his classes. Only the fear of tipping off his mom kept him from doing something crazy like standing up in the middle of science and turning cartwheels. *If I can even still do cartwheels . . .* But it didn't matter if he could still do cartwheels or not because tonight his mom and dad were gonna get it on!

Even in his own head, the thought was pretty weird, but when he considered the fact that having sex would put his parents one step closer to dating and therefore one step closer to getting back together, it stopped being so weird and traumatic and started being pretty stinkin' awesome! *Especially when the whole thing was my own idea!*

Lo initiated the first part of his plan as soon as he got out of last period. "Hey, Alex! Remember that tonight's when I need to crash at your place. Your mom's still okay with it, right?"

"Yeah, dude. I told you we were cool last night, and again at lunch—"

"And you know what the cover story is, right?" Lo ignored whatever it was Alex had been about to say.

"Yeah, yeah. 'I really need you to come stay the night at my house, so we can work on our science fair project. My ability to pass the class depends on how well we do, and I don't want to take any chances.'" Alex recited his speech somewhat robotically. "You know, this would be a lot more fun if you would tell me what you've really got going on tonight, and why we have to lie to your mom."

"It's for her own good, man. Trust me on it," Lo grinned.

"If somebody had asked me like six months ago, I would've never thought of you as adventurous, man, but now? Now I'm just wishing *you* trusted *me* enough to let me in on a few," Alex shook his head.

"It isn't like that, man! I'd let you in on this if I could. It would actually make things easier for me, but I can't."

"First you run away from your grandparents' and hitchhike all the freaking way to Raleigh, and now you're hatching crazy plans that involve lying to your mom about *why* you're somewhere, not *where* you are! I don't even know who you are anymore, Lo."

Lo could tell by the look on Alex's face that he was mad, and Lo wasn't sure J.J. would be a reliable cover, so he couldn't risk Alex backing out. "Look, have you ever seen that old Lindsey Lohan movie *The Parent Trap?*

"The one with the redheaded twins?" Alex looked confused.

"That's it!" Lo grinned.

"You mean you're gonna try something like that with your mom and dad? Dude! That's awesome! It'll never work 'cause your parents hate each other, and you don't have a twin, but it's awesome!"

"Thanks, bro," and this time Lo was the one shaking his head.

He moved on to step two when he got home from school. His parents were both there already, which was what he had been hoping for.

"Hey, Mom! How was your day?" he went to her and gave her his customary kiss on the cheek. "Did you have a good flight?" he turned to his dad and gave him a side-hug.

"Yes," they answered, one after the other.

He sat through half an hour of small talk before he asked what their dinner plans were. After some negotiation, he steered them in the direction of Anthony's Gourmet Pizza because he knew how much his mom liked it and that she tended to avoid it because she thought it was too high-priced for an everyday meal. He felt a tad guilty at the thought that his dad could've gotten off cheaper at a different restaurant, but in all fairness, the man had been warned.

When they got home, he popped into his room on the pretext of putting something away and shot an instant message to Alex. Five minutes later, on cue, his mom's cell phone rang.

When she picked up, she glanced at Lo and raised a brow. "Hello, Alex." A moment or two later, the glance became a glare. "I see. Well, now's not exactly the best time for a sleepover. Lo's dad just flew in from North Carolina, and he's only in town for the weekend, not to mention the fact that it's a Thursday, and you know Lo isn't allowed to stay over with friends on a school night."

At this point, he was carefully avoiding his mom's eye. Because she had her back to him, he braved a wink at his dad, who had been watching quietly from the couch. When Lo winked at him, Logan's eyes got huge, like maybe he hadn't taken Lo seriously on the phone the night before. Lo only grinned at him.

In a few more seconds, Lo knew that Alex had charmed his mom because she sighed really heavily and passed him the phone. The look she gave him said he was going to be paying for this for a good while, but he'd gladly take whatever punishment she chose if things kept going according to plan. *Heck, if everything works out, she may not even remember to be mad at me in the morning.*

"What's up, man?" he put the phone to his ear.

"Your mom's not happy, but I think she's going for it," Alex said.

"Yeah. I'm really glad you remembered the deadline, 'cause I *totally* forgot that thing was coming up," he said, taking a step or two away from his mom and turning his back.

"Be careful with the emphasis, dude. You don't wanna make her any more suspicious than she already is."

"I know, but the thing is, my dad's here, and you know I don't get to see him very much, man. . . I can't make any promises, but I'll ask and see what they say." Lo shrugged his shoulders.

"You do that," Alex laughed on the other end.

Lo turned to face his mom and covered the cell's speaker with his hand. "Mom, can I please go to Alex's tonight? You know it's the only night I'll be able to before Monday, and our initial project report is due in class that day."

"What about your dad? He flew in today especially so y'all could spend time together tonight," his mom reminded him.

"Dad, it's okay with you isn't it?" Lo kept his face blank as he asked the question. He could tell his dad was about to have a cow, and he didn't want to be the one to blow the whole operation by making his dad crack up.

"I can't believe I'm saying this," Logan paused and cleared his throat, "but school work is more important than hanging out, and we can always spend time together during the day on Saturday and Sunday."

Lo had to bite his cheek at the murderous look his mom was giving him and his dad.

His dad must've seen it too because he was quick to add, "But it isn't up to me. It's up to your mom."

~

Lillie was ready to kill both of them: Lo for being so irresponsible, which wasn't like him, and Logan for being an oblivious male who should have been able to see how awkward the night was going to become without Lo there as a buffer between them. *I can't take being **alone** with him! Not again! Lo'll just have to face the consequences of poor planning and have to explain why he wasn't able to do his assignment to Mrs. Kirk.*

*But he can't explain, can he? And it isn't his fault that he won't have time to do the project this weekend. **He** didn't choose to be born with lycanthropy. And Alex can't help that he's unlucky enough to be best friends with an actual teen wolf either. If anyone's at fault here, I am. . .*

"Mom. . . Alex is waiting," Lo's voice pulled her out of her ruminations.

"I'm going to regret this," she sighed. "Fine. You may go to Alex's."

~

Lo progressed to the final step in his three-tiered plan when he was sure his mom was pulling out of the Thompsons' driveway and he was safely hidden behind Alex's closed bedroom door.

He had been working on this since it had hit him, as he was waiting in that awesome hotel room his dad had gotten in Boston, that his parents were freaking in love with each other. The only problem was that his dad had no clue, and his mom was afraid of losing his dad all over again. *It's all or nothing now*, he thought and sent his dad a text:

SHE'S ON HER WAY. MAKE UR MOVE.

YOU SURE?

DAD…

FINE. THE SIGNAL?

IF SHE READS THAT MIDDLE AGES LOVE STORY IT'S A GO.

The signal had been the trickiest part of the whole thing. None of his cool secret plan would matter if his mom wasn't in the right mood, so he had to think of something he knew she did when she was lonely and wanted to be with his dad. The problem was, once he got himself to Alex's and out of the way, he couldn't watch what she did to see for himself.

When she needed distraction from something that was bothering her, she read for her PhD, but that wouldn't ensure that she wouldn't sock his dad in the eye if his dad made a move. She also watched her sappy old movies, but she wouldn't do that if his dad was in the apartment. He checked the Net for things chicks did when they missed their guys, and one of the articles he found said that if they were lonely, a lot of girls liked to read romance novels, the kind with half-naked dudes on the covers.

*Well, my mom doesn't read **that** kind of love stories, but I sure have seen her read that novel about the peasant woman who's in love with the duke more times than I can count. . . Come to think of it, she only reads that book here lately when she's talked to Dad on the phone or when she's seen him recently.*

~

Lillie had only *thought* she was nervous before. As she drove home from taking Lo to the Thompsons', she discovered her hands were shaking on the steering wheel. *It's fine. Everything will be fine. We're two adults, and Logan has given his word that he'll keep his distance. The only thing I have to worry about is keeping mine.*

She steeled herself for the ache, for the tension as she walked to her apartment. Lillie took a breath, shoved her key in the lock, and opened the door. Logan was sitting on the couch, staring at his phone. He seemed engaged in whatever he was doing, so she was quiet as she headed toward the kitchen to make a cup of coffee. It was, technically, too late for one, but she'd take insomnia over these nerves.

The pot was gurgling when she looked up and saw that he had joined her in the kitchen. Logan was a good three feet from her, and still she felt crowded.

"Would you like a cup?" she smiled.

"Why not? Did you get the kid all settled in at his friend's?" his voice was even, but her heartbeat wasn't.

"Yes," she tried to match his tone. "He's under strict orders to be on his best behavior, and he's to text me the moment he wakes up in the morning."

"Can't his friend's mom take him to school at the same time she takes her own kid?"

"Of course, but I want to make sure he doesn't cause her any trouble by sleeping in," she explained with her eyes on the glass coffee pot.

~

"He's a good kid, Lillie," he set his hand on her shoulder and felt her jolt as if it had been a brand. "You did a good job with him. Logan kept his voice friendly. *Are you sure you really want to do this?* He had his doubts, but the kid had worked so hard, and he had had a point with that reasoning for her behavior. And if Logan thought about it, the kid was right about something else too.

He did want Lillie. Had wanted her since the weekend in Boston—that much he knew—but now that he was considering, the wanting seemed to go even further back. *How long?* He couldn't be sure.

He took the hot mug from her hands and saw the wildness in her eyes, the nerves, but beyond that, there was need. *So it **wasn't** just Lo's imagination.* He saw it now as he looked at her, as clearly as he saw the light reflect off the pot as she poured her own cup.

To put her at ease, he took his cup and sat at the tiny dining table. When she relaxed fractionally, he knew he had made the right call. "Why don't we sit?" he asked because she seemed hesitant to join him.

"It would be like old times, right? Even if I don't remember."

She smiled at that and took her seat across from him.

"I wish I could remember," he said softly. "I wish I knew what it was that I first noticed about you. Logic would tell me that since they're the only memory left, it was your eyes, but I can never be sure." He put his hands up when the aforementioned eyes narrowed to green slits. "It's a legitimate question, and it's a perfectly acceptable topic for coffee and conversation."

"Just be sure to keep it that way, Logan." She was more wary now than suspicious, but he could see that she was guarding herself. *Are you sure?* he asked himself again.

He took a sip of his black coffee and let the dark taste absorb for a moment. "What did you first notice?"

"Your bearing," she said without pause. "You walked like you owned the world and were terribly bored by the whole arrangement."

"You had a relationship with me because I acted like a cocky rich kid?" He couldn't hide his disbelief.

"No, of course not! You only asked about the *first* thing I noticed, and I hated you for that bearing for quite a while. She smiled as she said this, and he understood that she was at least partially teasing. *Teasing is good. Teasing, I can work with.*

Half an hour later, Logan wondered why he'd ever doubted the kid. He'd kept his distance, just as he'd promised and kept the conversation light, just as she'd asked, but that was only the surface. Inside he was tensed, focused on his body language as well as hers.

He angled himself towards her, slightly off center in the chair and leaned forward, propping his elbow on the table and his chin in his hand. If her subconscious was paying any sort of attention, it should register that he was interested and listening. He was careful too about the places his gaze fell.

There was nothing so persuasive, Logan knew, as the power of suggestion, so he spent a great deal of time studying her mouth—the curves and dips that created it. Its color that stood out like a ripe raspberry against the cream of her chin and cheeks. Then the soft place just beneath her ear, right at the junction of her jaw, and sliding along that slant, back down to her chin. And at last, he dipped even lower, down the line of her neck to her collarbone, hindered by her blouse before he could even glimpse cleavage. Undaunted, he returned to his study of her lips and repeated the process again and again and again as they talked about Lo's grades and his extracurriculars, Lillie's load as a graduate assistant and how impressed Logan was with her for being mom and student and teacher simultaneously, his own business and the slight increase in profit the projections seemed to indicate. On the surface, friendly and open. Underneath, rapacious yet restrained.

Logan licked his lips and watched Lillie's pupils dilate. He smiled, unable to stop himself, and her cheeks colored faintly. Now he wasn't the only one leaning over the table, as near as politeness would allow. He glanced down at his empty cup, breaking the prolonged connection they had shared.

"Well, I think I'm going to change." He looked up and indicated the tie and button-down shirt he was still wearing, since he had gone to the airport directly from his office. His suit coat had long ago been spread carefully across Lo's bed. *After all, I've seen enough black and white movies know the value of a man in his shirtsleeves.*

When he came out of Lo's bedroom in his white V-neck T and gray NCSU sweatpants, she was wedged into the farthest corner of the couch from him, her nose buried safely in a paperback book. He nearly laughed but managed not to as he sat on the end opposite her.

She was still in slacks and the royal blue blouse she'd worn that day to campus. He could even see the parts of her flat beige shoes that weren't tucked beneath her. *If Lo were here, she'd have fuzzy socks and a p.j. set on by now.*

He raised his brow at her. "Don't you want to get out of your work clothes? It isn't as if you're going anywhere else tonight. Or do you think Lo might call any minute, wanting you to come get him because he's afraid of the dark?"

"I'm fine, thanks," she answered without looking up.

Logan gave her a few moments to get her bearings back before he spoke again, while he scooted infinitesimally closer to her. "Work or pleasure?"

"What?" her eyes snapped to his.

"The book you're reading, I mean. Is it for work or pleasure?"

She ducked her head shyly and tilted it up so he could read the title. It was *Katherine* by Anya Seton. From the cover, he could guess that it was fiction, and some kind of historical piece at that. *Well, I think that's just about as close to a green light as I'm gonna get, kid.*

"Don't you ever stop living in the past?" He tempered his words with a smirk.

"Not really. All the best things seemed to have already happened," she answered, eyes on the page once more.

"That's not true," he whispered, putting a hand on her left arm. She jumped at the touch, making him think of a skittish foal, but she wasn't the only one who'd been surprised.

Truthfully, he hadn't planned to say that. It wasn't how he usually got the hand started. *Then again, I'm not usually in a situation like this one, where I have a nearly sure bet, and yet playing these stakes come with an incredibly high risk.* There was only one way to go—with his gut.

"It isn't true, Lillie," he repeated, hoping Lady Luck was with his cards tonight.

~

Though her skin felt seared where his hand laid, she could make no sound, but neither could she move nor even look at him. Her whole being was ablaze, and doing anything to change her current state might cause irreparable damage. Even her hearing must have been affected, for there was no sound save the ringing in her ears.

When Lillie was calm enough to meet Logan's eyes again, she found that he was sitting on the cushion next to hers instead of on the other end of the couch, where he had been only a moment before, it seemed. His hand was still on her arm, and it was keeping her tethered. *He won't hurt you. He can't break his word. He won't hurt you, not like before.* She took a deep breath. "I'm sorry. I don't mean to be so melancholy." She had hoped that normal, innocuous conversation could dispel the tension that seemed to crackle between them—something had to; she was near explosion.

"Don't apologize. Not to me." He shook his head.

She peered at his face to be sure he was serious, and that was her mistake.

~

289

Capitulation. Logan saw it in the jadeite depths of her eyes. He knew he held the trump card. He watched her as he pressed his lips together briefly, and she shifted forward almost automatically—a tell if he'd ever seen one. She was terrified, he knew, but her body seemed to be at odds with her mind, and he was counting on that.

He leaned in, stopping just short of her mouth, and as if she were a wave caught in his gravitational pull, her lips came up to meet his, then sank quickly, having no choice in the matter.

## Chapter 29

Logan felt her tremble. *Was it fear? Pleasure?* He couldn't say, but he knew she needed more, more than the heat he felt beginning to build. She needed shelter and softness.

When he broke the kiss and surfaced for air, he scooped her up. She wrapped her arms around him and found his lips again, as if she had done so a thousand times before.

He cradled her and stood carefully, moving towards her bedroom, acting more than thinking as her mouth had yet to leave his.

When he bent to lay her on the bed and shifted her out of his arms, he hoped she wouldn't change her mind. Still, he pulled back a moment. *It's her turn to call or fold.* "Is this what you want, Lillie?"

"Yes," she nodded.

"I wouldn't blame you if you said no," he cupped the curve of her cheek with his hand, watched her eyes turn to liquid emeralds.

"I know." She reached for him, "But I would."

Lillie felt him shiver. "Cold?" she whispered.

He said nothing in answer other than drawing her closer to his side, her back and shoulders fitting snugly against his chest and her head beneath his chin. She didn't open her eyes. Didn't dare do anything that might make the moment pass. Perhaps, if she held her breath, she

291

could stay exactly where she was and feel exactly as she did for the rest of time. The years were gone. The pain was gone. She was empty again, empty and again so completely full.

~

Logan's fingers moved to brush over hers, lace into them. "Are you all right, Lillie?" He had waited as long as he could stand to ask. The satisfaction was fading gradually, and even though he couldn't remember a time that he'd ever felt more complete, he wasn't sure about her.

"I'm exquisite," she answered before burrowing her face into the sheet.

"What. . . What is it? Did I hurt you, doll?" *It's been so long for her, and I tried to be gentle, but what if I wasn't as restrained as she needed me to be?* For whatever reason, the question made her bury her face even more. "Lillie, what's wrong?" Anxious, he peered over her slightly shaking shoulder, trying to glimpse her expression.

Something in his tone must have caught her attention because she pulled away from the sheets and looked back over at him. "Nothing. Nothing's wrong," she wiped the wetness from under her lashes.

He pushed himself up on one arm so he could see her body better. "Tell me," he said, searching for bruises, anything that could explain her sudden tears.

"I'm fine, Logan. I promise," she smiled as if it would erase his worry. "I just got a bit sad there for a minute, that's all."

"Sad?" Now he was confused. *Was I **that** disappointing?*

"It was something we did . . . before," she sighed. "After our first time, you got concerned, just as you are now, and you asked me if I was all right. I told you I was exquisite, exactly as I did just now, and somehow that simple question and answer became the way we always assured one another afterwards. When I realized that I'd answered you automatically from memory a moment ago, it made me sad to think that you no longer share those lovely memories with me."

Logan watched as she blinked another tear away and pretended not to see. "So *that's* why it felt like you were reading my mind!" He lifted the side of his mouth into a smirk and hoped it would do the trick.

"How many times have you used *that* line?" She rolled her eyes, but at least she wasn't crying anymore.

"It's hard to say. . ." he grinned in earnest.

"How many times has it worked?" Her skepticism was evident, and though he couldn't see her face clearly as he lay behind her, he imagined she was lifting her brow in a way that probably made her students squirm.

"I'll get back to you on that." He pressed his lips to the softness of her shoulder.

"Ninety-eight percent success rate," Logan answered, sometime later, tired but content with the woman and the dark that surrounded him.

~

Lo sent his dad a text message as soon as he finished texting his mom the next morning.

TOLD U.

TOLD ME WHAT, KID?

U & MOM. I WAS RIGHT.

293

## AND YOU KNOW THIS B/C?

:)

~

Logan couldn't argue with the boy. He imagined his face looked a great deal like the emoticon Lo had just sent. It was even better, though, that Lillie's had looked the same a little while ago when he'd awakened with the feel of her snuggled into him.

He watched as she dressed and readied for work with a fascination he had never felt before. She was by no means the first woman he'd observed the morning after, but usually the routines that restored the façades that women wore out into the world held no interest for him.

This morning, he found himself thinking about the way she had kissed him one more time, hard and long, before she slid out of bed. How she didn't look back as she walked to the bathroom for her shower. How she came back to him twenty minutes later in a bright turquoise robe and carrying a cup of black coffee.

"Don't worry about me, Lillie. You're the one who has to be at work on time. I don't have to leave the apartment today if I don't want to," he smiled when she scowled.

"Isn't that nice? Not everyone can inherit his own company, you know." She handed him his cup.

"I do, and that's precisely why I'm telling you to leave me to my own devices so that you don't run late." He smiled again at his logic and the grumble he heard as she headed for her closet.

It was the first time he'd seen her in the morning when she didn't have to be the mom, and since she wasn't being the cheerful face that forced Lo to get up and go to school, she was free to be as cranky as she chose. It was surprisingly cute.

~

Lillie had been afraid of regret since the moment she woke up next to Logan and realized it wasn't just a dream. But here she was, almost ready to leave the apartment (a full fifteen minutes early), and there was no sign of regret. In fact, she was so content that she had to work not to start singing a song.

She looked at her reflection in the bathroom one more time and tried to turn her smile down a few notches. *Not everyone in the department needs to know that I had one of the best nights of my life last night.* Then she turned to examine the back of her loose bun to make sure there weren't any strands that had evaded her bobby pins. For once, she hadn't had to add any blush to her cheeks, and she was careful to downplay the brightness in her eyes with her choices of shadow and liner.

When she walked back into the living area, carrying the day's heels in one hand and her satchel in the other, Lillie saw that he had set two places at the table, poured more coffee, and made eggs-in-a-window. He turned at almost the same moment, and the sincerity in his expression took her breath.

This morning could have been any morning in that loveliest of spring terms of 2008. It was one of the first clues she'd found of the man that Logan could become—his need to bring pleasure to those who had brought it to him. She knew she wasn't quick enough to hide the tears when he set the serving plate down and came to her.

"Don't." His very act of wishing her tears away made it impossible for her to stop them. He took her in his arms then and pulled her close, as he had the night before.

Lillie tucked her face into the crook of his shoulder and felt the palm of his hand caress the back of her head. She was safe and whole here. She never wanted to leave.

"It's all right, Lillie," he whispered. "It's all right. I don't regret this. I don't regret a second of it, and neither should you. This wasn't a mistake. Listen to me." He held her a little away from him, lifted her chin from her chest so she would look at him. "It won't be like last time," Logan told her, and she knew he meant it.

"You can't know that," she managed.

"Yes, I can," he nodded. "This time other people in my life know about you. My parents have met you; Pres has met you, so even if I forget, there are others who will remember. And while we're talking about it, you've got to promise me something right here and now."

"I'm listening," she sniffed.

"If I do forget, you aren't allowed to take the kid and walk away again. You have to promise to make sure I remember."

"Everything?"

"Everything."

~

There was little time for Lo to be excited by the success of his plan or the fact that his mom really did forget to be mad at him. That night, he was set to start his Sixth Phase, and he wasn't the only one who'd been working on strategy. His parents had decided that the curse needed to be broken by next month, if possible. His mom had said something about seven being a "perfect number," but the reasons didn't matter to him as long as he didn't have to worry about spending the night in the woods and waking up with what he imagined a hangover would feel like. At this point, he didn't even care if it meant he would forget the past several months, his dad included. *That's* how sick of the whole thing he was.

~

Logan waited with Lillie outside Lo's bedroom window in the chill of that April night. He knew that the odds of them actually being able to track the wolf through campus and to its lair were slim. After all, Lillie had tried before during every phase. But if Lillie was right, and she was quite a bit more often than he would like, then figuring out the location of the den during this phase "was imperative."

Not for the first time, he wished for some way to attach a cell phone to the wolf. An app would do all the hard work that way. *Still, two sets of eyes are better than one*, he thought as he felt Lillie stiffen beside him.

There was a sudden scraping of claws against the floorboards, and then the wolf was bounding out the window. For a fraction of a second, Logan found himself frozen at the thought that the wolf could see him if it turned its head even the slightest to look back, but it did not.

"C'mon," Lillie whispered as she stood and headed for her car. "We can't afford to let it get out of sight."

Fortunately, Lillie was as agile as he imagined her to be, and the adrenaline that pumped through him allowed him to keep up with her, or nearly so. She made up for the few seconds they lost climbing into and starting her car by flooring it the moment they pulled onto the street from the parking lot. "I've got a pretty good idea of the direction it's heading," she said as Logan squinted into the darkness ahead and hoped for a glimpse.

They rode silently away from campus and the lights that kept its students safe, each concentrating on the view outside the vehicle. After a quarter of an hour, Logan didn't hold out much hope that they were going to find anything.

"It's too far gone," he said quietly, careful of the pronoun.

"I know," Lillie sighed. "I just keep praying that we'll see something and be able to follow it to its den. I can't stand to think about doing the same thing next month, and the next, and the next. . ." Though she tried to hide it, he was certain he heard tears of frustration behind her words.

"This isn't working. All that means is that we've got to find another way to keep up with the wolf before tomorrow night." He hoped his response would help calm her down. It might have been the post-sex phase of their relationship tinting his perspective, but he somehow felt bound to try to handle the problems she found to be overwhelming.

"What other way is there? And even if we do manage to find the den, how in the world are we going to get the wolf from there to a lake?" she shouted, and he feared that a full-blown crying jag was imminent.

*Crap! Do something, man!* "Maybe that's it. Maybe we *don't* have to track it and *then* lead it from there to water. Why can't we just lead it to water the moment it wakes up?" he suggested, pleased with how quickly the thought had struck him

"Are you *insane*? Just how do you think we're going to be able to lead it anywhere if it tears us to pieces as soon as it hops out of Lo's window? It isn't a horse we can tease with a carrot on a string!"

*Anger's better than hysterics,* he told himself when she turned her searing verdant gaze on him. "That angle might take a little work, but I don't see why we can't lay some sort of trail for it to follow."

"Like E.T.'s Reece's Pieces!" she mocked.

"Why not?" he shrugged and immediately regretted it.

"That was a *movie*, for goodness's sakes! Just because it worked for Spielberg doesn't mean it'll work in real life, Logan!" Judging by her expression, it appeared that he'd narrowly managed to escape having an eye-full of her fist.

"Well, if we can't lead it to the lake, then why can't we take Lo there instead? He can phase in some woods nearby, and then the wolf's natural instincts will send it to the nearest source of fresh water."

"That might actually work." The note of surprise in her voice was not an affront to his intelligence, Logan decided. "It would take a little doing, but it may actually work."

"It *is* a little astonishing that you haven't already considered that option," he grinned when her fist did tap his shoulder.

"You want to say that a little louder, mister?" she asked as her hand settled on his knee.

"Absolutely not."

~

Lo came to and knew without opening his eyes that he was in his mom's arms. He could smell her soft perfume. "Did it work?" he heard the rasp of his own words as if they were someone else's.

"No, my love," she whispered as he realized too late that they weren't soaking wet and freezing to death

299

outside. They were on his bedroom floor. "Don't worry, though. Your dad thinks he's come up with a better plan."

He eased his eyes open a crack and saw that both of his parents were with him.

"What happened? Did you at least find the den?" Lo tried to sit up but stopped quickly.

"It was too fast for us, kid," he watched as his dad shook his head. "But like she said, it's all good." Logan nodded at Lillie, and Lo saw the shared heat in their expressions.

"I guess it is," Lo agreed, and despite the throbbing in his head and the disappointment in his chest, he had no trouble smiling.


"How's your project going?" Lo's mom asked as they ate breakfast a little while later.

"Hmm?" Lo wondered around a bite of biscuit and gravy.

"The presentation you have to make with Alex at school in two days," his dad reminded him.

"Wha—Oh!" His brilliant plan came back to him. "I think it went pretty well. We should be good to go by the time we get to history on Monday."

"I thought you said you were working on something for science fair," his mom's eyes narrowed. *Crap!*

"Sorry. Science's what I meant to say. It's kinda hard to think with this headache." *At least that part's true*, he rubbed his temple.

Lo made sure to eat slowly and make eye contact with both his mom and dad for the next couple of minutes. He couldn't blow it now just by acting nervous. "Hey! How did the two of y'all manage not to kill each other while I wasn't home on Thursday night?" he widened his eyes and pretended to be suddenly super-shocked by the thought.

His mom cleared her throat. "I think we need to talk about that . . ."

"Are you sure now's the best time for that, Lillie?" his dad interrupted.

"Now's as good a time as any," she told him and tuned back to Lo. "The other night—"

"It's okay, Mom. I figured that would happen," he told her as fast as he could, so she didn't have time to say anything embarrassing.

"You figured *what* would happen?" she demanded, setting down the forkful she had been holding.

"I figured y'all would get back together eventually," he explained and watched both of their mouths drop open. "I just figured it would take a while longer than it did."

"Well, I wouldn't—" his mom began with pink cheeks.

"Just because your mom and I are seeing each other doesn't mean everything in our lives changes," his dad put in. "I'll still spend most of my time in Raleigh, and you and your mom'll spend most of your time here." Logan glanced quickly at Lillie for confirmation. She nodded.

"But everything in our lives *has* changed! Mom doesn't have to pretend she hates you anymore, and you don't have to pretend you don't care." Lo knew he had a crazy grin on his face, but it didn't freaking matter!

"Well, he took it better than I thought he would," Lo's mom announced.

"You think you're pretty smart, don't you, kid?" his dad asked and pushed out of his seat. "Let's see how well he takes this."

It seemed like Logan was standing on the other side of the table and drawing Lillie out of her own seat before she was able to draw a full breath. In the next moment, Lo saw both of his parents making out, full on, for the first time in his life, and it was hard to believe that the thing he had been wishing for his whole life was closer to coming true than ever before. He pinched himself just to make sure the headache wasn't making him hallucinate or something. But even after the sobering pain, he was still sitting at his mom's breakfast table, and his parents were still kissing. He watched in amazement for another few seconds, until he caught a brief flash of someone's tongue in the other person's mouth, and he had to look away before he threw up in his plate.

## Chapter 30

Lillie lay in bed on Monday morning. She listened carefully for the sound of the wolf coming back to Lo's room. Though she hadn't gotten a good night's sleep since Wednesday, she couldn't relax enough to even "catch a catnap," as her mother would say, in the half hour or so that remained before sunup. *I wonder if turning over will help?*

"Go to sleep, Lillie. It's your turn. I'll wake you when it's time," Logan murmured.

"I can't. I can never sleep until I know he's back safely."

"Nothing will happen to him. I phased twice as many times, and nothing ever happened to me, right?" The weight of his hand settled on her shoulder.

She rolled to face him. In the darkness, she could only make out the bridge of his nose and his forehead, but seeing didn't matter. Her fingers found his, and they laced together.

"It will be warm and dry enough in Raleigh this time next month for us to finish it."

"But what if it isn't the weather that keeps us from herding the wolf into a lake next time? What if it isn't just any body of water? What if it *has* to be Clark Pond? Or what if the wolf scents humans and refuses to go in the right direction?" *What good will avoiding pneumonia do, if we're torn to shreds by a wolf on the defensive?*

"Then we'll have to force its hand, so to speak. I'm sure it wouldn't like being shot at any more than you liked being attacked or chased."

"Logan, you can't! You can't use a gun! What if you shoot the wolf by mistake?" She shivered at the scene her question evoked.

"Try not to think about it now. May's phase is a month away. You have plenty of time to devise other methods of persuasion." He pulled her close against him. "Now, close your eyes and rest, doll. I've got you, and I'm not going anywhere."

Lillie was quiet once the three of them were up and moving for the day. In little more than an hour, she would be taking Lo to school and Logan would be leaving for the airport. She felt simultaneously numb and as if she was being touched with a live wire, her whole being tingling and electrified. Her limbs were restless. Even her thoughts refused to follow a sensible pattern and seemed to be as jumbled as the rest of her.

Lo, alert at least, was sipping the single cup of coffee he had been permitted and eating his Frosted Flakes mechanically.

"Mom," he said beside her and had her jumping in her chair. "Are you sure you're okay?"

"Yes, baby," she smiled. "I'm just tired. I'll hit my second wind eventually. I'm a PhD candidate, remember? I've gone longer than this without sleep before."

"You were younger then, Lillie," Logan reminded her. "You're not tired; you're exhausted. Why don't you call in sick at the University? I can take Lo to school on the way back to Detroit."

"It would be out of your way, Logan," she shook her head. "But I appreciate the offer."

When he opened his mouth, she stopped him. "I've been a single mom longer than you've been in the picture. I'm used to juggling several things at once on very little sleep. Go on to the airport like you planned. You can take Lo to school for me some other time."

"But that's the point. You don't have to do the juggling by yourself anymore. There are two of us now, and you don't hate me anymore, remember?"

*That's the problem*, she thought as she locked the apartment door behind them. The rental car was packed, but Logan lingered as she and Lo headed for her car.

"Be good, kid." Logan slung an arm around Lo's shoulders. "Take care of your mom."

"Yes, sir. I will," he promised, hugging his father. "See you next month."

"Absolutely."

When Lillie thought Logan would get in the car and pull away, he let go of Lo and came to her. She blinked up at him confusedly before he took her in his arms and kissed her until she felt her knees give. She was still clinging to his chest for support when he pulled back.

"I'll text you at the airport and call when I land in Raleigh."

She nodded, feeling more muddled than before. He opened the driver's door for her, and she got in and buckled up without a thought. Then Logan shut the door, gave her a rakish wink, and walked away.

~

He fell into bed that night and expected to be asleep momentarily. He was exhausted from the endless stream of meetings his position forced him to attend. If it wasn't the stockholders, then it was the board, and if it wasn't the board, then it was the attorneys representing his latest acquisition, and if it wasn't attorneys, then it was his own legal team. Times like these, he wondered if it wouldn't just save time to sleep in his suit, sitting at his desk.

*CEO ain't all it's cracked up to be.* Unbidden, an image of the kid filled Logan's thoughts. It had been two weeks since he'd seen Lo and Lillie in Ann Arbor, and it would be just under two weeks more before he flew them both to Raleigh for what everyone hoped would be Lo's seventh and final phase. That he missed the kid was natural, he supposed, but the longer he lay in the dark, it wasn't the kid he began to miss, and he decided that sleep would be a long time coming.

~

Lo was definitely sick. Sicker than he had been since he was little and they still lived with Ma and Pa. But he didn't dare tell his mom that the last thing he felt like doing today was getting on a plane because as soon as he did, she would call his dad, and the whole trip to North Carolina would be off, whether it was his seventh phase or not.

He had been nauseated all day, and he could only hope that he wouldn't need to use the stupid barf bags during takeoff. *How much more embarrassing could it get? At least if it did happen then, it would be too late for mom to make us turn around.* He put in his earbuds, pressed his forehead against the glass of the car's passenger-side window and closed his eyes.

~

Lillie glanced at Lo, sleeping peacefully in the seat next to her. Less than a year ago, he'd never been on a plane,

306

had no idea who his father was, and believed that werewolves and curses were just things that happened in people's imaginations. The time last month, she and he had been down the same road, heading to meet his father, and he was so excited about flying that he could hardly behave himself. *What a difference four weeks can make. . .*

*Lo isn't the only one who's changed, though.* There was no use lying to herself. Six months prior, she would have hauled off and slapped the face of anyone who dared to suggest that she would ever sleep with a man out of wedlock again, much less Logan Michaels. Yet she had, and last night, even Lo had been perceptive enough to know she was lonely when she hung up with his father.

"It's okay, Momma. You won't get hurt again. He loves you for sure this time." Lo had wrapped his arms around her with the words, and she'd prayed for the millionth time that love and hope would be enough.

~

Logan stood impatiently in the throng of others waiting for the passengers who were arriving from Michigan. He noticed that despite his height, he was pushing up on his toes to see Lo and Lillie even more quickly and shook his head. To the casual observer, he would have appeared to be just another husband, anxious to pick up his wife and son, he who had never once considered monogamy before Lillie, much less matrimony.

*And why should I? Philip and Ginnie set a sterling example for me of just how poorly the two concepts play out in reality, regardless of how pleasant things appear on paper.* He chuckled quietly. Ginnie Michaels, Lillie Thackery was not. He envisioned the icy blast of Lillie's temper and decided that had she been, his father would have already been dead.

He was still smiling at the thought when he caught sight of Lillie and Lo walking toward him, and for once, Lillie appeared pleased to be doing so. Lo was quick to hug him the moment they could reach one another, but Lillie stopped short.

Logan let go of Lo after several seconds and reached for Lillie, drawing her to him, so she had no chance to think about keeping her distance. He moved in quickly for a kiss for the same reason, or so he told himself as he felt her sink into him.

"Hey," he smiled again when they broke for air. "How was your flight?"

"Not too bad," Lillie moved toward the baggage claim.

"What about you, kid?" Logan punched his son's arm companionably.

"It was okay, Dad," he shrugged without making eye contact and reached for his bag as it came near.

Logan wasn't fluent in angst, so he glanced at Lillie to see if this was typical behavior.

"Don't ask me. He's been that way all day," she said under her breath.

"You okay, Lo?" he put a hand on the kid's shoulder. As Logan got Lillie's suitcase, Lo answered, this time looking at him.

"No." It wasn't his answer so much as it was the way Lo said the word that had Logan worried.

When he looked closer, he could see that Lo's color wasn't good. "What's wrong, son?"

"I feel like crap."

Lillie immediately put a hand to Lo's forehead, as if by virtue of being a mom she magically had the ability to read people's temperature using her palm. "You're a little warm, baby. Why didn't you tell me you didn't feel good?"

"I didn't think you'd let us come home if you knew I felt sick," Lo admitted.

*The poor kid **does** sound like he feels pretty crappy,* Logan thought. "Why don't we head back to my apartment, so you can lie down awhile?" he suggested aloud, then slung his arm around Lo's shoulders. "Do we have everything?" he asked, barely waiting for Lillie's agreement before leading them to the parking terminal.

~

Lo was positively green despite the fact that he'd been riding in the front seat of the car and had the air vents aimed at his face going full-blast. The joy Lillie had felt upon finally seeing and subsequently being kissed by Logan again had disappeared in light of the current situation. Now she sat in the backseat of Logan's Lincoln and kept a wary eye on Lo. "You don't feel like you're going to puke, do you?"

"No, ma'am," he told her but wasn't convincing in the least. *Thank goodness, we aren't very far from Logan's apartment.*

The moment they got inside, Lillie gave him Tylenol and a peppermint and sent Lo to the guest bedroom Logan rarely used. Then she tucked him in, pressed a kiss to his brow and shut the door as she went.

"What happens if he's still sick tonight when the sun goes down?" Logan asked when she sat on the couch next to him.

"To tell you the truth, I'm terrified to even consider it." *What's the point in hiding it?*

"I think we have to," he put a hand on her knee. "I'm not sure letting him take a leap into Lake Raleigh with a cold is a good idea, even if he is in wolf form."

"*I'm* not so sure that his changing into a wolf form with a cold is a good idea, period," she snapped. "He's lucky to have survived phasing as many times as he has. What sort of damage do you think something like that does to a healthy body, much less one that's ill?"

"Agreed. But we don't have a lot of choice about it, do we?"

She felt the tears forming in her eyes and looked at her lap. *I will not cry in front of him again.* She bit her lip.

"I'd do it for him if I could," he squeezed gently. "Knowing what I do, I'd do it again if it meant he didn't have to."

~

Lo lay in bed and tried to will himself to sleep. He only had a few hours before he phased. *As bad as it makes me feel to do it when I feel fine, I'd hate to think of how I'll feel in the morning if I don't sleep this crap off. No doubt, I'll be wishing I was dead . . . or maybe even **undead** because that way, it would only take one well-aimed shot to the head to put me out of my misery for good.*

The plan his parents had come up with was pretty freaking scary by itself, and he wasn't positive it would work without him or all of them getting killed in the process. *I mean, what kind of crazy parents plot to lead a wolf from some woods and into a lake by deliberately ticking it off?* It sounded like a sure fire way for him to wake up an orphan because he'd eaten both his parents like the wolf did the grandma in *Little Red Riding Hood.* Except this wasn't a fairytale, and there wouldn't be any happy ending or a woodsman with his trusty axe coming to their rescue.

He was still awake. *Thinking about bloodthirsty animals gobbling up Mom and Dad is a* **genius** *way to put yourself to sleep, Lo.* He rolled over and regretted the movement because now he felt like throwing up again. He wanted to cry, would have if he thought it would make things any better. *With my luck, it would just give me a headache on top of everything else.*

Lo closed his eyes and focused on being as still as he could be. *In the name of the Father, and of the Son, and of the Holy Spirit. . .* the standard opening for prayers filled his mind. *Hail Mary, full of grace. The Lord is with thee; blessed art thou among women, and blessed is the fruit of thy womb, Jesus. Holy Mary, mother of God, pray for us,* he thought. *Lord, I know it's sort of a long shot for me, but You were listening before when I asked for help, so if there's any way You can fix this situation, even a little bit, I'd appreciate Your help this time too. If Mom's right about You, then You've got some kind of plan in motion already, but from here, things aren't looking so good.* After second or so, he remembered to add, *in the name of the Father, and of the Son, and of the Holy Spirit. Amen.*

## Chapter 31

Lillie watched as the last of the sun's pink light faded from the horizon and knew that whatever fears she might have, there were only minutes before Lo's Seventh Phase began, and she could do no more to prevent it happening this time than she had before.

"Lillie," Logan touched her shoulder. "Come with me," his voice was quiet, but it pulled at her nonetheless. She looked at their son, unmoving beneath the blankets on the floor. He was sleeping for the moment, but the next—

"Come on, doll," Logan was tugging her away, and she went, trying not to think as she did.

She had attempted to make her peace with what was going to happen tonight, struggled to find that familiar comfort she took from her faith, but it was hard to do that when she was face to face with the truth that she had absolutely no control over Lo's ability to take his next breath.

Logan held her tightly in his arms. His back was pressed against the side of the apartment building as they sat waiting in the darkness. She tucked her face into the hollow of his shoulder when the familiar scratching reached her ears.

After feeling him tense and then exhale into silence, Lillie knew that the wolf had come. It had come out into the night, and with that coming, it had taken Lo, had taken him and might never bring him back.

~

Her tears fell, damp against the fabric of his shirt, and he held tighter, rocking her slightly. It was black despite the brightness of the moon and the lights of the building, so he only had a few seconds to watch the wolf lope away after it cleared the fire escape and that last floor. It seemed to move the same way it had any other time Logan watched it, but he was no zoologist. *What did a sick wolf look like as it climbed or jumped or ran, anyway?*

The two of them had decided, after about an hour of the quietest arguing he'd ever in his life been a part of, that just as there was a disconnect between Lo's mind and the wolf's, that disconnect would also be found between the wolf's body and his own, which meant that Lo's being sick would have no effect on the wolf and vice versa. And yet neither one could make the decision to leave the sick boy unconscious on the ground in the woods.

Logan had pointed out that this principle was the only way that he himself could have suffered from lycanthropy for a year without sustaining any physical damage to his human body. "Surely, the simple act of stalking and killing its prey would have involved a small altercation, even if the sheep . . . or cat didn't put up much of a fight."

Lillie had smiled then at his reference to cats, as his own wolf form had caused a scene on the NCSU campus when it had made a meal of the chancellor's cat, but the smile didn't last.

He tried to think of something now that might make her smile reappear but settled for kissing her head. After a moment more, he stood and carried her inside.

313

~

"We should have done it last night," Lillie sighed now that Lo was conscious and seemed no worse for the adventures of the night before. "We had already deduced that he would be safe."

"Deductions, my dear Watson, are by no means a guarantee of safety," Logan quipped.

"It could all be over right now," she shook her head, listening to the sound of the water running as Lo showered away the debris.

"Yes, and Lo could be dying of pneumonia right now, but he's not," he reminded her. "Last night, neither of us was willing to take that risk. Tonight will be different."

"How? It'll be just as dangerous if we move forward, but this time everyone will be at risk." Lillie resisted the urge to cover her face with her hands.

"Any risk I take is better than the one Lo's taking by continuing to phase indefinitely," he shrugged.

"It was easier when I still hated you."

"What makes you say that?" Logan turned from the cup of coffee he was freshening.

"It just was," she picked up the map in front of her and studied it a little closer.

"Not for me, it wasn't," he smirked. She could actually *hear* the way half of his mouth turned up with his words. *And ultimately, that's all that matters, isn't it?* He could be kind, considerate, tender, and supportive—to an extent, but when it came to the sticking point, what Logan cared the most about, even now, she was afraid, was his own well-being.

~

Logan knew what he had to do. *Lillie can think what she wants, plan all she wants, but it ends tonight.* He watched as

**314**

Lillie napped fitfully on the couch. He was glad that she had finally managed to calm down enough to sleep. If Lo had been worried, it didn't seem to be keeping him up, since he'd all but passed out in his bowl of Cap'n Crunch. *It must've been the combination of being sick and the usual exhaustion of roaming the woods all night,* Logan smiled. *Who wouldn't be tired after that?* But Lillie wasn't sick, nor had she prowled around on four legs recently. She had spent the night wide-eyed and worrying that her son wouldn't come home. *It's killing her.*

He saw the dark smudges beneath her eyes, the way she wasn't entirely relaxed, even in sleep. Her lean body seemed tense and ready to leap at even the slightest disturbance. He wasn't positive she'd had a good night's sleep since they'd "met" in December, and *that* was killing him.

He shook his head. *It's over.* Logan thought for a minute but couldn't remember a single time in his life when he had been this concerned about a woman other than Ginnie, and if he were honest, most of those times, he'd been more concerned about her reaction to something and how that would affect him than about his mother herself.

*It's **been** over.* He laughed at himself when he realized he couldn't even guess at how long it had been since he'd had sex with someone other than Lillie. Since that first time in her apartment in Ann Arbor, calling some other girl had never occurred to him, even on the nights when he was alone in his bed, wide-awake from wanting. *That's twice now. Twice, the woman's made me monogamous, and I have absolutely no idea how she does it!* Though his reasonable mind was still curious, the how of it was moot at this point. *All* *that does matter is what I manage to accomplish with the cards I've been dealt.*

~

Lo sat up and wondered what time it was. The sun was streaming through the window of his dad's spare bedroom, and he vaguely remembered eating cereal at some point, but who knew how long ago that had been?

He crawled out of bed and, seeing that he'd already showered sometime today and was actually wearing pajamas, headed for the living room.

"Hi, Dad," he said, finding Logan at his desk, shuffling through some reports or something.

"Hey, kid," Logan answered quietly and nodded toward the couch, where Lo saw his mom curled up, taking a nap. "Feeling better?"

"Mostly," Lo nodded. "Definitely better than I have since we got here.

"Good. Are you hungry?"

"Yes, sir. I guess it's lunch time?" Lo wondered.

"Try two o'clock in the afternoon," his dad grinned.

"Dang," he whispered emphatically.

"Tell you what, I'll make you an omelette, if you help me with a little plan I've been working on. . ." his dad offered.

The thought of eggs and melted cheese nearly had him, but Lo raised a brow when he remembered who was offering it. "What kinda plan? And how do I know it won't get me in trouble with Mom?"

"You don't." His dad cleared his throat, squinted, and added in a flat, gruff voice, "It looks like you're gonna have to ask yourself a question: 'Do I feel lucky?' Well, do ya, kid?"

~

316

Lillie woke and found herself stretched out on Logan's overstuffed couch. Lo and his dad were absorbed in one of those zombie games they both liked so much. She stretched contentedly and checked the time on her phone. 4:30. "Why in the world didn't y'all *tell* me it was this late? I've slept the whole day!"

"Oh, hi, Mom," Lo put down his controller. "Did you have a nice nap?"

"Apparently so," Lillie yawned. "What have y'all been up to all this time?"

"Just saving millions of innocent lives from the undead invasion . . . you know, the usual," Lo smiled sweetly at her.

Logan had yet to respond. "Did he beat you to a pulp again?" she prompted.

"Oh, you know it," he answered easily . . . almost too easily.

"You'd think you'd have improved your game after all the playing time y'all've gotten lately," she teased.

"I've tried. Trust me, but when the round is over, somehow the kid always winds up with the most kills."

"Yeah, it looks like Dad's just losin' his edge," Lo glanced at her and then at his dad. "I guess I've humiliated you enough for now. I guess I'll go listen to my iPod until it's time to eat," he added and began exiting the game.

By now, Lillie knew something was afoot. "Out with it," she said before Lo could slink off to his bedroom.

"Out with what, Mom?" he wondered.

"Out with whatever it is y'all aren't telling me," she narrowed her eyes so he knew that she meant business.

"What are you talking about?" the two of them asked at once.

"Lo*gan*. . ." she drew out the word and used her disappointed-mom/instructor tone.

"Ma'am?" Lo answered.

"Yes?" Logan inquired.

"I want to know exactly what it is the two of you are up to, and I want to know now!"

"We aren't up to anything, are we, Dad? Tell her." Lo promised.

"No, we aren't up to a thing, Lillie," Logan said solemnly.

"When I figure out what it is, you *know* there'll be consequences. . ." she played her ace and thought she saw Lo flinch.

"How can there be any consequences for Dad? He's an adult, and plus, how can there be any consequences for me if there's nothing going on?" Lo wanted to know.

"Hmm." Logan sat there next to him, smug as could be, and nodded. "Those are good questions, kid. I'd like to know the answers to them myself."

*I'll just bet you do!* "This is what I get for sleeping half the day away," she threw her hands up, acknowledging defeat.

"That's right, Mom. That's exactly what you get," Lo grinned, deception dripping from the curve of his lips. "You don't get to ask any more questions, and if you do, then Dad and I'll just take the Camaro and cruise without you, so we don't have to hear them."

She shot Logan her best are-you-sure-you-want-to-do this? glare accompanied by a hand on her hip for good measure, but all he did was give her the same grin that Lo had. "It isn't fair when the two of you go against me like this."

"Mom, you know the Eleventh Commandment: Thou shalt not whine," Lo quoted her own maxim to her, and as badly as she wanted to call him on it, she found that she could not.

"Fine. But you're taking me to dinner! You boys got that? There'll be no home cooked supper for a pair of tricksters who are plotting things and took advantage of a poor woman while she was trying to get some rest." Lillie stamped her foot for emphasis. "And it better be someplace nice!"

"That's a great idea," Logan brightened sincerely. "We can go anywhere you want! It can be a sort of pre-celebration since we're going to cure Lo tonight!"

"Yeah! Awesome idea, Mom!" Lo chimed in, nearly bouncing in his seat.

"Why do I get the feeling that somehow I've just done exactly what you wanted me to all along?" she eyed them carefully. When they didn't answer, Lillie did the only thing she could think of to punish them. She stood, deliberately turned her back on them, and walked into the bedroom to make herself pretty.

## Chapter 32

They waited in the dusk for the last of the sun's light to be overtaken by darkness, Logan and the mother of his child. Only a few yards separated them from their son's prone body. She reached for his hand, and he took hers, squeezing it.

Lillie hadn't spoken since they had moved away from Lo, and despite the merriment of their dinner, Logan knew better than to attempt idle conversation. Still, he shifted so that they were no longer side-by-side, and with an arm around her shoulders, he pulled her to his chest.

For a moment, he listened to the sounds around him, the crickets, the wind, the waves, the people who were too far down the bank to see. For a moment, he counted the breaths they drew, two of hers for every one of his own. For a second, he let the fear consume him, but her fingers were warm and solid in his hand, those slender bones that could bring life to things and people long ago lost to time. He focused on Lo's body and began.

"Six months ago you didn't exist for me. Neither of you. I still can't believe that. How I could wake up one morning and have a son."

She looked up at him, but he shook his head before she could speak. "It wasn't something I ever planned on. In fact, I did everything I thought I could to prevent it from happening, so when Lo came to my door that day, I didn't react the way he wanted me to or even the way I wish I had, looking back on it. All I could think was how

I wasn't cut out for it, not coming up the way I did, knowing what I do about fathers and sons and dysfunction. I thought he was a freaking fool to come all that way and be disappointed, and honestly, I was pissed beyond belief that he had put me in a position that gave me no choice but to disappoint him.

"My whole life, all I've ever wanted was to be free of Philip Michaels, and up 'til that knock on my door I'd done a pretty damn good job of convincing myself that I was my own man, whether I worked for him or not. But there Lo was, a carbon copy of the boy I had been, and it didn't matter that I'd spent my entire adulthood being the man Philip didn't care enough to be. It didn't matter that I had been careful with people, with myself. It didn't matter because there was Lo, and by existing, he had made me Philip. I had been my father all along.

"I can't do it anymore, Lillie. You see that, don't you? I can't keep letting Lo suffer because of my actions. As long as he does, I'm no better than my own father."

Her grip tightened on his hand, but she nodded.

"That's why I'm going now. I'm going, and you're going to stay here," he repeated as she began to shake her head in denial. "You're going to stay here and stay safe."

~

"No! No, Logan! That's not what we talked about! That's not what we planned! You know I'm faster. I've done this before, remember? I'll be fine!" she pushed the words out as fast as they would come.

Suddenly they were standing, and Logan was pulling away from her, making to head toward the shadow whose jaws had begun to snap. A pain like the shattering of glass burst inside her chest. *I can't do this. Not again. I can't watch*

*him die right in front of me. Not again. I can't! I can't! I can't
breathe! I can't live! Oh, Lord, I can't—*

"Lillie . . . Lillie, look at me," Logan's hands were
cupping her face. "Look at me, doll."

She managed to focus on his eyes, deep as death in
front of her instead of their usual gray. "Liar," she spat
and slapped him hard across the cheek. "You promised
me it wouldn't be like last time! You *promised!*"

"I told you long ago that I would never be able to give
you what you wanted." He met her eyes again even as the
blow seemed to echo around them. "Do you remember
that, Lillie? When I said that, it was because I didn't think
I wanted the same things you do, but I was wrong. I do
want those things. I want them with you and Lo." He
pressed a kiss to her forehead. "But more than that, I
want Lo to understand that I am not my father. I want to
show Lo that a father's love isn't reflected in a roll of
hundreds when he's pleased with his son's behavior, and
this is the way I can do it. This is the only way."

"Go," she whispered, and the air she drew to say it
sliced at her throat like a shard.

~

Logan let her go, knowing as he did that she sank to
the ground, wishing as he did that there was something
else he could do. But there wasn't time for anything
except Lo.

He moved swiftly over the distance when he saw the
wolf rise and shake its head as if to clear away the
grogginess of a long sleep. He ran until he looked back as
he felt the yellow glint of its eyes, sharp points of light,
focused hungrily on his shape. He turned his head slowly,
faced forward again, and took one step, two. Another.

Then one more before his feet rose and fell with instinct, so he was no longer able to count.

His breath was coming fast, and he ran towards a single thought: water. If he could reach the water, there was hope. His hand clinched the hunting knife he had kept hidden from Lillie. *The water.* The thought pounded through him with his heart and his blood. He looked back as he went, and the wolf was there, a few yards away. *I can't think now, not about anything but the water, not about anything but Lo's future.* And he pushed farther. *Just a bit closer. Almost there. Almost.*

Stretching himself, he fell forward into the waves, sucking in air with the shock of the cold and wet. *Deeper. I've got to be farther out.* So he pushed at the water with his arms and kicked out into searing pain. *Not deep enough.* For the first time, he wondered if he would be strong enough to finish it. *I have to be. I have to finish it. Lo*, he thought and pushed into deeper water. *Lo*, he pushed again. *Lo*, he tried once more, and then he couldn't think of anything other than pain. In his legs, in his arms, in his chest, in the fingers of his hand that gripped the knife. He felt the brush of fur and reached out, struck, and clung desperately to his last bit of hope.

~

Lillie sank to her knees on the sand. The wolf and Logan had entered the water together, and by the time she had gotten close enough to see, both of them were underwater. She watched anxiously for human heads to break the surface. *There have to be two. There have to be two.* She would take no less than that.

In the darkness, her mind drifted back to the night that had changed everything. He had reminded her of it only moments ago.

323

"It's too late for regret," she called out to the water. "I've thrown my lot in with yours, Logan, and I'll face the consequences. But we've managed to find each other again, even after all those years, and I believe there's hope for us yet."

## Epilogue

*Raleigh, NC 2022*

I gulped the air, pulling in as much as I could while coughing up water, and that wasn't nearly enough. I was somehow lying on my back and managed to roll onto my side and curl into myself. I pressed a hand to my chest, but that did nothing for my scorched lungs as the water that had filled them was expelled.

At last, I was able to catch my breath. I opened my eyes and saw the glint of the bright, round moon reflecting off the surface of the lake, which made me realize that my head was killing me, and the light only made it worse.

"Mom!" I called hoarsely and then sat up to look for her in spite of the wave of sickness I felt. "Mom!"

It took me no more than a second or so to spot her a few yards down the shore. I struggled to stand without falling or puking and then stumbled in her direction. She was kneeling in the sand, and I could see that something else was there with her. "Mom?"

"Here." She turned her head at her name but didn't move. When I got close to her, I could see that she was cradling someone's head in her lap. I fell onto my knees beside them and was near enough to hear the air hiss roughly with each breath the man drew. As I peered into his face, his lips started to move.

"Shh, Logan," Mom whispered close to his face. "I've got you. Don't try to talk just now, darling." She held his hand tightly in hers, as if she was keeping him from slipping away. "Not just now."

I touched her shoulder to let her know I was there, and her shirt was as wet as I was. "Mom, what happened? Where are we? Why is everyone so wet?"

". . . did it, didn't we, doll?" the man rasped, and it looked like he was trying to smile.

"Who is he, Mom? Is he okay?" I tried again. Nothing was making any sense. It was like I was having a crazy dream. I was standing in the sand with no clothes on and no idea how we'd gotten there, both Mom and I were soaked, and the poor dude she was talking to seemed pretty bad off.

"Lo, my love—" she began.

"Kid, would you believe me if I said I was your father?"